MW00824912

The MARBLE SEA

BY

BRIAN RUSSELL

ISBN: 978-1-66781-005-8
eBook ISBN: 978-1-66781-006-5

This book is dedicated to my Angel
and my best friend, Cheryl.

Special thanks to Karen Hunke for
her help and her friendship.

YEAR 2010

CHAPTER 1

The columns of mist furled tighter and tighter until they formed a dark curtain of gray. Then, for a moment, the curtain parted allowing just a glimpse of the prize. But as quickly as it appeared, the treasure was gone, faded back into the gloom, safely concealed from the invaders.

Peter Brandt stood wedged against the wheelhouse of the water taxi, balancing against the morning swells and gazing at the distant wall, waiting for the picture to reappear.

Sitting on the bench beside him was his wife, Nora. She sat perfectly still with her chin resting in her hands staring straight ahead. There was a hint of sadness in her gray-blue eyes but not enough to detract from her beauty.

The Brandts had flown all night from Los Angeles and Nora looked exhausted. Peter was grateful that their destination was within reach. He knew that with a little rest and a bite to eat, Nora would be back to her old self.

Then, suddenly, she was gone.

The water taxi had driven straight into a thick bank of clouds and the world disappeared. The driver quickly throttled back until they were idling in place, floating in near silence, save for the bells and horns from adjacent *taxi boats* warning of their presence.

Then, just as quickly as it had descended, the veil began to lift. The mist rose in lazy curls until finally Nora re-appeared.

Peter was strangely affected by how quickly his wife had vanished, but he brushed the disturbing thought aside and returned his attention to what lay ahead. Venice in the mist, he decided, was an apt metaphor for what was happening in their lives. He was hopeful though. The magical city had been their salvation before.

At that moment, the entire cloud dissolved like it had never been and there it was, the Campanile, the soaring scarlet steeple that had stood for a thousand years as the city's watchtower. It was a good sign and Peter was ready for a good sign. The Brandts had been fighting too much lately. Well not fights really, more like spats; tight-lipped little squabbles that occurred out of nowhere like a needy tot. But since they were working together, their personal gripes had had to take a backseat to other obligations.

They'd finished working just the day before and it had been a rigorous shoot. They were both exhausted, and more than ready to spoil themselves.

The taxi slowed and circled once through its own wake before coming to rest, bumping lightly against the landing in front of the magnificent Gritti Palace, one of the world's finest hotels and one of the Brandt's favorite destinations.

Peter hopped ashore before the boat was secured. He turned and extended his hand to his pretty wife. She skipped nimbly onto the pier, still girlish at forty. A shore attendant hurried forward to help, but he was too late. By the time he reached the taxi, the Brandts were already heading for the hotel lobby, laughing like children. The attendant watched the pretty woman and nodded his approval. As a long-time employee of the palace, the attendant knew he was not supposed to acknowledge such things. Who were they kidding? He was Italian.

"Mama, mea," he murmured, clutching his heart as the tether rope hit him square in the back, snapping him back to reality. He bent slowly to retrieve it, still shaking his head in approval. He had the feeling he'd seen the woman somewhere before. In fact, he had seen her before on the big screen and on the television. Nora Brandt was actually Nora James, television and film star but she travelled using her married name in order to enjoy some measure of anonymity.

Nora was indeed a beauty. Her auburn hair that hung in soft curls below her shoulders shone like burnished gold in the morning light. Her skin was lightly tanned, and her misty blue eyes sparkled with laughter. She was tall but not as tall as her companion, a good-looking man with salt-and-pepper hair and a brilliant smile. The pair was the picture of a Hollywood power couple.

The Palace of the Doge 'Gritti' had the air of a dowager, steadfastly refusing to relinquish her fading sensuality. Built in 1267 to celebrate the end of the Black Plague, the Gritti had stood for centuries as a symbol of life's finer things.

As expected, the old hotel welcomed the Brandts with open arms. As they entered the magnificent, gilded lobby an elegant older man dressed in a morning coat and pinstripes, hurried from behind the reception desk, bowing all the way, eager to bid his guests welcome.

"Señora Brandt," he stammered, "how happy I am to see you again. It has been much too long this time."

Nora reached out her hand. He took it and held it like it was a bird.

"Far too long, Leonardo," she smiled in reply. Her husky voice echoed softly around the room. "I'm happy to see you too."

Nora remained oblivious to the fact that grown men were often rendered speechless just by looking at her. It was once again the case.

"Señor Brandt," the manager managed to tear his eyes from Nora.

Peter stood smiling patiently. It was something he'd experienced countless times. The response was one of the drawbacks of being married to one of the world's 'most beautiful' according to *People* magazine from 2004 to 2006 and then again in 2010. It was something he'd learned to live with.

Brandt was attractive enough in his own right. He just didn't get noticed much when his wife was in the room. His was the kind of face plastic surgeons dreamed of. It was one that could be perfected with just a tuck here or there. His dark green eyes twinkled as he shook hands with Leonardo.

"Leo," he responded, "good to see you too."

"And you señor," Leo replied. "It's been too long."

"Yes, it has," Brandt agreed and turned to his wife. "Ready to head up?"

"Oh yes, please," she replied enthusiastically. "It's been a very long night."

A few minutes later they were in Room 9, arguably the most romantic suite of rooms in the entire world. Suite 9, where kings and queens and Hemingway had been regular guests, was the corner suite on the second floor of the palace. It was situated in such a way that it seemed to hang out over the Grand Canal, like the stern cabin of a schooner.

After a long nap and a hot bath and almost an hour of lazy lovemaking and yet another bath, and a short gondola trip, the Brandts were happily ensconced in a corner booth at Harry's Bar. Harry's, one of the most famous spots in Venice, had become a ritual. They always went there the first night in the city and always had the Steak Diane.

They'd been eating for almost two hours. The meal had been excellent as usual and the Brandts were euphoric, luxuriating in obscenely old port and spiced coffee.

"Do you really think we deserve all this decadence?" Nora smiled into her husband's eyes. They appeared almost black in the candlelight.

"Of course we do," Peter replied softly, "it was a tough shoot; I don't have to tell you."

"Yes," Nora sighed and nodded her agreement

"I wanted to throttle Ross by the last day," Peter continued. "He's more of a *pain in the ass* than ever."

"I know honey but it's the price you pay," Nora smiled. "He's got T.V.Q. The network's thrilled and he's a very good actor. I think the work was really good, don't you?"

"Yes, it was good," Peter allowed. "And by the time I get the film pasted together I'll have forgiven him for his damn tantrums."

Peter leaned back from the table and quietly studied his wife. He had the look of a man who was supremely satisfied. After ten years of marriage, he still enjoyed looking at her. She was painfully beautiful. Her eyes still managed to hypnotize him; her mouth to entice him, and her nose? It was perfect, so perfect that for three years running, it had been America's paradigm for rhinoplasty.

He signaled for the waiter, and an attractive young man hurried over. In passable Italian, Peter asked for the check.

The waiter nodded curtly and hastened away. Peter glanced back at his wife. She was gazing at him intently. Suddenly, she looked sad.

He reached for her hand. "What is it honey?" he asked quietly. "What's the matter?"

Nora looked away. She stared down at her tightly clenched hands and shook her head. She trembled slightly. "It's nothing," she murmured unconvincingly. "Really, I just had a funny feeling that's all, a feeling about . . ."

The waiter chose that moment to return with the check. He placed it on the table beside Peter and deposited a small, decorated box in front of Nora.

"Something for later, maybe," he managed in halting English, beaming at the pretty woman. "A special sweet from the chef; he says he is a very large fan for you. He loves all movies you do, as do I of course."

Nora smiled up at the young man. "Thank you, Marco," she said warmly, "It's nice to be appreciated, especially by a man as handsome as you, and one with such good taste." Her eyes were laughing again.

Marco blushed like a virgin bride, "Shall I get you taxi Mr. Brandt?" The young man was a bit flustered. "Sometimes is hard to find at this time. The gondolas are gone for the day, so water taxi is harder to find."

"No, it's alright," Peter replied, "I think we'll just walk back. It's a beautiful night and after that meal the exercise will do us good."

"Mr. Brandt," the waiter said softly, "is okay I'm sure, but do be careful. Don't go from what streets you know. It's very easy to be lost in the city. She is a . . . a maze, no? Don't go too deep, okay? Venice is not always so harmless she looks."

Peter offered his thanks and they made their way outside. The air was much chillier than when they'd arrived at the restaurant. A minute or two later, they crossed St Mark's Square, walking briskly, heading towards the Grand Canal and their hotel. Nora was very much aware of the quietness. It wasn't that late but there was not another soul on the streets.

An array of columns encircled the Piazza, casting long shadows across ancient stones. A cold mist began to mingle with the shadows. Within just a few minutes, the Brandts became enshrouded. The fog had descended quickly.

"Do you know where we are?" Nora whispered, sounding anxious and trying not to.

"I think so," Peter replied, sounding none too sure. "We're on Larga Street I think, so we should be turning left at the next square. It's got to be just ahead."

They continued on and a minute later, thankfully, they saw a brighter light just ahead. The fog seemed to thicken with every step, but Nora felt comforted. They were nearing the Piazza St Angelo, behind which they'd find the welcoming warmth of their hotel. She slipped her arm into her husband's and hauled him towards the light. A moment later, they were in the square and the fog dissipated for a moment. Just long enough for the Brandts to realize that there was something wrong. There was but one sorry light in the square and there was no street running to the left. Their way was blocked by the massive wooden doors of a church.

"I don't know," Peter muttered. "We must have gotten turned around by the fog. I don't recognize this place at all, do you?"

Nora shook her head bravely, but Peter could see the hint of worry, the fright in her eyes. He knew this was the kind of situation that terrified her. Being lost in the darkness was her worst nightmare.

"Should we try to retrace our steps?" she said tightly and searched his face for reassurance.

"No honey," he smiled "we'll be alright. Let's just head for the next square. It's bound to be one we recognize. We'll find somebody who can direct us. Come on."

Peter put his arm around his wife's shoulders, pulled her close and guided her from the square. They entered an unfamiliar street moving as quickly as possible and watched as the path before them slowly disappeared. The fog had returned with a vengeance. Neither of them said a word. A hundred yards farther and the street became an even narrower, no more than an alley.

Peter shrugged and moved bravely forward. His wife was close to his side, holding on for dear life.

It was then that they heard the music. It was opera, Verdi and it was an old record, one that was badly scratched. The music reached out through the mist as if to provide some comfort.

They followed the sound as if it could somehow lead them from the maze. Maybe that's why they were unaware of the cats. The cats, however, were very aware of them.

There was only one at first; a wretched-looking colorless creature with an awkward sidewinder gait. Soon it was joined by several others. Within a few minutes, there were more than twenty cats moving soundlessly through the mist on either side of the Brandts. They followed the couple closely, as if waiting for just the right moment.

Nora saw them first and started to panic. She'd been afraid of cats all her life and was now being stalked by a gang of the filthy creatures. To make matters worse, the street was almost completely dark. They'd long since lost the music. It had come from a place they couldn't quite reach. They were very lost now, in a labyrinth of streets and canals and stone bridges that all looked the same. The water they crossed was very still and smelled sour. The air was damp and cold.

A minute or two later, they found themselves in a small square. It wasn't a square really. It was more like a widening, where two alleys bisected a tiny canal. They stopped, breathing deeply, searching for any sign of life or light from the windows above. There was none.

The fog lifted for a moment, whisked away like a child's blanket. Nora gasped as she saw thirty or more cats standing or sitting around them, all perfectly still, watching. The cats had completely encircled them as if daring them to attempt an escape. One of the creatures rose to its feet and moved a couple of steps closer. The others immediately followed suit. A moment later, there was a repeat performance. The cats began to slowly circle. What had been complete silence was now being punctuated by loud hisses and throaty growls. A moment later, the terrible mournful wailing began. The cats were no more than ten feet away and moving closer.

"What are they doing?" Nora groaned.

"I have no bloody idea," Peter replied. "I've never heard of such a thing."

Nora turned to her husband and clutched him tightly. She really wanted to scream but somehow stopped herself. She whispered urgently, "The box! Peter, quick open it. Let them have it."

Brandt immediately tore the ribbon from the little cardboard box he'd carried from Harry's. He reached inside, grabbed a handful of pastry and cream and hurled it at the nearest cat. Bullseye! He then tossed the rest of the box as far as he could, grabbed his wife's hand and bolted. As one, the cats were on the sweets and on each other. Behind the fleeing couple, all hell broke loose.

The wails and screams gradually faded into the distance as the Brandts raced on through the darkness.

A moment later, bright lights appeared just ahead of them, and the sounds of life filled the dank air. They rushed forward and stumbled into a bustling street. The thoroughfare was filled with people. The shops were wide open, the cafés and bars alive with patrons. They'd reached the market at the foot of the Rialto Bridge. Venice was wide-awake again, refreshed from her evening nap, ready for commerce to resume. The city of merchants was alive.

Later, they lay in the vast canopied bed, listening to the sounds of the night through the open window. Nora lay in the crook of her husband's arm and smiled. "I don't know what it is, you devil," she murmured contentedly, "but you can sure get me stupid. My brains are gone, if you get my drift."

Nora pitched onto her side and lay for a moment studying her husband's face. She loved his face, certainly more than he did. He seemed to get embarrassed any time he was given the slightest compliment about his looks. His unawareness of his physicality made him even more attractive to her. Hell, she'd seen the effect he had on other women. She'd seen it for years. To Nora, the angular planes of Peter's face were quite beautiful. His eyes were closed tight. For a minute she thought he was asleep, but he turned to her, snaked his arms around her and pulled her close to him.

Nora took her husband's hand in hers and pulled his arm tighter around her. She snuggled in, butt to belly, until she was perfectly spooned, safe from anything and everything. She peeled open his fist and gently kissed the palm of his hand.

CHAPTER 2

The next morning, the sun was late breaking through the clouds but when it finally did, the city blossomed in its warmth. It was almost eleven when Peter and Nora, arm in arm, strolled from the hotel onto the dock where the attendant immediately beckoned for a gondola. A few minutes later, they were disgorged at the famous Hotel Danieli not far from St Mark's. They'd thought of staying at the Danieli this time, for a change, but at the last minute had decided to stick with the Gritti. Although the Hotel Danieli was fabulous, it was a bit touristier and a bit louder. They smiled independently as they watched people streaming in and out of the hotel's front door. Unspoken language was something they'd nearly perfected over the years.

The Brandt's crossed the square to the clock tower and disappeared through the small archway that led to Merceria and the great shops. As was his custom, Peter had agreed to help Nora find something special. It had become a habit for them. Great clothes had been supplied to her for the film but by the end of the shoot she was tired of wearing them. She craved something new.

They spent an hour or more sauntering around the district, checking out the shop windows but nothing compelled Nora to venture inside. The stuff was too Euro for her. She'd learned from experience that usually when something looked just right for an environment like Venice or Paris, it never looked right back in the States. She had stuff in her closet back home that hadn't seen the light of day since being hauled home from a shoot.

Suddenly Nora stopped, grabbed her husband's arm and pointed across the street. There in a shop window was something appealing. They crossed to the shop and Nora's face broke into a smile. It was a long flowing dress, burnished red in color, almost like her hair. The material appeared coarse but soft at the same time. The style was Arabic, Moroccan maybe. It was very nice. Peter agreed.

They entered the shop to the accompaniment of a little bell that jangled pleasantly above their heads. A moment later, a man stepped through the curtains, placed his hands together, offered a small bow and smiled in greeting.

"Good morning," he intoned, "welcome to my shop. It is a beautiful day, is it not?"

The man was middle-aged, overweight and of dark complexion. If he was Italian, Peter was thinking, he was from much further south. The man was no Venetian.

"How did you know to speak English?" Nora asked cheerfully, ready as always to engage in friendly conversation. "Are we that obvious?"

Ever the merchant, the man took a moment to consider his options and decided to fawn. "I'm afraid so," he replied softly. "Any woman as beautiful as you must be a film star or something comparable. That is why I assumed you were Americans, you see."

"Ah," she nodded solemnly, "that explains it. Now I understand." She then flashed a cheeky grin at her husband.

"What may I show you madam?" asked the round man. "Did you by any chance notice the dress in the window? Marvelous piece that one. One of a kind you know, it appears to have been made for you."

"Yes," Nora smiled, "I would like to try it."

Peter watched his wife enjoying herself. As always, he was pleased by her pleasure. It was something he wanted to last forever. He glanced around the shop, looking for somewhere to perch and spotted a chair in the corner. He crossed the tile floor and sat down to wait as the proprietor led Nora towards the curtains from which he had emerged earlier. At the last moment she turned, blew her husband a sultry kiss and disappeared.

Peter picked up a magazine and began leafing through it. Ladies fashion could hold his interest for only so long and he couldn't read a word of Italian.

The bell on the door rang and a young woman entered the shop and said something to the proprietor in Italian.

The proprietor responded and pointed to a rack on the back wall.

The woman crossed to the rack, pushed aside a couple of hangers and removed a dress. Peter looked up from his magazine just in time to see the woman disappear through the curtain.

A few more minutes passed, and it occurred to Peter that Nora was taking her sweet time. He looked at his watch. He could never understand what took so long with women. Any mirror automatically provided an opportunity to fuss. He glanced at the proprietor who was leaning on the counter reading a newspaper, totally unperturbed. Peter stood and crossed to the man.

As he did so, the young woman who had entered the shop just a few minutes before, emerged from the curtain and without saying a word, hurried out the door.

"Maybe I should give my wife a hand," he ventured, sounding a little uncomfortable. "Maybe she's stuck or something."

"If you like sir," the man replied calmly. "Please, as you wish," the man inclined his head toward the curtain.

The man was not Italian, Peter decided, Lebanese maybe or Turkish, something similar; definitely not Italian.

He parted the curtain and stepped through. The light inside was very dim and it took his eyes a moment to adjust. "Honey," he called softly, "where are you? Do you need some help? " He paused, "Where are you – Nora, I can't see you."

There was no reply. The only sound was that of his breathing which was getting heavier by the second. Suddenly, the hairs on the back of his neck stood straight up. He knew something was wrong. He moved farther in. "Nora," he called hoarsely, "what are you doing? Are you in here?"

He looked around and then spotted the door in the far wall. It was small, no more than five feet high. He quickly reached for the door handle, turned it and pushed hard. The door was surprisingly heavy and resisted slightly before giving way. Finally, it burst open, and Peter stumbled through. He found himself outside, behind the shop, standing on a dilapidated wooden dock. The dock didn't look like it got much use. The water that slid past was dark and oily and smelled putrid. There were one or two gondolas on the narrow canal, but none had passengers. As Peter turned to head back inside, he noticed a set of wet footprints on the wooden platform. The blood drained from his face as he ran back into the shop and pushed through the curtain.

"What the hell's going on here?" he growled. "Where is my wife?"

The proprietor blanched.

"What do you mean?" he stammered. "Where is the lady?"

Peter was about to reach for the man's throat but thought better of it. He stood glowering down at the man who was by now trembling. Brandt took a deep breath and struggled to keep control. He exhaled, turned away, walked to the front door and stepped into the street. He was immediately engulfed by the dozens of shoppers who crammed the narrow space. He shook his head and returned to the shop.

He re-entered just as the shopkeeper came through the curtains. The man was muttering to himself. "She really is gone," he murmured, shaking his large head. "How is that possible?"

"Telephone," barked Peter, snapping the man to attention, "I need the police."

"Yes of course the Carabinieri," he pulled a cell phone from his pocket, pushed a key and handed it to Peter.

The American took it with trembling hands. When the call was answered he realized that his Italian was not up to the task, so he handed the phone back to the proprietor.

In less than five minutes the cops arrived.

"We don't know," he repeated for the umpteenth time, exasperated. Since neither of the cops understood English, the shopkeeper had been acting as the translator until eventually Brandt was totally excluded from the conversation. The man told quite a story apparently. As he spoke, he became more and more animated and kept pointing at himself. Clearly, the man was intent on eliminating himself from any culpability.

A few minutes later, Peter was being escorted by the Carabinieri through the crowd towards the Rialto. It occurred to him that he was in the exact spot he and Nora had stumbled on when they escaped from the darkness. Last night he'd felt saved. Now he felt lost.

They reached the Grand Canal where a blue and white police launch was waiting at the dock. At the wheel was a young woman wearing the same light gray uniform as the two men. She looked at him blankly as he was ushered aboard. One of the male officers hopped aboard after him as the other cast them off and disappeared into the crowd, apparently heading back towards the dress shop.

"So, Mr. Brandt," said the officer who was seated next to Peter in the stern, "we have a problem here and I won't try to minimize it. That would do neither of us any good. We'll have to move fast if there's to be any chance."

"You're speaking English, damn it," Peter sputtered. "That whole scene was crap back there. What's going on here? What problem are you talking about?"

"Oh, I just wanted to find out if the shopkeeper was in any way a part of this. Having him translate told me much of what I needed to know. I would venture to say he's not involved."

"Involved in what, for Pete's sake?" Peter's heart was in his throat. He was very frightened. "Tell me."

"We see this from time to time," the young cop became thoughtful. He looked into Peter's face. "She's beautiful, right? With a lot of style, your wife, someone people would notice, a 'knockout' I think you Americans say."

"Yes,"" he was trembling, "a real knockout."

"Others, women like her, have been taken, abducted, five in the last several months. And we're not alone here in Venice, Mister Brandt, oh no. Women are being snatched from the streets of Rome as well, and Paris."

"But nobody told us," Peter's voice shook. "We were never warned about any of this. We should have been told damn it. How could they . . ."

The young policeman interrupted, "It's not something we like to advertise," he said simply. "I'm sure you can understand. It's the economy – we are the city of commerce you see, for over a thousand years – we are the *Merchants of Venice* and trade must go on. Someone here is involved in a terrible business and not such a new business. I'm afraid your wife may have become a victim."

The police launch hurtled across the dark water of the Grand Canal, flying past ancient palaces on either side. The female driver was on a cell phone apparently describing the situation to someone on the other end of the line.

"Where is she going?" Peter whispered. "Where are they taking her?" His teeth were clenched tight in his pounding screaming head.

"It's difficult to tell," the policeman replied thoughtfully. "Somewhere in the Middle East, we know that much, but by which route it is impossible to tell. There is so much ship traffic here in the Adriatic and the eastern Mediterranean. It could be any one of a hundred vessels and we can't stop them all. They know that."

"This is ridiculous," Peter was unaware that he was shouting. "I can't believe what you're telling me. It's like a bloody movie I've seen. It's a damn horror movie."

Peter suddenly leapt to his feet and screamed, punching the air above with his two fists. He lurched forward, almost pitching himself into the canal. If it wasn't for the quick reflexes of the much younger man, Peter would have been treading filthy water.

An hour later, Brandt was on the top floor of the Ronde di Polizia, having told his story to several police officers on two previous floors. He was now in an office with one desk and two older men dressed in plain clothes. One sat behind the desk. The other leaned against the wall just out of sight behind Peter's shoulder. It was an awkward arrangement that Peter knew was designed to make him feel uncomfortable. It was working. He refused to accept what he was hearing from the police. They were trying to tell him that his wife had just been snatched from the streets of Venice, pilfered like a piece of pretty jewelry to be delivered into God knows what.

His mind refused to allow the concept.

CHAPTER 3

A half-mile out, in the darkness of the Lagoon Basin of Saint Marco, an anchor chain slowly clanked its way upward. A minute later, the bow of the ship turned slowly into the breeze. The vessel slipped noiselessly into the channel and drifted on the outgoing tide. A half-hour later, the twin turbines came quietly to life. On the bridge, the lamps had been dimmed to almost nothing. No one spoke. Ship bells chimed softly as the captain set his course, the heading *east by south-south-east.*

After almost an hour, the captain handed over the wheel to his mate and proceeded to light a foul-smelling cigarette. He inhaled deeply, relishing the little catch in his throat as the smoke reached its destination. He could relax now, at least for a while. He had not yet been told where to go ashore, and wouldn't know for at least four days, when he was back in the waters of his homeland. Until then he would not be safe.

He thought about his special cargo and contemplated paying a visit later, just to see how she was feeling. The captain smiled slyly, pleased with the possibilities. She was one very beautiful woman, maybe the most beautiful he'd ever seen – at least in person. She was even more beautiful than the women on the pages of the forbidden magazines. When she'd been brought aboard, she'd been unconscious, but he'd still managed to see her exquisite face and the fullness of her breasts. He wondered if she was still asleep and felt the rising in his groin.

He raised the cigarette to his thick lips again and drew in deeply. The brass buttons on the sleeve of his naval uniform gleamed dully in the half-light.

CHAPTER 4

Peter sat curled up in the bay window of Room 9 staring out across the dark water of the Grand Canal. His mind was on overload, refusing to think, to postulate one more possible scenario. He'd left the police station two or three hours before. He wasn't exactly sure. Part of him was starving but the thought of swallowing food made him gag.

Hard rain spattered noisily against the windows.

This is it, he thought, *it's payback time.*

He'd often thought that his lot in life had been an easy one – maybe too easy. There never really had been any great struggle. He'd been lucky and he knew it. Doors had opened for him, and he had simply walked through. He'd never really had to make tough decisions. He'd simply taken the easiest path, the one that appeared before him. He'd often wondered what he had done to deserve what he had, a successful career in a very tough industry. Then there was the almost perfect marriage to the perfect woman, who'd asked him out in the first place.

The pain in his heart told him in no uncertain terms, that things had changed. Easy street had dead ended. And he wasn't particularly surprised. He'd known that he was going to have to pay sometime. Maybe in the next life, maybe in the next days.

He shuddered and turned back to stare into the gathering darkness, swung his feet to the floor and took a deep breath. Finding Nora was going to be completely up to him, and he knew it. It was a terrifying thought, and it was the first time in his life he'd felt real desperation. It was a feeling that changed his perspective on everything. He was painfully aware of how much he'd come to depend on her. In times of crisis he'd always had her to turn to.

He looked across the room to the phone sitting on the rosewood desk. He'd prayed it would have rung by now. He hadn't wanted to leave the police station but had been told there was nothing he could do, absolutely nothing. He had finally agreed to wait at the hotel once the police had convinced him that he was in the way and impeding their progress.

Captain Petero had begun an immediate trace. He had assured Peter that he'd call him as soon as the list of ships and smaller boats departing Venetian waters that day had been compiled. It was the best he could do.

"Why are you so convinced she's on a boat," Peter had asked.

"Well," the captain had replied, "you see this is Venice. Water is the only mode of transportation we really understand, or trust should I say, especially when it comes to a cargo as precious as Nora James. Your wife Mister Brandt is very important to someone; someone rich enough to have her taken. This was a carefully planned operation as well as a very expensive one. I'm afraid that her disappearance is no random abduction. You were followed to Venice, I'm sure of it."

Peter had been ready to call out the navy, to give chase immediately. He'd sat sullen and quiet as the cops explained the impossibility. He'd listened impatiently as they described the complexities of international policing. As soon as the craft had passed the six-mile limit, it had escaped Italian jurisdiction. It now would require international diplomacy before anyone could interfere with its progress.

Peter had crossed through the lobby of his hotel like a sleepwalker, ignoring the polite greetings from the staff. He'd climbed the one flight of carpeted stairs and slipped into his room. He was grateful that no one had stopped him. He had nothing to say, nothing at all. He couldn't answer the questions they were bound to ask. He could not and would not accept anything of what he'd been told.

He woke feeling a bit shaky. He rose slowly to his feet and moved towards the bed. He sat down heavily and lay back on the duvet until his sore and tired body was stretched out full length. He stared at the ceiling and had no sense of the moment until eventually, his thoughts became a dream.

He was inside the front door of their house in the flats of Beverly Hills dealing with a brute of a man on the other side of the door. He could hear the wood creaking. The heavy door was literally bulging at the seams, ready to give way. Nora was standing behind him panicked, clutching the phone to her ear. Suddenly the man was in the house behind him. He was huge and ugly and deranged. He was holding Nora like a rag doll, touching her, caressing her obscenely. Peter was trying his best to reach them. His brain was screaming but his feet refused to move. All he could do was watch helplessly as the awful creature dragged her away into the night.

Just then there was a sound at the door, a sound like the scratching of long fingernails on the polished wood or claws – like a cat's claws. Peter sat bolt upright. He was suddenly wide-awake. He heard it again. There was someone at his door. Peter slipped off the bed and moved quickly across the room. He reached for the door handle, turned it and pulled hard. The door rattled but didn't budge. He'd forgotten to unbolt it. By the time the door finally swung open there was no one there but at his feet was a carefully folded slip of paper. He picked it up and stepped into the hall looking around. There was no one there. He sprinted down the corner of the hall and hurried towards to the staircase. He flung the door open. Nothing! There was no one on the stairs.

He ran down the stairs to the lobby and headed for the front desk. Sergio, the young man on duty, offered a friendly smile. But when he saw Peter's face, the smile faded.

"Who the hell just left my room?" Peter barked angrily.

This was far from the Señor Brandt whom Sergio was used to dealing with.

"I have no idea señor," he sputtered. "I saw no one enter the hotel in the last hour and no one has used the stairs."

Sergio was doing his best to remain calm. His guest seemed to be overreacting, but it was his job to deal with such incidents.

"Are you quite sure señor that there was someone at your door?"

"Yes, I'm sure, damn it. They left me this." Peter held out the piece of paper for Sergio to see and it suddenly occurred to him that he should probably read it. He held the paper almost at arm's length to try to make out the scrawl, but it didn't work. He pulled it close to his eyes but still nothing.

"May I be of assistance señor?" ventured the young man.

"No damn it, you may not," Peter growled.

He held the paper underneath one of the desk lamps and just managed to decipher the scribble

The note read: *The Basilica. East portal. 10 o'clock. Be alone. Bring cash.*

Peter looked at his watch, spun on his heel and ran for the stairs. It was already past 9:30. He'd have to hurry.

A few minutes later, Peter was in the streets. The rain fell hard but Peter never noticed as he hurried through the darkness. It occurred to him that they hadn't given him much time. They must have known he was in his room. Apparently, he was being watched. He wondered how long they'd been watching him. He stopped and listened, his ears straining, searching the night air for the sound of footsteps behind him. There was no sound other than his heavy breathing. He took a long, deep breath and moved on. Seventeen minutes later, he was in St Mark's Square. He stood in the shadows and studied the façade of the ancient church directly across from him. He had no idea what to expect or who he was looking for. He glanced at his watch, but he couldn't see it. There was not enough light. He felt like he was about ten minutes early. He took another deep breath and started slowly towards the Basilica, staying in the shadows of the galleria rather than heading straight across the open square.

He reached the front doors and looked carefully around. There was nobody there. As a matter of fact, the square was devoid of humanity just as it had been the night before. He suddenly felt fear. He was really scared. It was an emotion he hadn't felt since the shock took hold. He'd been so angry, there hadn't been room for fear. Now, alone in the cold and dark, he felt more alone than ever before in his life. He shuddered.

The hand reached from the darkness like a claw and grasped his shoulder. Peter jumped a foot and almost screamed. He whimpered instead. He spun around and found himself face to face with a man. The man was somewhat smaller and younger than him. His black eyes glittered in a narrow compassionless face. He was dressed in pressed designer jeans and a red windbreaker. On his head was a Yankee's baseball cap of all things.

"Follow me," the man muttered thickly. He was no Yankee. He quickly walked into the darkness, without turning to see if Peter followed. A minute or two later, he ducked into a dark alley. The American was close behind.

"Where is she?" Peter demanded loudly.

The small man stopped and turned to him.

"In time," he muttered. The accent was Middle Eastern, Israeli maybe, or Lebanese. "First things first – what have you brought me?"

"All I could get my hands on," Peter replied breathlessly. "Nine thousand – some in cash, the rest in Traveler's Checks."

He pulled a folded envelope from his jacket pocket and thrust it towards the stranger.

The man took it, tore it open and briefly studied the contents. "Very good Mister Brandt," he whispered. "This is worth some information. Maybe two questions, eh? Yes, I think two questions."

"Wait a second," Peter felt the blood pounding in his temples, "I need to know, damn it. I brought enough for some real information. Where is my wife?" His fists were balled tight, his breath was racing.

"That will be question number one then Mister Brandt," the man replied softly. "Your beautiful wife is on board a vessel called the *Izmir.* She's somewhere in the Adriatic soon to be entering the Ionian Sea."

"Where is she being taken?" Peter blurted. "Who's got her?"

"Aah Mister Brandt," the man smirked, "that would be two additional questions, would it not? As I explained to you, I will answer two questions altogether and I will choose the next question. The *Izmir* is due to dock in Istanbul four days from now. Exactly were, I cannot be sure."

"Istanbul?" Peter was horrified, "Istanbul?"

He glared at the face before him. It took him a moment to find his voice. He swallowed, then said, "Tell me please, what the hell's going on here?" He heard himself whining, begging. He didn't care. "Who's got my wife?"

"I told you, no more questions. That's it." The man started to move past Peter to leave the alley.

Peter grabbed him roughly and spun him around. "Oh no you don't," he growled, "not until I've . . ."

The fist caught him right below the breastbone and he sank slowly to his knees, retching for breath and finding none.

He'd never in his life been in a real fight and the man he was facing had obviously been in more than a few. The toe of a black leather boot caught him flush on the side of his head and Peter slumped over onto his side. He lay in fetal position, gasping for life.

"I warned you." The smaller man spoke to him from very far away, although his face seemed very, very close.

"You're out of your element here Mister Hollywood Producer. You're overmatched. Go home and forget her if you can. There is nothing else for you to do. The police are useless, I promise you. There are forces at work here that have real power, too much power for you, Mister Brandt and if you bother them too much, you will die. They really don't care either way. And don't worry, she'll be treated like a goddess, like the true star that she is."

"How do you know all this?" Peter managed to whisper. "Who the hell are you?"

"More questions, Mister Brandt?" the man sneered. "That's not the deal, but I like you, so I will allow the question. I was driving the boat that collected your wife and delivered her to her destination."

And then just like that the man was gone. He was part of the darkness.

Peter Brandt lay huddled in the gutter for a long time. The rain fell softly now, and a few minutes later the tears joined in. They were hot and bitter and angry and afraid.

The next morning, Peter stood on the steps of the U.S. Consulate waiting for it to open. He'd placed one phone call home, to one very trusted friend. He knew that it was too soon to let the press get wind of this. He needed time and he needed help. Bob Rice was his oldest friend, his agent and sounding board whenever an opinion other than Nora's was called for.

Sure enough, they were expecting him at the Consulate. An eager young man by the name of Adam *something* quickly ushered him into a nice office where an older man looked up from behind a terribly cluttered desk. The man rose and extended his hand to Peter. The expression on his face said it all.

"I'm so sorry Mister Brandt," he muttered, "there isn't much to say really, is there?"

Peter shook his head and sat heavily in the nearest chair. He ignored the man's hand.

"The name's Welch," the man continued, "Ian Welch, Chief Attaché to the Consul General. The Consul is unfortunately on his way to Geneva today, but I've been instructed to provide you with any help you may require. This is a terrible thing that's happened Mister Brandt. Unfortunately, we're not very well set up to handle it."

"How do you mean?" Peter felt the anger again. He knew what was coming.

"Well, you see," the man was saying. He looked away from Peter's face and studied the wall. "This isn't New York or LA. These are not our police you understand. We haven't got much authority really. We're subject to someone else's priorities. At the same time, I realize that your wife is a rather famous person. In other circumstances I'm sure that fact would mean a lot and that the situation would merit special attention. Not here. Quite the contrary really – they want us to do things quietly. Any publicity about the situation right now, before we eh . . . really know what happened, whether there really is evidence of a crime here rather than just a simple, possibly temporary disappearance." The attaché took a breath.

"What the hell are you saying?" Peter was out of his chair, his hands grasping the edge of the desk.

"Please Mister Brandt," the man contended, "I'm on your side. Please understand that. We need the Venice police to help us, but it's got to be their way if you're ever going to see your wife again. She's high profile for them. The authorities here don't want this kind of publicity just as the tourist season is beginning. Do you understand? We need to play by their rules."

"Mister Welch," Peter said controlling his voice, "they have no intention of helping. They told me as much. They also told me that it's not the first time this has happened."

"Well yes and no," Welch responded. "There have been one or two other women, yes, but not like this. There was a model taken in Rome some time ago, but she was by no means as well known as your wife. At this point, we will need to proceed cautiously, Mister Brandt."

Two hours later, Peter was at the airport. He'd packed everything hurriedly and left Nora's bags with the Concierge who'd managed to acquire a ticket for Istanbul.

He'd been standing in line for twenty minutes and was getting frustrated. He didn't have much time to make the flight and the line was moving at a snail's pace. Finally, he reached the desk.

The woman behind it smiled, "Ticket please."

"It's here," said Peter. "I'm in the computer. Istanbul. 3 o'clock flight. Name's Brandt, Peter Brandt."

The woman smiled again and her fingers raced over the keys. "Aah yes here you are," she nodded. "May I see your passport Mister Brandt and your visa for entry into Turkey?"

"Visa?" he was dumbfounded. "What visa? No one said anything about a visa."

"Oh yes Mister Brandt I'm afraid that all foreign nationals require a visa for entry into Turkey. It's been this way for months now. I'm sorry, someone should have told you. I'm afraid that you'll have to go back to the city, to the Turkish Embassy to have your passport stamped."

"You've got to be kidding," he pleaded.

"I'm sorry sir. I don't know what else to tell you. Maybe I can book you on a flight for tomorrow. It only takes a few hours for the paperwork to go through."

"Yes, thank you," Peter mumbled and waited as patiently as he could until his reservation was set.

Peter sat alone in the stern of the water taxi. The city looked pale and lifeless across the gray water, far different from the last time he'd made the same trip. He'd decided to stay the night at the Danieli instead of Gritti Palace. There would be fewer questions. He needed to be somewhere where he was a stranger and could disappear. Maybe it was just as well he'd been turned back, he considered. Maybe it would be better if he had some kind of plan rather than rushing headlong into a perilous situation in a place he'd never been and people he knew nothing about.

He checked into the hotel, sent his luggage up to the room and headed for the bar. He stepped into the elegant room and looked around for a table. The place was busier than he'd expected. It was rather early in the day, but the room was more than half-full. He spotted a small table off by itself against the wall with only one chair. He made his way towards it. Just as he reached it, he was about to sit down when someone else slid into the seat before him. He almost found himself in the woman's lap.

"I'm so sorry," he blurted, "I didn't see you. Please. I'm sorry."

He turned and began to walk away.

"Please," said the voice, "you're welcome to join me. We're only sharing a table, nothing more. It's alright."

The woman laughed softly. "Although you do look like you've just lost your best friend," she continued, becoming serious. "Sit down. Have something to drink," she grinned. "You look like you could use one."

The woman was pretty, very pretty. She had glorious olive skin that looked like silk, and hair as black as could be. Peter thought he recognized the woman from somewhere, but he dismissed the thought. It was just too crazy.

The woman signaled for the waiter and asked for another chair. A minute later, the lad was back and Peter found himself sitting across from her. He wondered if he looked as shell-shocked as he felt. He felt numb really and he was finding it very difficult to gather his thoughts. No sooner would his mind light on something, something important, something he should be dealing with, when some other thought would invade, crashing into his consciousness only to be driven out by the next thought. His head was roaring and he couldn't stop it.

"Bring him a Bloody Mary," the woman commanded the young waiter, "make it very spicy and bring lemon not lime."

The woman said nothing as they sat waiting for his drink to arrive. The waiter reappeared shortly and with a dash of flourish, deposited a beautifully garnished Bloody Mary on the table before Peter.

"Drink," she smiled, and raised her glass to her lips.

Peter lifted the Bloody Mary and noticed that his hands were shaking. He reached with the other hand and managed to steady the glass and deliver it to his lips. He drank deeply and it took a moment for the shudder to come as the vodka and Tabasco sauce hit home. He blinked and it felt like he hadn't blinked in hours.

"What happened to you?" she was asking. "Are you okay really?"

Her accent was American, East Coast, Jersey maybe or Philadelphia. He wasn't sure, but he realized he should try to answer.

"Y . . . yes," he mumbled almost to himself. "I'm alright. I've got to be alright."

One hour and four drinks later, he'd told her the whole story. He'd needed to tell, to unburden himself, to anyone. He felt he was talking to someone who empathized, someone who cared.

"So, what are you going to do?" she asked calmly when he'd finished. "What can you do by yourself? You need help, you know that?"

Peter studied the young woman for a moment, leaned back in his chair and signaled to the waiter. He ordered yet another round of drinks. The woman firmly declined for the second time.

Half an hour later, she was helping a very drunk Peter Brandt to his room. The combination of the day's drama and lack of food had rendered him nearly senseless, not to mention the four and a half Bloody Marys.

He was vaguely aware of being placed on his bed, and of a soft voice speaking to someone on the telephone. She sounded like she was assuring someone about something. For some reason, he wondered if the assurance was about him, but the thought couldn't find focus. He took the aspirin the woman offered and collapsed onto his pillow. He didn't hear the door click shut as she left the room.

CHAPTER 5

The seas were rough, much rougher than the night before. The ship had rounded the tip of Pylos and was now battling the much heavier seas of the Mediterranean. She continued to move resolutely south-east heading for the Corinthian Canal, the shortest route to the Aegean Sea and Istanbul.

Nora had been fully awake for hours. She had no idea how long she'd slept but she'd begun to remember some things. It had taken her a few minutes to understand where she was, to realize that she was onboard a boat, a rather large boat. The way she got there though was hazy.

The last thing she could remember clearly was the shop and the dress she'd gone to try on, and Peter winking back at her as she'd left him. She'd found the dressing room and started to undress. Then there was a hand, a hand that smelled of garlic and limes. It was around her mouth and pinching her nostrils shut. She couldn't breathe. She was helpless as a baby.

She vaguely remembered being carried from the shop to the waiting motorboat where she was deposited rudely onto the floor and partially covered with the pretty dress.

Nora stared at the ceiling of her cabin and allowed her thoughts to ramble. Her first inclination had been to scream bloody murder but her stronger Nora prevailed. Why alert them that she was awake. Suddenly she remembered the dream, the dream in which someone, someone large and hairy had unlocked her cabin door and let himself in. She remembered his rough hands and the smell of him. He'd touched her, touched her all over. It became clearer now. She had been completely aware of what was happening to her. She could smell, she could hear but for some reason she couldn't get her body to move. She'd been unable to stop him. Had it happened more than once? She wasn't sure.

She then considered that it might have been a dream after all and decided that it must have been. She preferred it that way.

The ship was rolling strongly, and Nora wondered why she didn't feel sick. She'd never been much of a sailor. She rose from the bunk, crossed the cabin and pulled the curtain back from the porthole. Her eyes were just above the waterline. All she could see were gray swells and gray sky rushing past. She felt like she'd been buried up to her neck in a liquid grave. That did it. Suddenly, she did feel sick.

She made her way cautiously to the tiny bathroom, relieved herself and splashed cold water onto her face. She gazed into the filthy, cracked mirror, accepting that a cracked mirror was a sign of bad luck. She slowly shook her head. She had no idea about anything. All she knew was that the situation was not good. She thought of her poor husband and sighed deeply. *What must he be going through? Will they ever find me? Will I ever see him again*?"

She reached for a towel and patted her face dry. She knew she should be trying to formulate a plan. Hell, she'd done it often enough in movies. She turned away from the mirror and stumbled back towards the porthole. For a long moment she gazed out at the dreariness. There was no plan. She knew she was in big trouble. She began to cry.

CHAPTER 6

Peter packed quickly, checked out of the hotel and headed for the airport, visa now in hand. He knew what he had to do. Instead of waiting for his afternoon flight he'd decided to take his chances. Assuming there were regular flights into Istanbul, he was willing to go standby in order to get there as soon as possible. If Nora was being transported by sea and he was in Istanbul waiting, there was a chance, with the cooperation of the police, he might intercept the vessel and rescue his wife from the horror she'd been dragged into.

At the airport, there was good news and bad news. He managed to secure a standby ticket on the next Al Italia flight, but it wasn't due to depart Venice for another three hours. He pushed away the frustration and resentment, accepting that all he could do was wait. If Nora was on a boat like the man said, he had plenty of time. From what he'd been able to find out from the hotel manager, it would take days for a ship to reach the Sea of Marmara, the Marble Sea. Since terrorism had become woven into the fabric of Turkey, all ships were boarded by inspectors in the Marble Sea before being allowed to pass through the Bosporus Straits, the great passageway.

The three hours seemed like it took three days to pass, but mercifully there were enough cancellations to afford Peter a seat. So far, his luck was pretty good. Not only had he gotten a flight, but he was also seated in 1C in First Class. As the plane filled with passengers who represented just about every known nationality and body type, Peter barely noticed. He was busy running through his plan of attack once he reached his destination. The not too subtle cough roused him from his reverie, and he rose to allow his seatmate past. The man looked to be in his mid-thirties, had a swarthy complexion and a close-cropped beard. On his head he wore a Muslim skullcap. The man settled into his seat without a word and stared out the window at the flurry of baggage handlers who were busy loading the surrounding aircraft. Peter's immediate impression was that the man was nervous; very nervous. He alternated between rubbing his hands together and tapping his manicured fingers on the arm rest.

"Oh no," Peter muttered to himself, "don't tell me I'm sitting beside a damn hijacker. I'm not surprised. Life has certainly taken that turn." He stole a quick glance. It provided no reassurance. By now the man was sweating profusely. Peter tried to be rational. After all, the chances were one in at least a million and he refused to believe that his luck could really be this bad. It simply couldn't be. If the plane went down, he'd be unable to find Nora. She'd be left in the filthy hands of her captors. He did his best to dismiss his raging paranoia, but just then his neighbor launched into a prayer. The man began murmuring to himself in Arabic all the time rocking to and fro with his eyes tightly shut. This gave Peter the chance to steal another glance. It made him feel worse. He realized that the man perfectly fit the profile of an international terrorist. The words *shoe bomber* sprang to mind. He looked down at the man's feet and gasped. Although the man was well-dressed in a stylish Italian suit and a smart tie, his feet were adorned with Reebok sneakers that looked two sizes too big.

"My God," Peter whispered, "this is serious." He didn't know what to do. He was a stranger going to a strange land, facing problems that he could barely cope with. The last thing he wanted to do was raise the alarm and have the plane evacuated and the flight delayed. He determined though that he'd keep a close eye on his neighbor and if the guy went for his shoe, he'd be wearing Peter's right elbow between his ribs. In order to improve his plan, he signaled for the flight attendant and asked for a newspaper.

"Which would you like sir?" she asked in a heavy Italian accent, "English, Italian or Turkish?" she smiled demurely, indicating that she knew full well that he was an American and was probably a provincial monolingual.

"I really don't care," Peter snarled unaware he was being gruff.

"Yes sir," she replied testily, and disappeared into the adjacent galley. She returned with a day-old copy of the *Herald Tribune*. Peter snatched the paper from her and opened it wide. He placed the sheet strategically so that he could observe the movements of the suspected terrorist without being noticed. "Don't you dare," he mouthed silently.

As the plane taxied into position and the whine of the engines rose in pitch, the pace of his neighbor's genuflections increased, and the prayer sounded more and more frantic. By now the man was literally dripping great droplets of sweat onto his designer suit. What made the whole experience even more alarming was that during his prayer, the man repeatedly spat in his hands and wiped them on his face like a cat washing itself. It was getting to be too much. Peter dropped his newspaper, and tried to attract the attention of the flight attendant who was now strapped into her little jump seat, prepared for takeoff. She looked up and noticed Peter's gesticulations as he endeavored to draw her attention to the man on his right, tilting his head and using his eyes.

She glanced in the direction that Peter was indicating but her view of the window seat was blocked by the bulkhead wall. She smiled indulgently, as she would with a misbehaving child, ignored Peter's crazy behavior and returned her attention to the papers in her lap.

The plane lifted off the tarmac and climbed, roaring into the cloudless sky. For the next few minutes Peter continued observing his seatmate, while trying to slow his nervous breathing. Fortunately, the tuneless chant ended and the man leaned back in his seat, staring out the window at the beauty of Venice that was quickly disappearing from beneath them.

By the time the meal was served, Peter was almost calmed. He thought through his options and decided to take another tack. Maybe he should try to engage the man. If they were in conversation, it would be difficult for the bomber to execute his mission without being caught and beaten to a pulp.

Peter released his seat tray and waited patiently as the food was placed in front of him. He'd ordered the Chicken Parmesan as an entrée. His neighbor had opted for the fish.

Just great, Peter thought. As if things weren't bad enough, the smell of fish made him sick. *Although*, he considered, *maybe puking all over the guy would put a crimp in his plans.*

Trying to ignore the adjacent fish Peter took a bite of his chicken. It tasted like chicken. As he chewed thoughtfully, his thoughts were suddenly interrupted by the voice on his right.

"Tastes quite good, don't you think?"

Peter nearly choked. Trying to compose himself, he swallowed and turned to his neighbor. The man was smiling. "Well, yeah it is pretty good," he stammered, totally confounded.

"Are you heading for Istanbul," Peter asked, "or are you going on from there?"

"I'm staying in Istanbul," the man replied. "My family lives there. I'm an engineering professor at MIT and don't get to see my folks as often as I'd like to." The man spoke fluent English with just a trace of an accent.

Peter felt very foolish. He'd allowed his too fertile imagination to concoct a scenario that placed him smack dab in the middle of a terror plot and nothing could be further from the truth.

"I should probably explain what I was doing just before takeoff," the man was saying. "By the way my name is Demir Sorfo," he extended his hand, which Peter shook wholeheartedly.

"Peter Brandt," he responded.

"So let me explain," Demir continued. "First of all, I'm terrified of flying and I started to have a panic attack. That's why I was praying so fervently. But I'm a Shiite Moslem and we are forbidden to pray without first washing. Obviously, I couldn't go to the washroom during takeoff, so I did the best I could," he smiled sheepishly and returned his attention to his lunch.

Peter sat stunned, trying to digest Demir's explanation and was further confounded when his neighbor ordered a glass of wine to accompany his meal.

Noticing Peter's surprise, he took a long sip and placed his glass back on his tray. "I am Moslem, yes," he grinned, "but I'm no fanatic. I've lived in the States for fourteen years, so I'm half-American and I must confess I've picked up some bad habits. It's not something I intend to share with my family, however. They're a bit stricter than me."

By the time they were two hours into the flight, Peter had received an education in the fundamentals of Islam including the essential differences between the Shia and the Sunnis. Demir even told him a Muslim joke that he deemed was hilarious.

Peter laughed politely although he didn't get it. He found that his seatmate was a brilliant, kindly and sensitive man with a profound understanding of world politics. Peter was so comfortable that he felt compelled to tell Demir his story. The Turk listened without interruption as Peter explained the reason for his journey to Istanbul. Without a second thought, Demir offered any help he could provide and suggested a small hotel in the city center. He explained that the Gora Hotel would meet Peter's needs and place him in the heart of the community. The Hilton, he posited, would not provide any of the access Peter would require.

As they began their descent into the city, Demir insisted that they switch seats so that Peter could enjoy the view. It was certainly worth the move. Below, the ancient city of Constantinople, now Istanbul, stretched off into oblivion.

The sun was low in the sky and the sparkling waters of the Bosporus, that linked the Sea of Marmara with the Black Sea, were navy blue. Peter was gazing down at the crossroads of the world where Europe ended, and Asia began. He stared down at the gleaming palaces that lined the Straits on one side and the miles of concrete apartment blocks on the other, wondering which of these was to become Nora's prison. His musings were interrupted by Demir.

"Peter," he said, "I would very much like for you to come to my home, to meet my family. You must tell them your story. I don't pretend that there is much hope. As your people say, you're looking for a needle in a haystack. However, they might be able to set you on a path. My sister is a policewoman, and I'm sure she would be happy to provide whatever help she can. Should we say tomorrow evening? I'll be happy to come and collect you, otherwise, you'll never find our house."

Peter felt the tears welling up in his eyes and choked them back. The kindness that was being shown him stood in stark contrast to the suspicions he'd had about the man who had, within a few hours, become a true friend. Prejudice, he decided, is a deceptive and ugly beast.

At Demir's insistence, they shared a taxi into the city. As they crossed the gleaming Bosporus Bridge, the lights of the vast city began to come on. Within minutes, Istanbul was transformed into a blanket of jewels. In the distance, Peter could barely make out a cluster of mosques. The sun spread across the watery horizon and slipped from sight and at that moment, the calls to prayer began, floating on the evening breeze across the city's roofs from a hundred minarets. Peter was disappointed when Demir informed him that the muezzin no longer climbed to the tops of the minarets. Nowadays, they used microphones and loudspeakers instead.

The myriad smells that wafted into the cab were like magic. They were the exotic, spicy aromas of the ancient East. Once again, the tears threatened. He couldn't help imagining how heady the experience would be under different circumstances; with Nora snuggled close beside him.

They left the main thoroughfare and descended into a world that Peter could never have imagined. Narrow, twisted streets thronged with people bedecked in every conceivable form of dress. There were men dressed in Western-style suits with fezzes on their heads mingling with Arabs and Africans who wore flowing robes featuring all the hues of the rainbow. The color and vibrancy stood in stark contrast to the small clusters of women dressed in black burkas, hidden from the world behind their veils.

Spice and rug merchants cluttered the sidewalks forcing pedestrians onto the street to compete with automobiles, scooters, bicycles and donkey carts for space. On every corner, braziers sent plumes of smoke and the enticing aroma of roasting meat into the night air.

Peter had always prided himself in having an uncanny sense of direction, but he quickly recognized that his talent would stand no chance in this warren of activity.

They pulled up in front of a small, nondescript five-story building and Demir climbed out of the car, headed back to the taxi's trunk, hefted out Peter's bags and lugged them into the hotel. Peter took the opportunity to try and pay the cab driver, but the man would have none of it. Through some well-developed sign language, the driver managed to impart that Demir had already taken care of the fare. Peter pocketed his money and made his way into the hotel. He noticed that the Gora stood in the shadow of a small mosque, complete with four minarets.

At the reception desk, Demir was busy arranging a room. As Peter approached, his new friend turned and smiled. "All is set," he nodded enthusiastically, "you are a guest in my house now and you are my responsibility. It is a part of our teachings that we do not always adhere to as well as we should. This is a good place. You'll be well taken care of here. I have had a word with them. And let me add, you won't need a wake-up call. The morning prayers will make sure you don't oversleep."

He smiled and reached out his hand, which Peter shook with great gratitude. "I'll call for you at six tomorrow evening and it is probably best if you rest during the heat of the day. I can see that you're already very tired and with all you have to deal with, you're going to need all the strength you have."

With that, he bowed nominally, turned on his heel and headed for the door. As he walked away, Peter stood watching him. He felt alone again but not quite as much. He was grateful, grateful for hope and for his new friend.

He was shown to his room by a young boy who spoke passable English. The room was small but comfortable with a shower and almost as importantly, air conditioning. He unpacked in less than five minutes, stretched out on the bed and flicked on the television. After scrolling through the channels, he was disappointed to discover that there was no English programming, although four channels were devoted to belly dancing. He considered getting under the sheets and praying for sleep, but his mind was in an uproar. He was a lone traveller on a mission that seemed very unlikely, and sleep was not going to happen.

He felt another pang but this time, thankfully, it was one he could affect. His stomach was rumbling. He was starving. Recalling the enticing smells from the street corners, he decided he had to get something to eat. He put on his shoes, grabbed a windbreaker and left the room. Although he was on the fourth floor, he'd found the elevator far too claustrophobic on the way up and opted for the stairs.

He stepped out of the hotel and discovered that the air was still warm. He looked up and down the street, made a decision and turned right, heading for the sound of music coming from a brightly lit square. When he reached the square, he saw that it was teeming with humanity. All sorts of people were milling around, laughing and talking. Some danced to the music provided by a three-piece band that was playing a collection of instruments he didn't recognize. The sidewalk cafés were jammed with customers sipping coffee and people watching.

He made his way to a corner where a hollow-cheeked man tended a brazier that was emitting the most delectable smells. He joined a queue of people and when it was his turn, ordered what the couple ahead of him had chosen. He watched, salivating as the proprietor shoveled small chunks of meat into a piece of pita bread and topped it with diced onions and some dark seeds that looked like pomegranate.

The food was all that the smell had promised. The meat, though a bit tough was moist and flavorful; exactly what he'd been craving. As he savored his delicious meal, he strolled around the square, surveying the abundance of merchandise. He was reminded of a summer night at the county fair in his hometown in Ohio. Time passed quickly and before he knew it, he'd left the bright lights and was wandering a darker street where the shops featured hookahs and brass trinkets, cheap rugs and knockoff watches. He stopped to look at some authentic looking Rolexes and suddenly had the feeling he was being followed. He looked over his shoulder and caught sight of two men shrinking back into the shadows. He had spotted the pair earlier in the square as he'd waited in line for his sandwich. He had the same feeling then that they were watching him but he'd immediately dismissed his suspicions. How could anyone know about him or his presence in Istanbul? He figured they were simply curious.

One of the men was tallish and knife thin. The other was shorter but looked well-muscled like a fighter. He wore a white golf shirt that bulged in all the right places. The tall one wore a sports jacket and jeans and a Chicago Cubs baseball cap. It was the hat that Peter had registered in the first place, because he'd been a Cubs fan all his life and empathized with other loser baseball fans.

He moved quickly down the street, turned a corner and entered an even darker byway that had no shops and was almost deserted. As he walked, he repeatedly glanced over his shoulder, but the men didn't re-appear. Although he was a bit unnerved at the prospect of being followed, if it was that, he realized that being tailed was a positive development. If they were following him, he might be able to turn the tables; and use the situation as an opportunity. If the men had been assigned to surveil him, that meant they were reporting to someone who knew Nora's whereabouts.

His mind was churning with possibilities. He glanced back again – nothing. Damn! Maybe he was just being paranoid. Maybe he wasn't being followed at all. Maybe he was just losing his mind. Peter then realized he was lost; decidedly, completely, dangerously lost. The only thing familiar was the arrival of the cats.

CHAPTER 7

Nora was completely lost. For three days she'd tried to determine where the ship was heading. By tracing the arc of the sun, she'd determined that they had sailed south for two days before changing course and heading east. She'd always been pretty good at geography, so she was sure they'd navigated the Adriatic and Ionian Seas and had entered the Mediterranean. Maybe the Greek Islands was the intended destination, maybe Cyprus or Lebanon. She guessed they were travelling at about 12 knots. If she'd figured correctly, the distance they covered would be somewhere between 600 and 700 miles in the three days they'd been at sea. Not exactly a speedboat.

Since she'd been aboard ship, she had not set foot outside her cabin. She'd managed to open the porthole when the sea was calm and was grateful for the relief from the stink of diesel fumes. She had not sighted land, so she knew they were sailing in international waters, far from any country's patrol boats.

Now, halfway through the afternoon of the third day at sea, she'd completely lost her bearings. They'd been enveloped in a thick fog for hours and although she'd felt the ship change course, she had no idea which direction it had taken.

She heard the key being inserted and within seconds, the cabin door swung open. The same man she'd seen on previous occasions entered the room and set a tray of food on her bedside table. He stood for a moment and stared down at her and for some stupid reason it occurred to her that she looked like hell. Why it should matter was a bit troubling, but her appearance was important to her. Hell, it was part of the job. Her purse had disappeared, so she had no makeup handy. She figured she'd just have to make the best of it.

"So, the fog's pretty thick, huh," she attempted, "I sure hope we don't run aground. Might throw a wrench into your plan, don't you think?"

The man didn't react. Apparently, he didn't understand a word she'd said. He looked like he hadn't shaved for days and his black hair was stiff with grease. His jeans were filthy and the coarse woven shirt he wore was covered with stains. She decided that there was no need to worry about her appearance.

For the first time since the voyage started, she was hungry. She'd been terribly seasick the first two days and hadn't had an appetite at all. She looked at the food and failed to recognize what it was. It didn't smell too bad, so she took the tray into her lap, ignoring the presence of her warden and spooned some of the gruel into her mouth. It was actually edible, lentils in some kind of thin broth. She grabbed the hunk of dry bread, tore off a piece and dipped it into the bowl. The resulting morsel was quite good, or more likely she was starving. A few minutes later, she'd cleaned her dish. She took a long swallow of the water, trying to ignore the smears on the glass and handed the tray to the man.

"Thanks Omar," she muttered, "I must come back here again sometime soon. And may I say the service was nearly as good as the feast."

"My name is Salim," the man growled. He took the tray and hurried from the cabin. Nora listened as the key was reinserted and the door locked.

As she lay back down, trying to get a handle on what was happening, her thoughts turned to Peter. She couldn't imagine what he must be going through. One minute they were happily window-shopping on a busy street in Venice. The next, she was snatched from the dressing room of an elegant boutique and deposited in a stinking cabin aboard a tramp steamer bound for God knows where.

Knowing Peter, she could imagine him haranguing the Venice police, applying all the pressure he could bring to bear. And she knew in her heart, it was probably all for naught. She was now hundreds of miles from Venice, out of Italian waters, far from the reach of the Carabinieri. She wanted to cry, but for some reason the tears wouldn't come. She suspected she was dehydrated. God knows she'd puked a good amount of fluid into the filthy toilet during the first couple of days.

Abduction was something that she and Peter had discussed on several occasions. Although they didn't really believe it was a realistic concern, they'd talked about it more than once, particularly when they were far from the safety of their walled and wired Beverly Hills estate.

Her guess was that snatching her had not been a random act. She suspected that she'd been specifically chosen and tried to think back to any recent encounters that might have led to her present predicament. No matter how hard she tried, nothing came to mind. Then suddenly she recalled an incident that at the time seemed trivial, but now it took on a much more sinister implication.

A year ago, she and Peter had attended an industry party in LA where a wealthy Arab, who'd bankrolled several successful movies, had been a bit forward with her. Peter, as always, had rescued her from the man's unwelcome attentions and until now she hadn't given the encounter a second thought. Now she wasn't so sure. She knew she couldn't rule out any possibility and felt that the more she could construct about her abduction, the more prepared she'd be when she reached her destination. She tried to picture the man's face, but it wouldn't quite come into focus. She hadn't actually paid that close attention. She'd been more intent on searching over his shoulder for a glimpse of her husband.

She did remember that he'd worn a garish blue ring and that his breath smelled of cloves. And his eyes, aah yes, his eyes, they had been very bloodshot, so much so that the edges of his pupils looked ragged and more tan-colored than brown. She recalled that his skin was badly pockmarked, and his goatee was thick, coarse and black as the Steinway he had her pinned against.

When Peter had appeared on the scene and extricated her from the situation, she'd glanced back to see the man scowling at her with something like venom in his dark eyes. At the time, she'd felt a shiver of fear and she'd completely forgotten about the unsettling incident until this moment.

She tried to remember the man's name, but it didn't come to her. He'd told her where he was from, but she'd forgotten that too. Nora was generally proud of her powers of recall. Years of memorizing scripts had left her with a keen ability to remember names and details. She continued to rack her brain, trying to rouse any other recollections with no luck.

She awoke to the flat light of early morning and was immediately aware that the weather had changed. The ship was pitching and rolling dramatically and occasionally the waves splashed hard against the glass of the porthole. Surprisingly, her stomach was unaffected, and she figured that she'd probably found her sea legs. She rose, swaying from her bunk, crossed to the little window and stared at the angry whitecaps that went on forever. The sun was still low in the sky off the starboard side, so she determined that they were steaming north-east. Her memory failed her again. She couldn't determine what countries lay in that direction. She thought that Israel was out there somewhere but had a feeling the Holy Land was not where they were headed.

She heard the key scraping in the lock and returned quickly to her bunk, drawing up her one blanket around her. She wanted to provide no display whatsoever. This time a different man entered. He wore a shabby khaki uniform complete with a faded, gold-braided cap. The man was so tall that he had to stoop to avoid scraping his head on the low ceiling.

"I am Musa Arim, the captain of this ship," he announced in halting English. "I've come to inform you that our voyage is almost completed." He placed a cup of steaming black coffee and a bowl of something white on her bedside table, took an item from beneath his arm and tossed it on the bed and took a seat on the cabin's only chair. "We will make port sometime in the middle of the night and tomorrow morning, you'll be transported from the ship to your destination. Now, you have three options as to how the rest of your journey will proceed. Number one, to eliminate any possibility of unpleasantness, I can drug you as before. That will be easiest for me but not so comfortable for you. You remember how sick you felt last time when you awakened. Number two, I can bind you tightly and wrap you in sailcloth. You'll be handled like cargo, also uncomfortable. Thirdly, and I think this is your best option, you can promise to remain peaceable and make no effort to either escape or draw unwanted attention. I'll leave you to consider the options. Please have your decision by the time I return. I will personally deliver your evening meal at sunset and expect an answer at that time."

He rose and crossed the cabin floor giving no indication whatsoever that his ship was bucking like a mechanical bull. He paused at the door and turned back. "You might want to put on the shirt," he indicated the clothing he'd tossed on her bunk. "A bit more practical than that lovely dress you have on." With that he left the cabin and locked the door behind him.

When he was gone, Nora reached for her half-empty mug and took a sip. The coffee was thick and dark and quite delicious. When she'd drunk it all, she inspected the contents of the bowl and discovered that it was yoghurt. She liked yoghurt and had a bit of an appetite in spite of the constant motion. She ate it all and lay back to consider what, if anything, she'd learned. She carefully listed the information she'd been given. She was a good listener after years of practice and went about piecing together the facts. If they were to dock during the night and were heading north-east, they could be headed either for Bulgaria or Turkey or maybe one of the Aegean Islands in between. If they were to reach land in the middle of the night that meant that there were about 300 miles left to travel. She settled on Turkey, probably Istanbul or one of the resort towns further south. The irony did not escape her. She'd never been to Istanbul, and it was a place she and Peter had often talked of visiting. This, however, was a far cry from the arrival she'd dreamed of. She knew she looked like hell. She hadn't showered in days and had been brushing her teeth with her finger and the salt she'd purloined from her dinner tray. The only clothes she possessed were her Versace jeans and the dress she been trying on over them when she'd been abducted. After five days of wear in the foul-smelling cabin, the dress was no longer the stylish number she'd fancied in Venice. Rationally, she knew that her appearance was not an issue, but it was something she always considered. It was part of being an actress and someone who was constantly in the public eye. She decided that the denim shirt was the better choice.

The other decision was easy. Of course, she'd promise to behave, and then look for any opportunity to bolt. Her captors were ruthless but she'd most likely been bought by someone powerful, someone the captain would fear. There was no way he'd be allowed to kill her or hurt her badly. She was resourceful and knew she'd find a way out of this mess.

The day passed slowly and by mid-afternoon the waves had calmed. They'd entered a more protected sea and the surly Mediterranean had been left in their wake. As the sun fell, her door opened, and the captain bowed his head to enter the cabin. He put down a tray, which contained an unappetizing-looking sandwich and the now familiar grimy glass of water. "Have you reached a decision?" he asked without sitting down.

"Yes," she replied scornfully, "much as I hate to accommodate you. I'll take option three."

"This is a good decision. And I'm confident you'll keep your word. You see, if you decide at any time to raise the alarm or endeavor to escape . . ." He paused to remove a wicked-looking knife from a leather sheath on his belt. "I will slice open both sides of your face. As a result, you will no longer be of any worth to the man who is so desirous of you. You may, however, still have some value on the darker streets of our city."

CHAPTER 8

Peter hurried through the shadows, grateful that the moon had made an appearance. The sheer darkness had lifted, allowing him to see something of the street ahead of him. Although it was lined with buildings that looked like houses, there was not a light in any of them. He rounded a corner and as he did, he saw a figure a half-block away slip into a doorway in an effort to conceal himself. Peter's heart, which was already racing, thumped even faster. He stopped in his tracks, unsure of what to do. Should he turn back, or were his watchers still behind him? The other possibility was that they'd split up and he was now trapped between them.

Just then, he spotted a dark alley a few feet away and considered ducking into it, hoping that it wasn't a dead-end. The gunshot and the sound of a bullet zipping over his head helped make up his mind. He bounded into the alley, in full knowledge that the men's evil intentions were not just a figment of his imagination. Behind him, he could hear footsteps running hard. There were definitely two sets.

As he ran, the alley became even narrower until, he could reach out and touch the walls on either side. Then his worst fear appeared in front of him. He'd reached the end of the road. Before him was a blank wall, too high to scale. "Damn," he whispered, "now what?"

He realized he had no choice but to try and get over it. He leapt as high as he could, but still couldn't reach the top of the wall. To confound the problem, it was made of some smooth stone that provided no purchase and the footsteps were getting closer. He backed up a few paces, took a deep breath and launched himself at the wall, praying that some superhuman, adrenalin-induced power would propel him high enough to reach the top. No such luck. But as he collided hard with the obstacle, a small portion of it seemed to give way.

"My God," he murmured, "thank you." On closer inspection, he saw that it was a small doorway that had ruptured from his 200-pound onslaught. He shoved the door open and bolted through, praying that he'd found an escape. He was in a small, walled courtyard, on the far side of which was another door. He sprinted toward it, paused and booted the door with all his might. The old wood splintered into a dozen pieces and Peter stepped through into a street with both pedestrians and vehicle traffic. As he appeared seemingly from nowhere, people scattered in all directions as if fleeing a bomb. He turned right and barreled on without looking back. People quickly moved out of his way like he was a madman.

Two blocks later, he slowed, gasping for air and chanced a look behind him. Small clutches of people eyed him suspiciously, but he saw no evidence of the hounds. He made a quick right onto an even busier thoroughfare and managed to flag down a taxi. As he gratefully collapsed into the backseat, he turned and looked out the back window and watched as the two men emerged from the crowd, the Cubs baseball cap shining like a beacon.

The men raced after the cab but were seconds too late. The driver pulled away from the curb, apparently unaware of the drama unfolding behind him as the chasers tried to commandeer another taxi. Within seconds, Peter's cab had merged into a stream of identical blue and white Fiats and Peter knew he'd escaped – for now.

"Hotel Gora," he said.

The cab driver peered at his strange passenger in the rearview mirror, grunted his acknowledgement and proceeded to light a foul-smelling cigarette.

To Peter, nothing had ever smelled so sweet. He was tempted to ask for one but decided that his life was already getting too short.

Ten minutes later, having successfully negotiated the clogs of traffic, the cab pulled to a stop in front of the hotel. Peter handed the driver a fifty-lira note, which he pocketed without a word or any offer of change. He waited impatiently as Peter hauled himself out of the backseat and stumbled to the hotel entrance. Peter's legs were still shaking so he opted for the cramped elevator and held his breath as it creaked slowly upwards.

His room felt secure as a palace. He took off his shoes, collapsed on the bed, and carefully relived the events of the last hour. There was no doubt, his presence in Istanbul was unwelcome and the forces he was up against were much tougher than him. He wondered if they knew where he was staying and prayed they didn't. They had obviously followed him from somewhere. He considered the possibility that his new friend Demir had sold him out but decided that if that was the case, his usually reliable judgement of character had been completely faked out.

He awoke with a start, convinced that the hounds had found him, broken into his room and now stood over his bed screaming at him. It took him a second to realize that the terrible squawking was the sound of the muezzins screaming the call to morning prayers. The sky was just beginning to lighten. He peered at his watch. It was only six-twenty. It was going to be a long day. The events of the previous evening came flooding back. He wondered if the chase had really happened or if it had been a dream. His throbbing legs provided the answer. It had been years since he'd run that hard; or run at all for that matter.

He rose from the bed and headed for the bathroom making sure to avoid the mirror. He returned to the bed, lifted the telephone receiver and ordered coffee and a sweet roll. He clicked on the television and scrolled through the channels hoping for any piece of English programming. Much to his relief there was a *BBC News* broadcast, and it was in English. He wondered if there would be any mention of Nora's abduction but there was none. Instead, the news segment focused on the evils of America and its imperialist foreign policy. The program ended with a piece on the inhumanity of fox hunting before the channel reverted to the ubiquitous belly dancing. Fortunately, the sweating bellies were interrupted by a knock on the door. Peter's heart leapt into his throat then he remembered. He grabbed the robe from the closet and squinted through the peephole. He was relieved to see a friendly looking young man holding a breakfast tray aloft. He grinned at his stupid paranoia. As the boy placed the tray on the desk beneath the window, realizing he couldn't remain locked up in his room; Peter asked where he could do some sightseeing.

"Well," the boy replied in English, "this is Tuesday and the Topkapi Palace shouldn't be too busy if you get there before the bus tours arrive. It's no more than a fifteen-minute walk and it's a truly magnificent complex. If you decide to go, be sure not to miss the Harem. It's a most interesting look into our past." The boy smiled broadly, "You see, we're no longer allowed to imprison our women here in Turkey, even if they do deserve it."

The irony of the statement was not lost on Peter. Feeling a sudden wave of helplessness, Peter tipped the lad and showed him out. He crossed to the desk, poured his coffee and sat staring at the ship traffic plying the Bosporus. He couldn't help wondering if his wife was imprisoned on one of the passing vessels. He munched on the sweet roll, although he was not at all hungry. As he watched the busy waterway, he was reminded of Fifth Avenue in New York. The traffic was almost as bad except that the yellow cabs here were ferries and gaudily painted sailboats, gleaming yachts and small steamers. The boats wove among each other with no apparent rhyme or rhythm or collisions. Peter did, however, witness half a dozen near misses.

The sun was now well up and the straits sparkled in the bright light of summer. Much as he would have loved to crawl back into bed and pull the covers over his head, he had to get out; to get a feel for the city; a city that would soon be concealing his wife. He grabbed a pair of clean jeans from his suitcase, pulled them on and laced up his sneakers, trying to ignore the throbbing in his legs.

Peter descended the stairs to the ground floor and crossed the lobby to the front door. As he prepared to step outside, it occurred to him that the hounds might be watching, and he decided to alter his plans. He re-crossed the lobby and proceeded down a hallway to the left of the reception desk. At the end of the hall, he found a door, pushed it open a crack and peered through. He was looking out onto a quiet street and there was not one person in sight. He took a deep breath and stepped out into the brilliant sunshine, surprised by the warmth of the early morning.

As he walked, he glanced repeatedly over his shoulder and was relieved to discover that he was not being followed. He rounded a corner, making for the main street that would convey him to the Topkapi and stopped in front of a shop window that was crammed with brass cymbals of all sizes; something he had never seen before.

When no reflection appeared in the window, he continued on, walking as quickly as he could, waiting for the stiffness to leave his legs. By the time he reached the museum, the throb had subsided. He entered the Imperial Gate and joined a short line at the ticket booth. Ticket in hand, he strolled into the second courtyard and immediately felt like he'd been transported to the time of Suleiman the Magnificent. He was surrounded by opulence the likes of which he'd never seen. Even the capitals of Europe paled in comparison to the splendid beauty of this palace. Roses and shade trees added a sweet smell to the air, which was so still that not a leaf moved. He felt like he was the only thing moving in a still life painting. After touring the royal kitchens and the Chinese porcelain exhibit, he joined a guided tour preparing to enter the Harem.

For some reason, he felt compelled to see the place where a hundred women at a time were imprisoned.

The Harem was a maze of rooms and terraces and small cubicles, which the guide explained were the rooms for the concubines. They were small and sparse, and stood in stark contrast to the opulence of the palace itself. Peter was struck by the number of fountains that adorned the place and remarked on their proliferation to the guide.

The man smiled and nodded. "Oh yes," he said, "there are countless fountains in the Harem's 400 rooms. The sound of water, you see, made eavesdropping very difficult. Their presence cut down on palace intrigue. Most ingenious, don't you think?"

When he'd completed the Harem tour, Peter stepped back into the sunshine and became aware of a delightful aroma and followed his nose to a terrace restaurant that had a fabulous view of Old Istanbul and the Golden Horn beyond. He was led to a shaded table and was relieved to find that the proffered menu was in English.

He ordered a dish called *Adana Kebab* which was described as spicy lamb patties on a bed of rice with roasted eggplant. The dish sounded truly delicious and as he sat waiting, sipping on his iced tea, he began to salivate in anticipation.

He and Nora had always loved people watching but this parade of humanity was beyond description. He was particularly intrigued by a small group of women seated in a circle on a nearby patch of grass. All of them were covered from head to toe in traditional black robes and veils, but he could tell by their body language that they were young, probably teenagers. What he found surprising though was that at least half of them were smoking. It was comical to watch as they inserted the cigarettes up under their veils from which billows of smoke would rise into the air as if the girls were sending smoke signals. The visual was so entertaining he determined to use it in a movie.

As his eyes flicked back and forth absorbing the endless medley of tourists, he became aware of her. He had noticed her before, but he'd paid her no attention. This time though, his eyes lingered. From a distance, she looked young and very pretty, with long black hair gathered into a loose ponytail. She sat on the edge of an elaborate fountain, with her legs crossed and she seemed to be watching him. He turned to see if she was focused on someone sitting behind him but there was no one else there. Although there were no real physical similarities, for some reason the girl reminded him of a younger Nora, but as he continued to study her from behind his sunglasses, the resemblance melted away. A sudden wave of sadness welled up and reality hit him like a brick. He was compelled to look away. Fortunately, his food arrived and he was able to concentrate on something else. As he ate, he continued to steal glances and was surprised to see that the girl remained in place, watching him.

Feeling very satisfied, he paid the check with a credit card. As he left the restaurant, he noticed that the girl was still there. His curiosity was now piqued and he wandered in her direction, eager to get a closer look. For a minute or two she remained seated but when he was halfway to her, she stood up and hurried away. A second later, she'd melted into a guided tour, and he lost sight of her. Feeling strangely disappointed, he stopped and waited, hoping that she'd reappear. Much to his amazement, she did just that. She emerged from the throng, walking quickly away in the direction of the main gate. Without a second thought, he took off after her. As he fell in behind her, he saw her glance back. He quickly ducked behind an extremely corpulent man wearing a multi-colored kaftan; pretty sure he hadn't been spotted. For some reason, though, she picked up her pace. Peter did too and soon the distance between them closed.

The girl looked back again but gave no indication that she'd seen him. He saw her disappear around a corner and he walked even faster, now determined not to let her escape. He had no idea what he was doing or what he'd say if he did manage to catch up to her, but now, in the heat of the chase, he was beyond any rational thought. "What the hell is she up to?" he muttered. He wondered why she had been spying on him. And even more importantly, was she working with the other two who had so far not appeared?

He reached the corner, slowed to a stop, and carefully peeked around. She was gone –she'd disappeared. He was in a small courtyard featuring flowerbeds, stone benches and several more fountains splashing in chorus, but there was not a single person. He crossed the tranquil little square, looking behind every bush and water feature but the girl was not there. Disappointed, he continued out of the courtyard and made for the Imperial Gate. He'd seen all he wanted to and decided to head back to the hotel. He was to meet with Demir that evening and thought that a nap might serve him well. After all, he'd been up since six or so, from the moment the muezzins had so rudely invaded his sleep.

As he entered the hotel, something made him look back. He would have sworn he caught a flash of long dark hair pulling back into the shadows. He considered giving chase again but dismissed the idea. He had no chance of catching the girl if she didn't want to be caught.

CHAPTER 9

Nora heard the whine of the turbines subside. There was light in the sky but from her porthole there was no sign of land, and she knew they hadn't docked. She listened to the clatter of the heavy chain as the anchor was lowered and a minute later, she was enveloped in silence. She hadn't realized how noisy the ship was during the days at sea. The quiet was a welcome relief. She felt the ship swing into the wind, tugging on its bonds as it tried to break free.

She was then surprised to see that they were not alone. A dozen other ships, mostly tramp steamers, except for one large oil tanker, were anchored at various distances from them. Beyond the ships was land, dry land, land completely blanketed with buildings of all descriptions. Sprawled out before her, a sea of apartment blocks stretched up and over the hills. Closer to the shore dozens of modern glass skyscrapers rose from among the countless rows of shabby houses. In the murky distance sat a hulking mosque flanked by four towering minarets. "Istanbul," she breathed, pleased that her calculations had proved right. She hurriedly cranked open her little window and was immediately assaulted by the clamor and pervasive reek of the city.

She felt a flutter of excitement, aware that her terrible adventure was about to move to a different stage. A part of her wondered how much worse things could get after the days of solitary confinement in her tiny cell.

By the time the key finally scraped in the lock, she was ready. The door swung open to admit the captain, who'd shaved and was now dressed in a worn blue serge suit, an almost white shirt and a poorly knotted tie. Behind him was the fat pig who had played the role of jailer for her first three days at sea. He looked like he'd also tried to clean up a bit but from the smell of him, a shower had not been part of the process. He now sported wrinkled khakis, a different pair of dirty sneakers and a lime green Polo shirt, which was stretched to the limit across his belly.

"Sometime in the next hour," the captain announced, "a tender will arrive to transport you to your next stop. The two of us will accompany you, and please remember your assurances. Any attempt to disrupt our journey will be met with severe consequences, as I have already warned you. You will cover yourself with this." He tossed a shapeless black garment onto the bed and left the room with his henchman close behind.

Nora lifted the black robe, shook it out and recognized it immediately. It was an abaya or a burka. She wasn't exactly sure, but she knew she wasn't going to like it whatever it was called. She knew it would cover her completely, even her face, but as if that wasn't enough, it stank of sweat.

She sat down on the edge of the bunk and dropped her head into her hands. Although things were looking bleak, she refused to cry. There would be plenty of time for tears later. Her new wardrobe, she realized, would certainly limit any opportunity to bolt and she knew that if she tried and failed, the captain would carry out his threat. She had assumed the man would be loath to risk the wrath of the buyer, but having listened to him lay out the threat, she wasn't sure. The thought of being a disfigured American woman cast out on the streets of Istanbul was something she didn't want to contemplate. She'd have to wait for another opportunity.

The bumping of a vessel against the side of the ship roused her from her reflection. She sighed and rose bravely to her feet. It was time. Scrunching her nose against the smell, she pulled the burka over her head. As expected, reached right to the ground. She adjusted the headgear until she could peer through the tiny holes that allowed her to see the cabin in fragments and was almost overcome by the sensation. Never had she experienced anything so dehumanizing. She felt like she'd been dropped into a deep dark well.

Gasping for breath she ripped the head cover away and flung it across the cabin. It struck the wall and slid to the floor where it lay still, like a dying bird. She fell to her knees and this time she couldn't stop the tears. "Oh God," she sobbed, "I can't do this."

By the time her door opened again, she'd changed her mind. God had helped. Hell, Muslim women had worn the dreadful things for a thousand years. And nuns, nuns had been bound in black for centuries and somehow managed to survive. They hadn't had their faces covered of course, but still. She took a deep breath and felt better. She was an actress. She knew she could do this.

The captain stepped into the cabin. He was tight-lipped and appeared nervous. "The head cover," he ordered, "put it on, now. It's time to go."

She picked up the head cover, resolutely pulled it over her head and immediately the world closed in around her. The panic descended like a fever. First, she started trembling. Next the sweat broke and she had a sudden, clear understanding of why the thing smelled so foul.

She didn't remember the screaming, or the prick in her arm as the needle was inserted.

She awoke to a sound she didn't recognize, although the stink of her clothes had been overpowered by another, more animal smell. Horses! She smelled horses. And the sound, she knew what it was. She was listening to the rhythmic clip-clop of hooves on pavement. For one feverish moment, she decided she'd been transported back into a movie she'd shot years before in London. It was a period film, a remake of Jekyll and Hyde and featured lots of clip-clopping.

She opened her eyes and was relieved to discover that her veil had been removed. She was reclining across the backbench of a small carriage, which had a fringe on top. Oklahoma, she decided. She'd been wrong about Jekyll and Hyde. Suddenly, the horse farted loudly, and she was wide-awake, gasping for breath. This was reality. As if a trumpet had announced their arrival, the carriage slowed to a stop. Nora sat up and looked around. Captain Arim eyed her carefully ready to grab her should she make any effort to escape. His fat ugly pal was seated up beside the driver. He was staring down at her like he was willing her to bolt which would provide him another opportunity to get his hands on her.

They'd stopped on a leafy lane in front of a huge shingle house that had been painted a soft yellow. All of the surrounding houses were similar in size, all Victorian, boasting large, shaded porches and gabled roofs. The homes were painted in a variety of pastel hues, from pale blues and greens to rose pink. Most featured filigree and dormer windows.

Nora decided that she must have been mistaken. This bucolic scene couldn't possibly be part of Istanbul. The posh neighborhood was more like a wealthy suburb you'd expect to find in Connecticut or the Carolinas.

Without a word, the captain stepped down from the carriage and reached for Nora. He pulled her towards him, and she struggled to her feet surprised at how lightheaded she felt. As she reached the little step, the horse took a step forward, which resulted in Nora falling into the captain's arms. As he held her close, he leered down at her and she recoiled, revolted both by his closeness and the stench of yesterday's beer on his breath.

He took her by the arm. He wasn't exactly rough, but his grip was determined. He led her up a brick path to the front door of the house and rang the bell.

"Where am I?" Nora murmured. "What are you doing with me?"

She got no response.

The door swung open, and a middle-aged black man dressed in white livery gestured them inside. Instead of entering the house, the captain shoved Nora in the direction of the black man, spun on his heel and hurried back down the path as quickly as his long legs could carry him. Nora reeled and nearly fainted. If the houseman hadn't managed to grab her, she'd have hit the floor.

A woman, also dressed in white appeared from a room off the foyer and crossed to Nora and the obviously flustered man. She put her arm around Nora's waist and steered her towards a sweeping staircase. The woman who smelled vaguely like medicine was also dark skinned, but it was Nora's opinion that she was Arabic. The woman had short-cropped hair and white shoes and the demeanor of a nurse.

The house was cool and airy and as Nora did her best to climb the carpeted stairs, she couldn't help but notice the rich furnishings and wall hangings. She wondered if this elegant home was to be her new prison and if she was about to meet her abductor.

She was led down a long, wide hallway to a doorway at the far end. The woman continued to hold onto Nora as she pushed open the door. Unlike the rest of the house, the room was sparsely furnished; more utilitarian than plush. Against one wall was a hospital bed with a white enamel table and a stainless-steel cabinet next to it. On the far wall was a chest of drawers on top of which was a small television. Nora had the impression she'd entered a hospital room. She felt a twinge of fear and tried to swallow but her mouth had gone dry.

The woman pointed to a doorway.

"The bathroom is in there," she said in accented English. It was an accent Nora didn't recognize.

"There are fresh towels and all the toiletries you'll need. In the closet there, you'll find some clothes, all in your size as well as pajamas and a robe. I'll leave you to clean up and will return with something for you to eat."

The woman left the room and Nora heard the sound of a key turning in the lock. She crossed to the large window and looked out. Behind the house was a perfectly manicured lawn bordered by brick paths. Beyond the garden was a stand of tall evergreens through which she glimpsed a sparkling sea and what looked like a ferryboat struggling against a heavy swell. Miles away, across the vast expanse of water lay Istanbul. She noted the skyscrapers and the pall of smog that hung over the hills. "I'm on an island," she whispered, "I'll never get away from here."

The shower felt like a paradise rainfall. She stood beneath the spray for a good fifteen minutes in an attempt to wash away the grime from her days at sea. Brushing her teeth with toothpaste and a real brush was ecstasy. She put on the pajamas and the crisp cotton robe and stretched out on the bed. For a long time, she stared at the ceiling, praying that her vivid imagination would come up with something. She had to find a way out of this horror. Living the rest of her life as a sex slave was unthinkable. The possibility of suicide entered her mind. She briefly considered the idea, but she dismissed the thought. It was not yet time for that.

She heard the key being inserted into the lock and a second later, the nursey-looking woman walked in carrying a tray. Despite the numbness Nora felt, the food smelled delicious. The meal was comprised of roast chicken, rice and a side dish that she suspected was eggplant. She ate every scrap. Dessert was a sectioned orange, topped with honey. Although she didn't really care for honey, she ate it all. As she was sipping the hot thick coffee, the nurse returned. This time she was accompanied by a man. The man was young, late twenties maybe. He was slim and dark, dressed in neatly pressed slacks and a pale blue sports shirt that complemented his almond skin. The man's deep brown eyes, framed by lashes that were at least half an inch long looked much too large for his face. His expression was somber.

"My name is Ishmael Shamir," he announced, "Doctor Shamir. This is Nez, she's my surgical nurse."

Doctor! Surgical nurse! The panic rose in Nora's throat, followed immediately by the sickly-sweet taste of honey. She almost vomited but managed to choke back the sensation. Doctor?" she demanded. "Why do I need a doctor? I'm not sick."

Doctor Shamir studied her for a long moment and sat down in the chair by the window. He then answered, "I've been asked to perform a procedure. I assure you it will be painless, nothing more than discomfort for a few days. You see, your new husband insists that all of his wives be virgins." He almost smiled. "So, it's my job to reconstruct your eh ... virginity."

For the first time in her forty years, Nora was struck dumb. Her mouth hung open like that of a hooked fish. She'd heard the stories of medical procedure abominations like female circumcision, but what she'd just heard was the sickest by far. "You've got to be kidding," she whispered, "you're ill."

He shook his head resignedly, "I'm afraid that I'm not kidding. The operation will take place tomorrow. The Emir wants you repaired as soon as possible. He's most eager to have you with him."

Desperate for any information she could glean, Nora managed a question. "Is this where I'm to stay then? Is this house to be my prison?"

"Oh, no," the doctor replied, "this house is far below the standards you will be enjoying. You will be moved to the city when you have recovered. Your host is an extremely wealthy man. You will be living in a palace, one of the most beautiful in Istanbul."

With that, Doctor Shamir stood and made for the door. "Please, try to get some rest," he advised. "Tomorrow will be an important one for you." He walked out of the room.

Nez the nurse collected the used towel and Nora's soiled clothes from the bathroom.

Nora moved back to the bed and sat down on the edge, watching her. "Nez," she asked quietly, "will you please tell me who the man is who has stolen my life to make me his whore?"

"I can't tell you that. I really can't," Nez replied. "I don't know who the man is. I was simply hired to care for you for a few days and to assist in the operation. I was told nothing else."

"Then I have another question and I know you can answer. Please Nez, where am I? It's terrible not to know." She watched the woman as she considered the request.

Nez lingered for a moment in the center of the room, gazing down at her patient.

Nora thought she almost looked sympathetic and maybe a bit remorseful.

"Well, I suppose it would be alright for you to know. After all, you have no one to tell, do you? You're on Buyukada Island. The body of water you can see through the trees is the Sea of Marmara – the Marble Sea." Without another word, Nez picked up the tray and left the room.

Nora stretched out on the bed and listened to the inevitable scraping of the key in the lock. She was suddenly exhausted. "The Marble Sea," she murmured, "how soothing."

CHAPTER 10

Peter waited in the hotel lobby until he saw Demir's car pull up. At first, he wasn't sure it was a real car. The vehicle was tiny. He hurried down the steps and climbed quickly into the miniature car.

"Hi," said Demir, "how are you holding up?"

"Well, not too bad, I guess, considering. Your city is actually very interesting."

As Demir weaved through hopelessly snarled traffic, Peter felt like he was strapped into a recliner atop a motorized skateboard. During the infrequent breaks in the action, he filled Demir in on what had taken place during his foray into the city the night before.

Demir listened without interruption and when he'd finished, took some time to respond. "Well, in a way it's not all bad. If they're watching you, we may be able to find a way to watch them. Can you describe them?"

Peter described the men as best he could. Demir nodded thoughtfully and continued to drive like a NASCAR driver. Because the car was so tiny, he managed to navigate the traffic almost unseen. Twenty minutes later, they pulled up in front of a nondescript building, the ground floor of which was a flower shop. There was no house to be seen. Demir locked the car and headed for the shop.

"So, what kind of car is that?" Peter asked. "I've never seen one."

"It's called a Smart Car," Demir replied. "They're becoming quite popular in the city. Best defense against the traffic jams. And you can park them anywhere."

"It's great. I wish we had them in LA."

"Oh, don't hold your breath, my friend. It'll be a long time before they show up in the States. They're far too practical."

Beside the flower shop was a small door. Demir climbed two steps and pressed a buzzer in the wall.

Sure doesn't look like much, Peter speculated.

A voice crackled from the speaker. Demir answered and they were buzzed in.

They climbed three flights of worn stone steps and arrived at another door set into a peeling painted wall. Demir knocked and the door opened almost immediately. A small smiling woman reached up to embrace Demir.

"This is my mother, Tati," said Demir.

He turned and spoke to his mother in Turkish. The only word Peter recognized was his name. Tati reached out her hand and smiled shyly. “Welcome,” she said softly. Peter took her hand and smiled back. The tiny woman reminded him of Demir’s car.

He entered the apartment; it was like stepping into another world. The space was large and airy, with high ceilings and pale walls. The furniture was simple but elegant. The artwork was of very good quality, but the most impressive part of the décor was the pervasive arrangements of flowers. They made the place smell exotic.

Seeing Peter’s reaction, Demir smiled. “Family business,” he explained, “we get to enjoy what we don’t sell.”

He proceeded to introduce his guest to the others in the room. Peter met Demir’s sister Iza, who looked very pregnant, and her husband Bak, a jovial young man. They both spoke very good English. The other man was a well-built, athletic-looking fellow, with a perfectly manicured beard and piercing green eyes.

“This is Mahmet,” said Demir. “He’s the fiancé of my second sister, who’s around here somewhere.”

Mahmet shook Peter’s hand. There was not a hint of a smile.

Tati approached and handed Peter a glass filled with pale pink liquid. “For you,” she said hesitantly. “Enjoy please.”

"Try it," said Demir. "It's called daisy tail. You probably won't like it but it's my mother's specialty, I'm afraid."

Tati continued to smile, obviously unaware of what her son had just said.

"Please follow me," said Demir, "I have something to show you."

Peter followed his host down a short hallway and through a narrow door. What stretched out before him was truly incredible. They were standing in a large roof garden, beyond which was the Bosporus, where a hundred boats of all shapes and sizes vied for position. The sun was just setting, and the water was liquid gold.

"It's called the Golden Horn," said Demir. "I guess you can see why."

As Peter stared at the bumper boat armada before him, he became aware of a person standing at the railing nearly in shadow. From the long dark hair, he assumed it was a woman.

"Sofi," Demir called out, "please, I'd like you to meet my friend Peter."

Slowly, the girl turned to face them. As the light reached her face, Peter's eyes widened. He clutched his glass more tightly so as not to drop it. It was her; the woman from the Topkapi; the woman who had been watching him. And up close, she was even more beautiful than he'd first thought. Her dark eyes were almond shaped and filled with laughter.

Unsure as to what he should say, he waited for the woman to speak.

"Good evening, Peter," she said and started towards him with her hand outstretched. He took her slim hand in his.

"It's nice to meet you Sofi," he responded. "So, you're Demir's sister?" he continued, restating the obvious.

"I'm afraid so," she replied, her eyes twinkling. "But it's okay. It's not as bad as you might think."

Peter smiled in response, unaware that his gaze had not left her face.

"It's a beautiful evening, isn't it?" she went on, turning back to look at the water.

" So, what do you think of our view?"

"The view's amazing," he replied, "absolutely beautiful." She moved back to the railing and stood perfectly still, gazing out at the teeming waterway.

Peter looked over his shoulder and was surprised to discover that Demir had left. He was alone with the woman. He walked across and joined her at the rail. "I know this sounds tacky, as we'd say back home, but I have a feeling we've met before. Have we?"

`She continued to stare at the water. It took her a moment to respond. "I don't think so Peter. I'm sure I would remember."

He stole a glance, sure, she was teasing him and saw that he was right. Her face had broken into a mischievous smile.

"You're sure?" he pressed, "didn't I see you earlier today at the Topkapi?"

"That's highly unlikely. I was working all day. I had no time for leisure pursuits."

` "I see," he replied, not at all convinced. "So, you're a policeman …er, person. I understand."

She dragged her eyes from the bustling waterway and focused them on Peter. The twinkle was back.

"Yes, I am," she replied, "and policeman is okay with me. Correctness hasn't reached us yet."

"I like that," Peter replied, grinning. "I won't get in so much trouble."

The banter was interrupted by Demir's return. He appeared carrying two glasses filled with a dark liquid.

"Here," he said, handing Peter a glass, "that stuff my mother serves is a bit challenging. I think you'll like this better."

Peter smiled and took the proffered glass, grateful that Demir had made the switch.

Demir raised his glass. "Sofi doesn't drink except for emergencies but don't worry, she doesn't judge." Sofi turned to her brother, raised one eyebrow and said nothing.

"Cheers," he offered, "welcome to our home and to our country. My only regret is that your visit isn't under more happy circumstances."

They solemnly clinked glasses and Peter took a long swallow, whereupon his throat spasmed. He choked and nearly spewed the whole lot, but somehow managed to keep it down.

"Sour Cherry Vodka," Demir smiled, nodding. "They make it here locally. Smooth, eh?"

"Wow," gasped Peter, wiping his eyes, "yeah, real smooth, kinda like Drano."

"Don't worry," said Sofi, "the next sip will be painless. You'll get used to it."

Sofi turned and looked at Peter. There was sadness in her eyes. "Please, Peter, let me say how terrible I feel about your wife. My brother told me your story . . . I'm so sorry. Please know that I will do all I can to ..."

She was interrupted by the appearance of her fiancé, Mahmet, who looked irritated. He ignored Peter and growled something to Sofi in Turkish.

Her face flushed. She turned away and followed Mahmet back into the apartment.

"What was that?" Peter asked Demir once the two were gone.

"Oh, it's just his way," Demir replied apologetically. "He can be a bit possessive sometimes. You see he's a private ... eh security consultant and is inclined to be suspicious of strangers. We should go in. Dinner's almost ready.

Peter cast one last glance at the amazing view and followed Demir inside.

Dinner was a wonder. Peter counted at least seven courses, several of which he didn't recognize but was too polite to question. When the meal was done, they all retired to the roof top for coffee and port. Peter was full to bursting. He'd eaten everything set before him. The evening was balmy and the conversation, most of which had been conducted in English, was light and very enjoyable. Peter learned more about Istanbul in three hours than he could have gleaned from an entire college course. Not surprisingly, the surly Mahmet hadn't joined in. His entire contribution to the evening's discourse consisted of smug asides delivered to Sofi in Turkish.

As they sat enjoying the coffee and the cool evening air, Demir steered the discussion to Peter's plight. At Demir's request, Peter recounted his entire terrible tale. The others listened without interruption and when he was done, no one spoke. Sofi had translated for her mother and when she was finished, Tati looked horrified.

"I know this for you," she managed in English, then turned to Sofi and spoke to her in Turkish. She turned back to Peter and with tears in her eyes began to speak. Her English was not good, but her daughter helped when Tati got stuck.

"Three years ago, my dear husband disappeared," she began haltingly. "They found his body days later floating in the Sea of Marmara. He'd been shot and the fish had made a mess of him. To this day we don't know why he was killed. It's the reason Sofi joined the police force. I understand, Peter what you are going through. I know your pain and I am very sorry."

Although Tati's English was very difficult to understand, Peter managed to get the gist of the story.

They sat in silence until Tati stood and with a nod, walked away.

Demir took it upon himself to break the silence. "Before Sofi joined the police force, she was going to move to Italy to become a model," said Demir proudly. "She was signed by the biggest modeling agency in Istanbul, and they planned to send her to Milan. The death of our father changed everything for her – for all of us."

"I understand," Peter murmured softly. "What a terrible thing." He felt it was time to change the subject but couldn't think of what to say so he threw out a question to no one in particular. "So how come you all speak English so well? I must say it has made my evening enjoyable. I wouldn't have been able to offer much conversation otherwise."

Demir took it upon himself to answer. "Well, as you know, I've been living in Cambridge for four years. Sofi came to join me for a while. She'd considered going to school there, but she was too homesick. What a baby. She didn't last a year."

He grinned at her. She scowled back.

"Now of course, my baby sister could whip me with one hand."

Everybody laughed everybody but Mahmet. Peter wasn't sure if Mahmet understood what was being said. but he got the impression he did and was simply being rude.

"Anyway," Demir continued, "when she got back from the States, Sofi took it upon herself to teach mother and Iza. Iza did great. Mother not so much."

Everybody laughed. Peter saw that Mahmet showed a hint of a smile. "Aha," he thought.

The evening was a real blessing for Peter. For a few hours he was able to push the horror into the background. The only thing that bothered him was Mahmet. The guy made Peter nervous. Several times during the evening, he'd caught Mahmet regarding him with obvious dislike. He decided that he'd try to avoid making Mahmet angry. There was something threatening about the man.

Feeling weary all of a sudden, Peter decided it was time to leave and made the suggestion to Demir. After saying his good nights, he and Demir headed downstairs. Sofi led them down while Mahmet stood at the top of the stairs and watched as Sofi opened the door for them. She kissed her brother on the cheek and offered Peter her hand. As he shook, he felt something being slipped into his hand and quickly palmed it.

Demir dropped him at the hotel, promising that he'd call first thing in the morning. He explained that the ship would either be in port by now, or just outside. It was time to begin the search. "Sofi will help, I'm sure. She seemed to like you and she doesn't like just anyone. She'll gather the information we need about ship arrivals."

"You know, speaking of Sofi. I thought I saw her yesterday at the Topkapi. Is there any chance she was there? Could she have been following me?"

"Entirely possible my friend. I told her all about you and your dilemma as soon as I got home. Knowing her as I do it wouldn't surprise me if she wanted to observe you for a while before becoming involved. Without giving you the details, I can tell you that helping you might not be the most popular decision. It could hurt her professionally."

Peter unfolded himself from the Smart Car and hurried up the steps to the safety of the hotel. As he prepared for bed, his head was swimming. He wondered if the four or five tumblers of Sour Cherry Vodka might have contributed to his condition.

CHAPTER 11

The insistent crowing of the Muezzins saved him. They'd awakened him from a terrifying dream, one in which he pulled Nora from the water, riddled with bullets. Her body was so badly decomposed she was nearly unrecognizable. He was able to identify her only because of the ring she was wearing.

When he rolled over, he discovered that his pillow was soaking wet. Tears or sweat, he wasn't sure, maybe both. He rose from the bed on trembling legs, staggered to the bathroom and vomited in the sink. He'd tried to make it to the toilet but didn't quite reach it.

A long, hot shower followed by an ice-cold rinse helped him feel better. As he pulled on his jeans, he remembered the paper Sofi had slipped him. He found it crumpled in the pocket of the slacks he'd worn. The paper contained a phone number and a short message which read: *Call me tomorrow between 3 and 4.*

He refolded the note and placed it in his wallet behind a credit card. At that moment the phone rang. He picked up the receiver to hear Demir's voice.

"I'll be there in fifteen minutes. There's someone I want you to meet."

Peter headed downstairs and managed to down two cups of coffee before the Smart Car pulled up. Peter climbed in and buckled up as Demir headed into the traffic, ready to wage war. It took them almost twenty minutes to travel three miles, where they arrived at a huge complex that resembled an Eastern European rail terminal.

Demir parked in a crammed lot and bribed the attendant to guard his vehicle. They entered the building, which felt like a city within a city. The Grand Bazaar was exactly what its name implied. Narrow alleyways, as far as the eye could see, lined with shops of all descriptions. At the shop doors, insistent hawkers intercepted any pedestrians they could in any language, insisting that their merchandise was by far the best and certainly the cheapest. The two men made their way through the throngs of people, doing their best to avoid the hawkers, the cats and the pervasive pigeons.

They continued up a major thoroughfare for a quarter mile where they turned right onto a narrower lane where the shops were smaller, and the cats looked meaner. They stopped at the door of a tiny carpet shop called *Omar's*, whose gaudy banner proclaimed in English that they were going out of business, their prices were rock bottom and that they would be happy to ship anywhere in the world.

Demir rang a bell and waited patiently.

"Going out of business, are they?" Peter asked, curiously. "Too bad."

"Oh yes. Omar has been going out of business for thirty years."

A small peephole opened in the door and Peter listened as three locks were undone. The door creaked open and they entered the shop. The space was dimly lit, cramped and smelled strongly of mildew, black tea and tobacco. In the corner, a very old man sat puffing on a water pipe. Demir shook the hand of the heavy-set, middle-aged man who had opened the door and presented his companion.

"Omar, this is my good friend Peter Brandt. He's American and I'm afraid he has a very sad tale. I'd appreciate it very much if you'd hear him."

Omar smiled, revealing a set of gold teeth that made him look like a cheap ornament. "Would you have tea?" he asked.

"Please," Demir replied, "that would be very nice."

Omar snapped his fingers and a young boy dressed in a dirty robe appeared from the shadows in the corner. The lad crouched down and rolled up a rug in the center of the floor. He then lifted an exposed trapdoor and retreated into the shadows.

"Please," said Omar indicating a set of rickety-looking steps.

Demir went first and disappeared through the doorway. Peter took a deep breath and followed. Behind him Omar climbed down pulling the door shut behind him. Peter reached the bottom of the steps, only slipping once and whistled as he took in what lay before him. He felt like he'd entered a sultan's tent. The room was large, sixty feet long or more, well lit, and airy. Air-conditioning, Peter decided. Stacked against the walls were piles of carpets, six or seven feet high. The floor was covered with a huge deep blue carpet and as Peter crossed it, he couldn't decide whether he was walking on water or floating on magic. The room contained three ornate desks, each of which held a state-of-the-art computer and behind each one was an operator, hard at work. As Peter followed Omar across the room, not one of the workers looked up. He wondered if they ever looked up.

"Carpets are just one of Omar's businesses," Demir explained. "He has many interests, and he may be kind enough to help us in our search. They were shown to a corner of the room where an elegant couch and three chairs surrounded an iinlaid table. The three men sat and within moments a silver tea service appeared, presented by a young woman dressed in a long, striped robe and gold sandals.

As she poured the tea, Demir smiled up at her. She completely ignored him.

"Story of my life," he shrugged, "as they say in America."

The young woman finished pouring and strolled away. As she did, she turned and flashed a shy smile over her shoulder in Demir's direction. Grinning in response, he tapped his heart with his hand.

"Omar was a good friend of my father's," Demir began as they sipped the hot sweet tea. "As fellow merchants, they had much in common. As a matter of fact, Omar was at one time married to my mother's sister. I've known him since I was a small boy and I trust him with my life. So, why don't you tell him your story."

Peter recounted the events of the Venice abduction, his journey to Istanbul and the subsequent chase through the dark streets.

Omar listened in silence and when Peter finished, he sat shaking his head. "Unfortunately, your tale is not so uncommon as you would think. Every year, it seems, more and more women and children are stolen from streets in the West and brought to countries where the law is inclined to look the other way. Our own country is often a destination. The Arab world and the Far East are often the destinations for such prized merchandise.

"There are people I can talk to, and I will. However, I must caution you, I think it would be unwise to be overly optimistic. This city is one of dark secrets and muted whispers. Give me a day or two to make inquiries. I will report my findings as soon as there's anything to tell. And please, Mr. Brandt, try to be patient. On the surface, our modern society moves quickly, but in truth much has remained unchanged here for centuries. Rest assured though, I will do my best. I am indebted to Demir's family and any friend of his is welcome in my humble tent."

The meeting concluded and the visitors rose to leave. Demir looked around, hoping to have a word with the girl who'd served them. He spotted her sitting in front of a computer and approached shyly. From afar, Peter observed the brief conversation and smiled. He watched his friend scribble something on a piece of paper and head back beaming triumphantly.

As they waited, Omar grinned up at Peter. "Please don't tell him that Layla is the youngest daughter of my oldest sister. If he finds out he'll be too nervous to ask her out. He's afraid of Massla. We all are and in truth, Layla needs the company of a young man like Demir. She works far too hard and has no real social life."

`The trapdoor opened above them, and the subterranean room plunged immediately into darkness. Peter and Demir climbed the steps while Omar remained below.

"So," said Peter as they exited the bazaar and crossed the street, heading for the car, "things seemed to go pretty well."

"Oh yes, very well indeed," Demir responded. He grinned and patted the pocket of his jacket. "I got Layla's phone number.

CHAPTER 12

Mohammed Hassan al Caribe reclined on the silk divan waiting impatiently for the new girl to complete his pedicure. She'd bathed him tenderly, provocatively, but he'd experienced no flush of passion. As the girl labored, he watched CNN, curious to see if there was any further news about the abduction of Nora James. He knew that she'd become Nora Brandt upon her marriage to Peter Brant, the arrogant producer of Hollywood trash.

He was surprised the story hadn't engendered more coverage. For two days after she went missing, there had been no mention of her disappearance. Then he caught a couple of brief blurbs on Fox. Now, six days later, nothing!

"Oh, the attention span of the Americans, he sneered. They require new grist for their horror mill every day or they are bored. Such children they are." He glanced down at the mane of dark auburn hair and scowled with impatience. The girl had buffed his fingernails, squeezed out his overnight blackheads, the consequence of his greasy complexion, and was now buffing his toenails. One of his minions had joked one day that Hassan's bad skin was the result of screwing camels as a young man. Hassan had the man flogged within an inch of his life.

Hassan allowed his imagination to wander and fantasized that it was Nora James kneeling before him. The thought brought with it a slight stirring and he felt his manhood begin to stiffen. But he knew it was an exercise in futility. Fulfillment was a fleeting experience these days. He sometimes wondered if all men had a limited number allotted for their lifetime. If that were the case, then he was well past his limit. He closed his eyes, trying to concentrate on images of Nora but the images soon faded, and he was back to reality

The girl who was now smiling up at him, hoping for some more intimate demands, but he ignored her. Without a word, she gathered up her instruments and her lotions, bowed deeply and scurried from the room.

Hassan sat still for a moment, wondering how soon Nora would be his companion. He knew that he'd eventually tire of her as he had with all the others, but still he was looking forward to the time she'd excite him. He didn't dwell on the fact that when he was done with her, she'd suffer the same fate as all the others had.

Except for his first wife, Beta, who'd borne him three daughters and a son, his women had been shipped to Bahrain when he tired of them. Their talents would continue to be exploited, with none of the benefits of course. He despised Bahrain, although the wretched little country had been good to him. He'd been born into an upper middle-class family. His father was a doctor who had risen through the ranks to become one of the Sultan's personal physicians. Through hard work and his father's connections, Hassan had managed to acquire several properties. He'd used his cunning to build a thriving business until eventually he'd built two of Al Manama's most luxurious hotels. His piece de resistance was the Grand Mosque, the largest in all the Gulf States. Although he was one of many contractors in Bahrain, he'd outsmarted all of them and had left there a very wealthy man.

Manama, Bahrain's capital city was a dreadful place, in his estimation, but it had provided him with riches like he'd never imagined. While building his hotels and mosques, he'd encountered many dealers in art and antiquities, who'd introduced him to the world of pirated artifacts. He discovered instantly that he had an eye for these rare and beautiful objects and had become one of the Middle East's most successful dealers and one of the world's most avid collectors.

Although he still had a home in Bahrain, he seldom ventured there. Instead, he preferred to inhabit any one of his other four domiciles. He had an apartment overlooking the East River in New York City; a showy beach house in Malibu, California and a grade one listed country house in

Hampshire fifty miles outside London, but his favorite by far was the glittering white palace on the shores of the Bosporus. He loved Istanbul for its variety of cultures and its dearth of taboos. The teeming city provided all that a man's heart could ever desire, with few questions asked. It was a place of mystery, an ancient metropolis with a foot resting in each of two worlds. It was where the wealth and promise of the Wild West rubbed seductively against ancient civilizations and the violent history of the East.

Bahrain frustrated him. It was like the Gulf that surrounded it; polluted beyond repair. Although, from the marble verandahs of his house, the sea looked vibrant and alive, it was, in fact, as lifeless as the Dead Sea. The waters were thick with oil; an environment in which nothing could live. It was like modern-day Islam, a religion rife with hypocrisy. Not that Hassan was a religious man, but he was ashamed of the behavior of the powerful Arabs who claimed to be devout.

On more than one occasion he'd asked the wealthy Saudis who frequented his hotels, why it was permissible for them to come to Bahrain, where liquor was legal, drink themselves into stupors and proceed to shame themselves in the sleaziest bars and strip clubs the city had to offer. The answer he'd received had horrified him. No wonder he had no faith. Islam had become a blueprint for failure and despair and hypocrisy. The Saudis had responded that their behavior was of no consequence because Allah couldn't see across the water.

His mind drifted back to the present and he rose from his musings and crossed his exquisitely furnished bedroom to gaze out over the sapphire straits of the Bosporus. Displayed behind him was an entire wall of ancient weaponry, priceless relics from civilizations long since passed, some dating back to the reign of Nebuchadnezzar. The palace was a museum of rare artifacts, the value of which exceeded fifty million dollars. Al Caribe was a jealous collector of beautiful things and was about to add to his collection.

Suddenly he felt hungry. He pulled a tasseled cord beside the window, alerting the kitchen staff that he was ready for something to eat. Within fifteen seconds, there was a soft knock on the door and a teenage boy entered the room. The boy was slim and very good looking, almost girlish. His dark eyes flickered with fear. "What is your pleasure, Pasha?" he asked in Turkish.

"Oh, Tarik, I think I'll have eggs this morning. Yes, I'll have the eggs with caviar and a pot of English tea." With a wave of his hand, he dismissed the lad, crossed to an ornate desk and flicked on his computer. He pulled up the *Wall Street Journal* and perused a few pages. As he scanned the stock moves, he nodded with satisfaction. Next, he checked his e-mail and was pleased to see that his latest film project had been green-lighted by Universal. "Good," he breathed.

He would have a reason to fly to California for a week or two. Of all his businesses, aside from his collecting, the film industry was his favorite. It provided him with easy access to beautiful women who were happy to accommodate his most intimate desires. The promise of stardom opened all doors. In truth he enjoyed even more the few who attempted to refuse his advances. They inevitably provided him with even more satisfaction. Hassan was not a heartless man. He'd arranged for several of his conquests to be cast in films he'd financed; all were minor roles, mind you. But it was the thought that counted, after all.

After a soft tap on the door, Tarik wheeled a silver trolley into the room. Hassan moved to a small table in anticipation of his morning nourishment. The boy presented him with a napkin and removed the covers from the food. After tasting each dish, he bowed deeply and hurried from the room. Hassan dug into the first of his three eggs and smiled with pleasure. He'd first tasted eggs with caviar served in the shell at L'Orangerie in Los Angeles. It had remained one of his very favorite dishes.

As he ate, half-a-dozen cats emerged from their hiding places and circled his legs in anticipation of a treat. Halfway through the feast, his cell phone chirped. He picked it up. "Yes," he barked, irritated that his meal was being interrupted.

A moment later the frown furrows disappeared from his brow. "That is excellent news, doctor," he beamed. "So, the merchandise can be delivered in three days." He paused, listening intently. "I am pleased everything went well. You will be handsomely rewarded."

He finished his breakfast, pulled the cord button to summon a servant and disappeared into his dressing room. When he'd dressed in his robe, a flowing kaftan embroidered with gold, he stepped into a pair of butter-soft sandals and left his bedroom suite. He much preferred Arab dress. It was so much less confining than the stiff, constrictive Western clothing that he was compelled to wear on occasion.

He floated down the grand staircase and swept through the marble colonnade past the main salon. Six Persian cats scurried along in his wake, ignoring the frightened fluttering from the birdcages that lined the corridor. Every forty feet or so, a fountain splashed contentedly. He was pleased with his ubiquitous fountains. It was a design idea he'd incorporated from the water features at the Topkapi. Just as the old palace had been in its day, Hassan's mansion was also a house of secrets, and the splashing water was an effective deterrent for eavesdroppers. He entertained often and his guests wished to be able to converse, confident that their words would not be overheard.

There were several shadowy causes to which Hassan contributed that he preferred to keep secret, but he'd learned that a little well-placed cash, whether to militants or freedom fighters, facilitated his access to artifacts that would otherwise be unavailable to him. He was a strong believer in profits but didn't subscribe to the theory that money was the root of all evil. Money was not the problem. Greed was the real monster. He, of all people, should know.

He strolled down a long skylit corridor, removed a key from his pocket and unlocked the very last room. The room was comparatively small, almost cozy. It was his inner sanctum, the place that protected his darkest secrets. He allowed his cats entrance, closed the door behind him and locked it. He crossed to his desk and removed a manila envelope from the top drawer. He emptied the photographs onto the desk and began sifting through them.

They were all pictures of Nora James in a variety of outfits and locations, from the Gucci store on Rodeo Drive to the boat landing of the Gritti Palace in Venice. Any shot that included her husband had been altered. Peter Brandt had been carefully clipped out of her life.

Hassan was a bit bothered that his people hadn't yet managed to eliminate Brandt. That he'd figured out that Istanbul was the *Luxor*'s destination was a bit disconcerting, but it was a mere hangnail in the scheme of things. He'd been advised by the ship's captain to change the ships name, just to be on the safe side. The name change would provide an additional allayer of protection.

After a little paperwork and a little paint, and a lot of cash the Izmir was now the Luxor and more difficult for any investigators to identify. And they'd remove Brandt soon enough, just like he'd been removed from the photographs. It would have been Hassan's preference to have the man die a painful death for having pawed and penetrated Nora's body but capturing and torturing him was not worth the risk. Having him killed would have to suffice. Soon there would be no trail for anyone to follow.

CHAPTER 13

Nora was awakened by the pain. She tried to move but the effort only intensified her discomfort. She managed to reach down beneath the sheet and discovered that she was wearing a pair of heavy underpants the likes of which she hadn't worn since she was a girl. Inside was an industrial size sanitary napkin that felt like it was soaked with blood. To add to her suffering, she was dying of thirst and her lips felt as dry as sand. So, they'd done it. Somewhere deep inside the pain, she felt a surge of anger. How dare they, she groaned. They'd mutilated her.

She became aware of someone else in the room. She moved her head and groaned and a second later there was a face looking down at her. When she managed to focus, Nora recognized the nurse, although she couldn't remember the woman's name. It seemed to Nora that the woman looked sad, maybe even a little guilty.

"I imagine you're thirsty," the woman said softly. "Let me sit you up a bit and I'll bring you some water." She wrapped her arms around Nora's back and gently pulled her higher onto the pillows.

The rush of pain was so intense, Nora nearly passed out. She was immediately soaked with sweat.

The nurse crossed the room and returned a moment later with a glass of water and a straw.

Slowly the pain subsided, and Nora managed to take a sip of water. Nothing had ever tasted so good. She nodded her head with gratitude and drank some more. "What's your name?" she whispered. "I'm afraid I can't remember. I'm sorry."

"Don't be sorry," said the nurse kindly. "It's me who should be sorry. Things did not go as well as we'd hoped. There was a complication, and you lost a lot of blood. You have so much pain. I'd like for you to take a pill. I will change your dressing and you'll go back to sleep. God-willing you'll have less pain when you wake. And my name is Nez."

Nora gratefully accepted the little pink pill and a minute later, the room started swimming. Her eyes closed and she slipped into the welcome relief of sleep.

When she awakened the room was dark. She lay still, trying to remember where she was and slowly the reality of her plight came flooding back. She felt a cramp in her back and concluded it was from lying in the same position for so long. She tried to roll onto her side and managed with some effort to complete the maneuver. Although she was still in pain, it wasn't nearly as bad as it was the last time, she was awake. She lay on her side for a few minutes and when it became uncomfortable, managed to roll to her other side. In this position she could see the door and the narrow border of light surrounding it.

She became slowly aware that the ribbon of light was wider on one side than the other. Her heart leapt into her throat. Had someone left the door ajar? And if they had, was it by accident or on purpose. Was this the chance she'd prayed for since her abduction? Or was it a cruel joke? The prison was unlocked. Freedom was staring at her, but the terrible irony was that she couldn't walk – or could she.

She breathed yet another prayer and slid to the edge of the bed. When she tried to place her feet on the floor, she nearly passed out, but she discovered that the reaction was more from lightheadedness than from pain. She sat for a moment waiting for her head to clear and when it did, she tried to get to her feet. On the third attempt, she was up. She hobbled across the room to the closet and noticed that the sky was getting light. In an hour the sun would be up, as would her jailors. She knew that getting dressed would take too much time, so she reached for the white robe and slipped it on. Her head was swimming, and her heart was pounding like it would burst.

She found a pair of slippers on the closet floor, slipped them on and crept towards the door. Gently she pushed it wider open, hoping it wouldn't squeak. Soundlessly, the heavy door swung on its hinges, and she peered out into the hall. She strained her ears listening for any activity but mercifully the house was silent. She assumed they were all still asleep; but for how long. The pain between her legs was intense, but bearable. She knew in her heart that it was now or never.

She moved into the hallway and headed for the stairs grateful for the thick carpet that masked her footsteps. Hugging the banister like it was a long, lost friend; she navigated the staircase and finally reached the foyer. It seemed like her painful descent took forever. As she reached for the front doorknob, it occurred to her that the house might have an alarm system. She realized that if it did and she tripped it, her salvation would be short-lived. With a sinking feeling, she searched the adjacent walls, figuring that if there was an alarm system, there'd be a keypad somewhere close. There wasn't one. Suddenly she was lightheaded again; she could hear her pulse pounding in her ears.

At that moment, there was a noise behind her. The clatter of pots reached her from what she assumed was the kitchen. There was no choice. She reached for the door handle, turned it and pulled hard – nothing. The door wouldn't budge. Fighting tears of frustration, she stood trying to gather her thoughts. Should she try for another way out? Should she return to her bed and wait for another opportunity? No way in hell, she decided. It was then that she noticed the dead-bolt knob.

"Dummy," she whispered to herself. Breathing heavily and sweating like a lineman, she reached for the knob. It turned easily, silently. The door handle was next. Trembling, she turned it and pulled the door. It opened. She was met by a rush of cool air and the sweet smell of jasmine.

She stepped out into the garden and pulled the door shut behind her. As it closed, the lock emitted a loud click. "Damn," she cursed. But there was no immediate response. She wasted no time making her way down the brick path to the street. She stood for a second, trying to decide which way to turn, which direction would provide the help she so desperately needed. She'd walked a block or so before she realized that the pain had lessened. Was the adrenalin blocking it or was it the magical pink pill? Either way, she'd take it.

Somewhere behind her she heard the clip-clop of horse hooves coming closer. Wondering if she should flag down the driver, she quickly decided against it and ducked behind a hedge until the carriage passed. She knew that she was on a small island and had no idea who were allies and who were enemies. She concluded that if she could make her way to the harbor, she'd either find a way off the island or else some port official or policeman who could help her.

Suddenly, there were shouts behind her, accompanied by the sound of running footsteps. She knew it was her captors.

Her escape had been discovered and they were after her. She glanced back and determined she was right. There were two men, running hard, and heading in her direction. She was pretty sure they hadn't seen her, but she knew that if they did spot her, she'd never outrun them. The idea of finding a hiding place crossed her mind, but she dismissed the idea. She didn't have time for that. If they knew she hadn't escaped the island, they had all the time in the world to comb every inch of it.

She upped her pace and was immediately aware of the pain returning. The adrenalin that had masked it was now running out. She reached an intersection and looked both ways, praying that she'd see a car to flag down. Then it struck her. There were no cars. She'd heard no sound of traffic since arriving on the island. The horse-drawn carriages were the only means of transportation.

She turned left, trying to run but her legs refused to co-operate. She stumbled and nearly went to her knees. Through the grace of God, she remained upright and hobbled on, her heart in her throat and her lungs screaming for air. She glanced over her shoulder and groaned. The men had rounded the corner and were now no more than a hundred yards behind her and gaining fast.

She spotted a narrow lane just ahead and ducked in, hoping she'd find a place to hide until they passed. Instead, she found something entirely different. Standing in the middle of the little alley, facing her and munching away on the contents of its morning feedbag was a sorry-looking horse with a carriage attached. There was no human in sight. She recognized that the surrey was a Godsend and knew she had no choice. She hurried to the side of the carriage and clambered aboard.

It was not entirely unfamiliar territory. Several years back in one of her movies, she'd had to wrestle a team of six runaway horses while perched atop a stagecoach. Her stunt double had done the real work, but Nora had learned how it was done. She unwound the reins from the carriage strut, slapped the horse's rump hard and held on for dear life. The horse jumped in its traces, totally amazed that some crazy person was intending to drive him while he was feeding. Completely spooked, the horse took off at a gallop. They reached the roadway just as Nora's pursuers appeared. She slapped again and the horse plunged right towards them. The men had no choice but to dive out of the way. The one Nora recognized as the doctor landed in a hedge. The dark-skinned houseman flew over a strategically placed garbage can and fell flat on his face. Neither of them had a chance to recognize the driver of the runaway rig.

Nora hauled hard on the left rein and the terrified nag complied without question. She raced on down the hill towards the water, which she could now see in front of her as the sky lightened. As she drove, she became aware that she was wet, very wet. She glanced down and was horrified to discover that the front of her legs were wet with blood. The incision had no doubt burst open from her exertion.

She reached a small harbor where several boats were tied to the pier. She pulled up, searching for anyone who might be able to help. There were no officials to be found. The only person present was another cart driver, sitting on a bench, and smoking. When he spotted Nora, he leapt to his feet, pointed in her direction and yelled something in Turkish. Nora concluded that he'd recognized her rig and had assumed she'd stolen it. He dropped his cigarette and ran towards her. From the looks of him the man was angry.

It didn't take Nora long to decide that he wasn't going to be of much help. He was not her savior. She spun the carriage as fast as she could and raced off in the direction she'd come. She looked over her shoulder and saw the man running for his own cart, apparently intending to launch a pursuit.

She was aware that somewhere ahead of her, two desperate men were searching for her. When she approached the lane where she'd found her getaway cart, she slowed to a trot and made a left. She proceeded down the narrow roadway until it spilled into a wider road. Guessing, she turned right.

A mile up the road, she came upon a broken-down shed and had an idea. She steered the now sweating horse along the rutted lane and drove into the building where they were well hidden. It was a place where she could rest for a while. It would give her an opportunity to think.

She spotted a rusty tap protruding from a broken wall and when she'd caught her breath she searched around until she came up with a suitable vessel. She filled the leaky bucket with fresh cool water and after removing the feedbag, presented it to her actual savior. She'd loved horses all her life, but never had she loved one as much as this sorry-looking creature, her knight in shining sweat.

When the horse had drunk its fill, Nora decided that she should try to have a look at the damage she'd done to herself. She sat down on a broken bench and began removing the under pants. They and the pad were soaked. As she peeled away the pad, she had a macabre, irrational thought. She wondered if, now that she was a virgin again, she'd still be able to use tampons. "You're crazy, you know that?" she whispered to herself.

She was relieved to discover that although the wound continued to ooze blood, it was no longer flowing like it had been. She rinsed the underpants under the tap and hung them up to dry. Then, using a jagged piece of tin she found on the floor, she cut two strips of cloth from the hem of her robe. When she was done, she was overcome by a wave of nausea, which she assumed was from the loss of blood. She took a few sips of water from the tap, soaked the cloth strips and washed herself, then climbed back up into the surrey. She curled up on the cracked leather seat, wrapped one wet cloth around her forehead, placed the other between her legs and closed her eyes.

She woke in a panic. She could hear the distinctive sound of hoofbeats, and they were getting closer. Ignoring the pain, she climbed down from the carriage and peeked out of her hiding place through a crack in the wall. She sighed with relief when she discovered that no one was heading for the shed. Instead, there were several carriages moving on the nearby street. The town was now wide-awake, and everything appeared normal.

She realized though, that she was trapped in the shed at least until the sun went down. If she appeared, either in her carriage or on foot, she'd be noticed, and she couldn't risk it. If she was going to move, it couldn't be before nightfall. Maybe if she altered her appearance, she'd have a chance to move around without drawing attention. The carriage was a problem. After all she'd stolen the thing and was sure the owner was searching for it. If she was caught with the carriage she'd surely be arrested and there was no guarantee the cops would be interested in helping her. She could just imagine telling her crazy, unbelievable story to people who didn't speak English and probably worked for the bad guy.

She offered the horse some more water, which it drank and responded with a steaming gush of foul-smelling urine. Avoiding the spreading puddle, she collected the now dry cloths, climbed back into the carriage and re-wrapped herself.

When she was done, she leaned back in the seat, closed her eyes and thought about Peter.

CHAPTER 14

Demir drove them to a small outdoor restaurant, which he promised served the best fish in the city. It was no lie. Lunch was delicious. As they walked back to the car Peter looked at his watch and was surprised to see that it was past 3 o'clock. It was time to call Sofi.

When they arrived back at the hotel, Peter thanked Demir for the lunch and the ride and slid out of the car

He hurried up the stairs to his room and removed the phone number from his wallet. After three rings, she answered.

"Evet," she said sounding impatient.

"Hi," Peter responded, "it's me, Peter Brandt. You asked me to call. Sorry I'm a bit late. I hope I'm not disturbing you."

Her tone changed immediately, "Oh yes Peter. Hi. How are you?"

"Oh, pretty good, considering."

"I understand," she said softly. "Listen, Peter why don't you meet me later today. I have a couple of ideas."

"Sure. That would be fine. Do you want me to come to your office?"

"Oh no," she replied firmly, "you can't come here. My fiancé has friends here and if he finds out that I was meeting you, he'd be furious. He doesn't like you for some reason. He won't tell me why, but in truth he's never happy if I speak to another man."

"So, do you want to come here?"

"That's not a good idea either. You may be being watched still and I can't be seen with you."

"Well, how do you want to meet?"

"I have an idea," she said, "near the big bridge on your side, there's a small mosque. It's set in a beautiful garden right on the water. It's called the Şemsi Pasha Mosque. Meet me there at six o'clock. I'll come straight from work. Any taxi driver will know where it is."

"Great," Peter replied, "I'll be there."

"Okay and be sure you're not being followed. Maybe you should change taxis a couple of times . . . just to be sure."

"Okay, I'll see you later. Bye." Peter hung up the phone feeling excited. He was anxious to hear what Sofi had come up with. He also wondered what he'd done to upset her fiancé. "Oh well," he muttered to himself, "there's nothing I can do about it. And he's got no cause to be jealous. I'm a married man for Pete's sake."

He felt his excitement waning and decided that a good stiff drink might help. He washed his face, combed his hair and left the room.

In the bar, he chose a corner table and sat with his back to the wall. The waiter had followed him to the table.

"I'll have a Sour Cherry Vodka, please – on the rocks. And do you have any chips or nuts or something?"

The waiter nodded and made his way back to the bar. A few minutes later, the young man returned, set down the cocktail and a bowl of pistachios.

"Thanks," said Peter. He took a deep breath, anticipating the impending fire and lifted the glass to his lips. He was not disappointed. The vodka hit him like a ball-peen hammer. When he caught his breath, he ventured another sip. It was certainly gentler than the first.

After two vodkas, he was feeling better. The warmth in his belly translated to a mounting sense of hope. He was eager to hear what Sofi had to offer and was looking forward to seeing her again.

At five o'clock, he decided he'd better get going. Even if he arrived early, he was happy to wait. After all, Sofi was going out of her way and risking Mahmet's wrath to help him. He left the hotel by the backdoor, glanced around for any sign of trouble and seeing none, took off at a brisk pace. Halfway down the block a shot rang out. He dropped to the ground like he'd been poleaxed and crouched there frozen with fear, his heart hammering. A second later, a dilapidated truck trundled by, belching black smoke. As it passed, it backfired again. Peter sighed with relief and managed to draw a breath.

He got to his feet, brushed himself off and headed for the main thoroughfare and eventually flagged down a taxi. He changed cabs twice and arrived at the mosque just before six. The garden appeared to be deserted. Apparently, he was first to arrive.

At ten past six, a small motor launch pulled up to the seawall. He watched as Sofi leapt off and the police boat sped away, heading back into the marine traffic. Sofi looked over her shoulder once or twice as she made her way across the gardens to where Peter waited on a stone bench. As she approached, he rose and stuck out his hand. She gripped it firmly and smiled up into his face.

"Hi Peter," she began, "sorry I'm late. I was waiting for a response to one of the e-mails I sent. It finally came."

"So, what was it about? Did it have to do with Nora?"

"As a matter of fact, it did." With that, Sofi reached into her purse and pulled out a package of Marlboros."

"You smoke?" Peter asked, surprised.

"Yes, I do," she replied, smiling. "Does that make me a bad person?"

"No, no, nothing like that," he stammered, feeling like a yokel. "I mean . . . well it's just that I don't remember you smoking last night."

"No, I didn't smoke last night. My mother would kill me. As a matter of fact, Mahmet doesn't approve either, but his concern is not for my health. He fears I've become a little too Westernized; too much of a modern woman. I must say he is a bit of a traditionalist." She rummaged around in her purse and emerged with a disposable lighter.

"Would you like one?" she asked, offering him the pack.

"Thanks. Yeah, I would actually." He pulled a cigarette from the pack, placed it between his lips and waited as she lit her own and handed him the lighter.

"What the hell am I doing?" he wondered. He hadn't had a cigarette in over ten years. He pushed aside the guilt, lit the thing and took a long drag. It tasted pretty good.

"I don't remember seeing you smoking last night either," Sofi said, her eyes twinkling. He could see she was teasing him.

"Well, I don't really smoke," he replied. "I quit ten years ago. But with all that's going on right now, I don't see how it could hurt."

They sat for a moment without speaking; smoking like the act required all their concentration.

"So, tell me," Peter began, breaking the silence, "what's Mahmet's problem with me? I don't remember doing anything to annoy him."

"Oh, it's not you," she replied, sighing deeply. "He's employed by a very wealthy man as a . . . she searched for just the right word . . . *a protector.* He's sort of a bodyguard. His employer is one of Istanbul's untouchables; one of our super rich multi-nationals who drift in and out of here and feel that they're above the law. It's true. We, the police, are discouraged from interfering with them, no matter what they do. They all know someone in the government who's willing to exchange protection for a contribution. The untouchables live in their palaces right on the shore of the Bosporus, right across the water from my mother's flat.

"If your wife has been taken by one of them, which I fear might be the case; it will be very difficult even if we discover where she is. As I said, these people are protected from the law and their homes are impenetrable. The neighborhood is protected by a cliff that must be two hundred feet high and all the residents have armies of guards who are paid to shoot before asking questions. Mahmet is a guard for one of these untouchables. His employer is a truly terrible man"

Peter took the last drag of his cigarette, dropped it onto the stone path and ground it out. He was suddenly depressed. If what Sofi had just told him was true and if Nora had been taken by one of the people she described, the chances of getting Nora out were slim indeed. This place was not like the States. Going to the police would be of no help whatsoever.

Seeing Peter's deflation, she touched his arm. "But that doesn't mean the situation is hopeless. This is a complicated society and there are many ways to skin a cat. Don't give up hope."

He turned to face her, appreciative of her support. "So why are you doing this?" he asked. "What's in it for you?"

She considered for a moment, finished her own cigarette and answered softly. "This is personal for me Peter. It's a long story. I'll tell you about it when the time is right. In the meantime, let me tell you what I've been up to. Now as you can gather, I had to go about collecting information in secret. You see, half of my co-workers work for the bad guys and will stop at nothing to protect their patrons."

"So what have you found out?"

Sofi lowered her voice and started to answer. As she did, she glanced over her shoulder and stopped. Behind them on the path a man was taking pictures of the mosque, which was turning gold in the evening light. She was immediately suspicious. "Not here," she whispered, "follow me."

She got up and walked quickly towards the water. Peter was right behind her. They circled around behind the mosque, where Sofi headed for a small door. She turned the handle and breathed a sigh of relief as the door swung open. She, pulled a pale blue silk scarf from her purse, covered her head and removed her shoes. Peter removed his shoes as well, placed them on the step beside hers and followed her inside.

The interior of the mosque was breathtaking. The cool, quiet space was bathed in gold light that emanated from the stained-glass windows and hundreds of candles that flickered contentedly. Every inch of the soaring walls was adorned with blue and gold mosaic tiles arranged in intricate patterns. The tiles reflected the light and directed it up into the dome that towered 60 feet above them. It occurred to Peter that the job of setting the tiles must have taken forever.

"Fifteen years," Nora whispered, reading his mind, "and more than a hundred artisans. It's one of the most beautiful mosques we have, but it's hidden away. Tourists seldom come here. It'll be safe to speak now. It looks like we're alone and if we are being followed, we'll see them enter and there are several ways out. And don't worry, I'm armed and I'm a very good shot."

Despite the circumstances, Peter couldn't help but smile.

Sofi led him to a darkened corner where they sat down on an ivory and gold inlaid bench and resumed their conversation.

"So," she continued, "I thought I'd check all the marine traffic that has entered port over the last couple of days, as well as the ships that are due to arrive over the next few. Of course, I looked specifically for any vessels that departed

Venice around the time of your wife's abduction. There are eight ships that fit the bill. Five of them are already here. I have their names. She retrieved a folded piece of paper from her purse and handed it to Peter.

He eagerly scanned the list and shook his head, obviously disappointed. "It's not here," he sighed.

"What do you mean?" she asked, sounding surprised. "You know the name of the ship? How did you get that information?"

"Well, actually I paid for it. I got a message in Venice and met with a man who gave me the ship's name. It's called the *Izmir*." He indicated the list, "But it's not here."

"Peter," she said patiently, "what makes you so sure the man gave you reliable information. You were an easy target at that moment in time; willing to believe anything. You were desperate for any hope."

"Yeah, but he was right about Istanbul, wasn't he?"

"There's no way to know that, is there? Maybe you're on a wild bird chase."

Seeing his shoulders slump, she changed her tack.

"On the other hand, this is an obvious choice. It's the kind of thing that happens here all the time. It's a big business. Some of the untouchables have been suspected of trafficking human beings in the past. Let me tell you, my instincts are very good, and, in my heart, I believe that Nora is here somewhere."

Peter realized that she was trying to make him feel better. He touched her arm. "Thank you, Sofi," he whispered. "I really do appreciate all you're doing for me. You're a good person. But I think we're going to need more than just instinct."

"Well, actually, it is more than instinct. I'll tell you if you promise not to laugh."

Intrigued, Peter promised.

"The fact is I have a psychic, a true mystic whom I trust completely. Three years ago, she directed us to where we'd find my father's body. She was right and she's been right about everything else I've ever asked her."

Peter stared at her, his face a study in disbelief, "You're serious?"

"Oh yes, I'm very serious," she nodded. "Anyway, I paid her a visit during my lunch hour." She paused for a moment, "she told me that Nora's here in Istanbul and that she arrived on a ship from Venice. She almost came up with the name of the ship but . . ."

At that moment, the peacefulness was shattered by a loud screeching that sounded like it was being blasted through a cracked speaker. Peter nearly jumped out of his skin.

"The call to prayers," Sofi chuckled. "It won't hurt you. But we need to get out of here. The faithful will be arriving soon and we don't want to be caught in here. They will be suspicious, and we don't need any of that."

They hurried to the door, slipped on their shoes and walked quickly away from the mosque.

"Are you hungry? Would you like to grab something to eat?" Peter asked when they reached the street.

"I'd love to, but I can't. I'm meeting Mahmet for dinner and I can't be seen with you. Remember?"

"Oh yeah," he grumbled, "so when do we get together again?"

"I'll call you when I have something and don't worry, Nora's somewhere here in Istanbul and if anyone can find her, we can." With that she patted his arm and strode away.

As he watched her leave, the streetlights began to come on. The weight of sadness descended upon him again. Was he being a fool? Was there any real chance of finding Nora in this alien world? He listened to the sounds of music and children's laughter coming from the houses around him. Finally, he stuffed his hands in his pockets and trudged towards the busy street in the distance where he figured he'd have a better chance of finding a taxi.

CHAPTER 15

As darkness descended over the island, Nora awakened to an awful stench. The oats the horse had consumed that morning had apparently outlived their usefulness and were now departing the nag's back-end in resounding plops.

She clambered from the carriage as quickly as possible and stuck her head outside to gulp some breathable air. There was nobody on the street and she decided it was time to move. She couldn't stay hidden forever. The poor horse was growing increasingly restless, and she was afraid it would bolt. It was nervously tossing its head and stamping its hooves, causing the harness to jingle loud enough for any passing pedestrian to hear. She needed to find help and she was running out of time.

Trying not to breathe, she returned to the carriage and climbed aboard. The horse seemed very eager to get going. It backed willingly out of the broken-down door and as soon as she turned it around it broke into a trot without being asked.

She knew that it was the horse's intention to get home to its own barn and a much-needed meal but realized that it would be close to the house from where she'd escaped. Too close! She decided to give the horse its head for a while until she was sure which way it wanted to go. She would then force it to go in the other direction until she found a safe place to ditch the carriage. She had no idea which door to knock on, but there was no choice. She had to try.

"Faith," she whispered to herself, "you gotta have faith, girl."

She reached an intersection where the horse did its best to turn right. It took all of Nora's strength to haul its head around the other way. She managed to negotiate a left and found herself heading up a steep incline and away from town. The houses were fewer and further between and the trees seemed taller and fuller. The darkness thickened around her and suddenly, she felt a chill. The horse tossed its head and repeatedly tried to reverse course.

She reached the top of the grade where roads fanned out in all directions. She had no idea which one to take but concluded that it made no difference. She hauled back on the reins and pulled the horse to a stop. As she sat trying to decide, the horse continued to toss and stamp. It was almost time to part ways. Suddenly, she heard the sound of an approaching carriage. It was moving fast, and she knew that it was time. Hurriedly, she looped the reins loosely around the carriage's roof support and climbed down. The horse, seeing its opportunity, spun in place and bolted, heading back the way they'd come.

Nora slipped into the shadows under a huge elm tree and waited for the new arrival to pass. As the carriage swept past, she got a glimpse of the driver's face. The man's skin was as dark as the night around him. She couldn't be sure, but she had a feeling it was the houseman she'd escaped from that morning.

When he'd passed, she started looking around looking for any place that looked safe enough to hide her for the night. She was standing beside a high stone wall that was topped with barbed wire. She knew there'd be no scaling the wall, so she took off to her left, hoping to find a gate. Darkness was gathering quickly, and she'd have to gamble. From the looks of the wall, she surmised that the inhabitants of the house were wealthy – and cautious. She decided that taking a chance here was as good as any.

Fifty yards from where she started, she reached a gate. It was not exactly welcoming. She peered through the iron bars and could make out a large house at the end of a long tree-lined drive. The house was in darkness. She sighed deeply and decided to take the chance. After all, things couldn't be any worse.

She took a step back and studied the gate. The prospect of climbing it looked daunting, but not impossible. She took a deep breath, stepped up to the iron barricade and began her climb. It was not easy and her wounds hurt like the devil. She climbed past a large bronze plaque, which was unreadable in the gloom, but since the sign was written in Turkish, it didn't much matter.

If it had it been written in English, she wouldn't have taken another step.

Eventually, she reached the top of the gate where she was forced to rest for a moment in order to catch her breath. She hung there praying that no one would pass by and catch her breaking and entering. Mercifully her luck held.

The descent proved a lot easier than the climb, but when she reached terra firma, she was exhausted. She considered making the trek to the house but decided that arriving unannounced at the front door would not be a good idea. Instead, she searched for a place that would hide her until morning.

Behind one of the trees, she found a mossy bank. Gratefully, she collapsed onto the ground and stretched out on the bed that felt like a cloud. Slowly, she felt her body let go of its tension and that's when the tears came. They were not little girl tears. They were the product of sheer exhaustion and the damp cold and the feeling of utter hopelessness. She lay shivering and weeping until sleep rescued her.

She had a fitful night. The cold and the pain kept waking her. During one of her bouts of wakefulness, she wondered if the estate had guard dogs. She prayed they didn't, because if there were dogs on patrol, she'd be easy pickings. She wasn't afraid of dogs, but this was different. Guard dogs were trained to ask questions later.

It was only after the sun rose that she fell into a real sleep. The air had warmed quickly, and she descended into a wonderful dream. In the dream, she was a little girl spending the summer at her uncle's farm. She was playing with her cousins in a freshly built haystack. It was heaven.

She was awakened by the sound of children's laughter. For a moment, she thought she was still lost in her dream. She sat up, rubbed her eyes and peered around the great tree that had kept her hidden. What she saw drained away the last vestige of hope. They were not children at all. What she'd heard was the sound of full-grown people, dressed in different-colored robes, cavorting and laughing, engaged in some bizarre game of tag, acting like lunatics. When she spied their keepers dressed in blue uniforms, she realized that her determination was right on the money.

"Oh God," she whispered, "what have I gotten myself into?"

If she'd been able to read the sign on the gatepost, she'd have known she'd descended into hell; a hell that was named the El Mahdi Hospital for the Insane.

CHAPTER 16

As Peter crossed the lobby of his hotel, he heard the receptionist calling him.

"You have visitors Mister Brandt; two men. They're waiting for you in the bar.

Should he flee? Should he call Sofi? He had no clue, so he decided to flee. As he made for the front door someone else called his name. He glanced over his shoulder to see Demir standing at the entry to the bar, shrugging. "Where are you heading Peter? We're waiting for you. Didn't the receptionist tell you?"

Peter allowed a sheepish grin, re-crossed the lobby and shook Demir's outstretched hand.

"Good to see you," he said, sounding relieved. "Who's with you?"

"Oh, I've brought Omar, you know, from the carpet shop. He has some information that might be helpful. He brought you something else as well."

They entered the bar, where Omar stood from a corner table and flashed Peter his golden smile. As Peter approached, the merchant reached down and picked up a small, cylindrical package. He shook Peter's hand and handed him the package. "A small gift," he murmured. "It may be small, but it's of the best quality. I hope you like it. I do hope your wife will enjoy it as well."

The sheer kindness of the gesture brought a lump to Peter's throat. He turned away and dashed a tear from his eye before it gave him away. "Thank you, Omar," he replied, "you're too kind. You didn't have . . ."

Demir's raised palm silenced him, "You must never question a Turk's generosity. It would be taken as a terrible offense."

Noticing Peter's chagrin, he chuckled. "No big deal," he said, grinning, "just accept the gesture with grace. Everything will be fine. And please, sit. Omar has another gift."

Peter faced Omar, eager to hear what the rug merchant had to say. As he did, the waiter approached the table, but Omar waved him off.

"I have made a discovery," he began, when the waiter was out of earshot. "The ship called the *Izmir* that you told me about during our last meeting did indeed sail from Venice on the day your wife disappeared. Since my business involves import and export, I have some very good contacts within the shipping industry. My sources tell me that the *Izmir* made an unscheduled stop in Cyprus. She was docked there for twelve hours. I'm told that during her stop, she underwent a bit of a transformation. Her manifest was altered but even more interesting, she was re-flagged, and she departed Cyprus with a new name. She's now called the *Luxor*, she's registered Egyptian, and she made port here in Istanbul three days ago. Currently, she's anchored in the Sea of Marmara awaiting dock space so that she can offload. Supposedly, she's carrying Egyptian cotton, but I'm told her cargo is Italian wheat, which means she needs to await a specific dock which is equipped to handle grain."

Peter's eyes were as big as golf balls. His heart had ascended into his throat. Omar and Demir watched his reaction looking very pleased with themselves. Peter eventually managed to speak, "So we need to go to the police, or the harbormaster or whatever. We need to get onboard. Nora's probably there. Let's go; right now." He watched them shaking their heads and his heart sank back into place. "What?" he demanded.

"Well," Demir responded, "I wish it was that simple, but getting permission to board a foreign ship, even by our police, involves a sizeable pile of paperwork plus a sizeable pile of cash. Things don't work here quite like they do in your country. Besides that, I'm afraid that if we go through official channels, by the time the police get permission to board, your wife will be long gone. We don't know where she's headed, but let me tell you Peter, if she reaches the Black Sea, she'll never be seen again."

Peter's shoulders slumped and he slid back in his chair. He dropped his head into his hands. "What can I do?" he mumbled. "What the hell do I need to do?"

"Don't give up Peter," said Demir. "Let me talk to Sofi. She may have an idea. I'll call you once I've talked to her."

"Okay," Peter said softly, sounding deflated, "I think I'll head upstairs. I'll wait for your call." He pushed back from the table and stood. He felt lightheaded and was afraid he was going to cry. And he sure didn't want to break down in public. "Thank you, Omar, for your help," he managed, his voice trembling. "I'll never forget it."

Omar rose and stuck out his hand, but Peter never saw it. He was already heading for the door.

He wearily climbed the stairs and entered his room. He locked the door and started peeling off his clothes. When he was done, he stumbled to the bathroom, turned on the shower and climbed in before the water was even lukewarm. As the water cascaded over his head, the tears began. He'd tried to be strong. He'd tried to push reality into the recesses of his mind so as to cope with what he had to do, but his bravado had reached its limit. He wept like a baby and allowed the fear he'd been holding in check to flow over him. He collapsed to the floor, curled into a ball and lay sobbing as the water rained down on him.

After a few minutes, feeling completely drained, he stepped out of the shower and dried off. He wandered to the bed and collapsed in a heap.

He woke to the jangling of the telephone. Before reaching for the receiver, he glanced at his watch. It was just past midnight. "Hello," he whispered hoarsely.

The voice on the other end of the line was Sofi's. "Hi Peter," she said. She sounded nervous, "Meet me where you last saw me, in an hour. Make sure you're not followed and wear something warm." With that she hung up.

She must have been calling from a place where she had to be careful not to be overheard. He lay for a moment staring into the darkness wondering what he was in for. He discovered after a moment or two of contemplation that he was no longer depressed, no longer defeated. His determination returned. Action was so much better than the waiting game, he concluded.

He got up, dressed in the same jeans he'd worn earlier, donned the only sweater he had and grabbed his windbreaker from the closet. He knew he had time to spare so he stopped in the bar, which was still filled with patrons and the acrid smell of Turkish tobacco. He found a vacant stool and ordered a double Sour Cherry Vodka and a pack of American cigarettes.

By the time he'd finished his drink and another single plus four cigarettes, he was ready to go. His throat felt like sandpaper and his head was a bit light, but he felt great. He was a man on a mission.

He boldly left the hotel by the front door, figuring that anyone watching him would be long gone. He found a taxi almost immediately and directed the driver to the Şemsi Pasha Mosque.

Twenty minutes later, he reached his destination, thrust a wad of bills at the driver and leapt from the cab, ready for anything. As he crossed the gardens towards the mosque, he noticed that the shadows cast by the minarets fell across the lawn like an eagle's talon. He glanced to the sky to see a full moon. There was nearly enough light to read by.

He reached the doorway that he and Sofi had used to gain entry and startled as a person emerged from the shadows. He saw immediately that it wasn't Sofi. The person moving towards him was a man.

"Peter," he called out, "it's me Demir. Quick, follow me."

Breathing a sigh of relief, Peter hurried after his friend as he headed for the water. Tied to the dock was a small motorboat. This one however, had no police markings. He smiled at Sofi as he climbed aboard. It was hard to believe that it was only five hours ago he'd left her. It felt like a week had passed.

Demir untied the launch from the iron cleat and hopped aboard.

"Hi Peter," Sofi said. Her voice sounded tight and for the first time since he'd met her there was no smile in her eyes.

"So where are we going?" he asked, although he already had a pretty good idea.

"It's time we had a look at the *Luxor*, don't you think? If we wait any longer, I'm afraid we'll be too late."

Peter nodded enthusiastically. "Oh yes Sofi. Thank you." He nodded in the direction of Demir, "Thank you both. I still don't know why you guys are doing this, but I'm indebted for life."

"We'll it's personal for us, Peter," said Demir softly. "We also have a debt to repay. Our father was not just a flower merchant, you see. We think he was found out. That's why he died."

Peter was tempted to ask more but decided that this was not the time.

The powerful launch carved through the heavy chop of the Bosporus and in a few minutes, they left the turbulence behind them. They entered a sea so calm that the moon reflected on it like a giant pumpkin. Before them, a path of gold stretched across the surface of the flat water. It seemed to be leading them to their target.

"We're in the Sea of Marmara," Sofi explained. "The *Luxor* is anchored out here somewhere. It may take some time, but we'll find her."

Peter stood next to her gazing at the flotilla of ships that floated like giant geese on a mirror pond. There were dozens of them. He studied each one of them wondering: *Could she be there*? *Could she be this close*? He knew that whoever had bought her would not want her hurt. He knew she was alive. He just had to reach her before it was too late, before she was lost and gone forever.

His thoughts were interrupted by something poking his ribs. He looked down to see the butt of a gun being jabbed into his side.

"Do you know how to use one of these things?" Sofi smiled. "I sure hope so. You never know, you might have to use it. Can you use it if you have to, Peter?"

"Oh yeah," he growled, "no problem. Don't you worry." His jaw set and his eyes shining in the moonlight, he continued studying the fleet of ships that were looming larger by the second.

The first ship they approached was an oil tanker, which from their vantage point looked like it was a mile long. Sofi cut the engines back and floated towards the hulk. The ship was so immense that it appeared monstrous as it towered above them, ready to engulf them at a moment's notice.

They tucked in the shadows under the vast stern and Demir picked up a pair of binoculars. The others waited in silence as he glassed other adjacent sterns. The eerie sound of

Arabic music floated down from high above. Someone was playing the radio very loud.

"The music's a blessing," Sofi whispered, "it'll cover the sound of our engine."

After a few minutes, Demir dropped the glasses from his eyes and shook his head. "Not here," he announced, "maybe she's in the next pod."

Sofi gently nudged the throttles and they emerged from the tanker's shadow back into the moonlight. They headed slowly in the direction of a group of five ships that were clustered tightly together.

Right smack in the middle of them sat the *Luxor*. It was as if the other boats were providing her protection. She was a rusty old tub and unlike the others, which had a few lights on, the *Luxor* was completely dark.

Sofi again pulled back on the throttles until the launch was drifting silently towards the foul-looking scow.

Nora and Demir used paddles to bring the launch under the *Luxor*'s stern. Demir looped a rope around the anchor chain and turned to his sister, ready to hear what she had in mind.

"Well, this is it," she whispered, "we don't know what's waiting for us up there, but I think it's time to find out."

The men nodded grimly.

From the stern of the boat, she and Demir launched a tiny inflatable dinghy. From Peter's point of view, it looked too small to handle all three of them, but Sofi had other plans.

"Okay, let's go," she ordered, sounding very much in command

They managed to climb aboard the little dinghy where Peter was relegated to the floor between the other two whose job it was to paddle. They slipped down the port side, looking for any way up top. There was none. Peter felt like Jonah, thinking that at any moment he could be swallowed up.

They crossed under the bow and began searching the other side. This time, they were in luck. Halfway down the starboard side was a set of steps. Peter wondered why the steps had been left in place, hoping that it signified the crew was ashore and that Nora was up there waiting for him. The thought that she might be no more than a few feet away was almost overwhelming.

Demir secured the dinghy to the steps and led the way. Peter was right behind him. Sofi brought up the rear.

"Oh, please God," Peter whispered as his feet reached the filthy deck.

CHAPTER 17

From her hiding place, Nora watched the antics of the patients. For a while, they continued with the game of tag but eventually got bored. Some sat down on the lawn, refusing to participate further. One of the keepers called them together and apparently made a suggestion. Nora almost laughed when she saw the inmates join hands like obedient children and began a rousing round of *Ring-around-the-Rosy*. It sounded no better in Turkish. The robes they wore were all different colors, which made the circle look like the flower chains she'd made as a little girl.

They soon petered out and collapsed to the ground, apparently exhausted from their efforts. Next was a game of hide-and-seek. This suggestion seemed to be met with enthusiastic approval. All went well for the first couple of games but on the third game disaster struck. A heavy-set man, in a dirty pale blue robe, covered his eyes as his playmates scattered in all directions. Nora watched, horrified, as one of the women turned her back on the seeker and headed right for Nora. There was no doubt her game was up.

The woman laughed and squealed as she got to Nora's tree. She raced behind the trunk and dropped to her knees. When she looked to her right and saw Nora kneeling there too, staring at her, she looked like she was about to burst into tears. The women studied each other silently until the newcomer blinked. She smiled shyly, took Nora's filthy hand in her own and pressed a finger to her lips.

Amazingly, she just assumed the new girl was one of them. Nora didn't know whether to laugh or cry. She was both relieved and horrified.

So intent were they on each other that they didn't notice the fat man approach. Hearing heavy breathing close-by, Nora looked up to discover the man smiling down on them, "Aha," he crowed.

Nora groaned. They'd been caught.

Blueboy grinned; spun away and skipped triumphantly back to home base, robe flapping in the breeze, providing total exposure.

Nora's new friend shrugged, looking very disappointed at having been found. She rose slowly to her feet and pulled Nora up behind her. Hand in hand they made their way back to the group. Nora began to panic. She was about to be discovered. When they reached the others, one or two of them noticed the newcomer but most of them paid her no mind. More importantly, the keepers didn't seem to notice they'd acquired a new patient either. It occurred to Nora that the fact that she was wearing a robe was indeed a Godsend. She only hoped there would be more, many more.

Nora and her friend sat quietly waiting for the game to end. When playtime was over, the inmates formed a line and marched towards the big house. Nora fell in behind the others and followed along like she was supposed to be there. She accompanied her new pal into the hospital and up the staircase where the men turned right and the women turned left.

At the end of a long, wide hallway, an attendant unlocked a heavy wooden door and the women walked past her into the ward. Holding her breath, Nora continued and mercifully the attendant noticed nothing out of place. She entered a huge, richly paneled room with tall windows that looked like it had been a ballroom before the mansion had become an asylum.

Some of the patients, who had not participated in the activities were sitting around the room in clusters or alone, some engaged with each other, and others not. A few lay on narrow beds, either sleeping or staring into space, lost in their own worlds. Although there were at least thirty beds, there were only about twenty-five women. Nora's heart leapt. Was it possible she could stay here, undetected and out of harm's way until she came up with a plan?

"Thank you, God," she whispered.

She chose a bed that looked like it had no occupant and sat down. Her mind reeled with crazy thoughts. Among them, she found herself praying that the condition surrounding her was not catching. For the first time that morning, she became aware of the pain between her legs. She turned away from the others, opened her robe and noticed that her bandages were bloody again. As she sat wondering what to do about it, she realized she was being watched. She looked up to find her new friend gazing at her from the adjacent cot. She glanced down at Nora's bandages and smiled knowingly. She immediately stood up and signaled for Nora to follow her. As they walked through the ward, Nora noticed that only one or two of the women paid her any mind.

They reached a door at the end of the room and walked through into a large, white tiled bathroom. There were half-a-dozen toilets and sinks plus a communal shower. Smiling shyly, her friend opened a cupboard beneath one of the sinks and emerged triumphantly with a handful of sanitary napkins. She handed them to Nora, who smiled with gratitude.

"Thank you," she whispered.

The woman nodded her head and bowed slightly.

Nora pointed to her chest. "Nora," she said.

Nodding excitedly the woman responded. She pointed to her own chest, "Talya," she announced. Solemnly, she stuck out her hand.

Nora took it and shook it warmly. "Thank you," she said softly.

"*Tesekkur ederim*," Talya replied.

It was apparent to Nora that communication was going to be somewhat limited.

As Talya watched unabashedly, Nora washed her hands and face and then her wound. Although there was no hot water, she was grateful there was water at all. She applied the sanitary pad and realized there was a problem. She had no way to keep the pad in place. She turned to Talya and shrugged. Recognizing the dilemma, Talya opened another cupboard and pulled out a shallow box. She handed it to Nora, who opened it to discover a variety of underpants, some paper, and some plastic. She decided on a nice pair of the green plastics in something close to the right size and pulled them on. Talya grinned, proud of her contribution.

As Nora smiled back, she noticed that Talya no longer had teeth. She could have sworn she had teeth earlier. Then again, after what she'd been through over the last few days, she didn't have much faith in her powers of observation.

They returned to the ward and again went mostly unnoticed. These women had enough problems of their own to give a newcomer much attention, Nora concluded. She stretched out on the bed she'd commandeered while Talya sat down on the one next to her. She refused to take her eyes off her new friend. It was as if she was worried Nora might disappear.

Nora smiled reassuringly. Talya immediately smiled back. This time there were definitely teeth. Nora stared at Talya's mouth. She was very confused. Maybe she was losing it after all. As she watched, disbelieving, the teeth moved. Suddenly, they were no longer attached to her upper gums. Instead, they sat proudly on her lower gums. Nora burst out laughing, relieved she hadn't gone nuts after all. Apparently, Talya had mastered the ability to switch her single denture around without removing it from her mouth. Obviously, the poor soul had far too much time on her hands.

At that moment, the big door swung opened, and two orderlies entered the ward wheeling trolleys. From the accompanying smell, lunch was being served.

As the orderlies went about serving trays to the patients, Nora slid from her bed onto the floor and disappeared. Although she wasn't convinced these people would recognize that there was a new patient, they'd certainly be able to figure out that they were one meal short.

When the trays had all been distributed, the attendants wheeled the trolleys out of the room and locked the door behind them. Nora decided that escaping the psych ward would prove more difficult than gaining entry had been. She slipped out from under her bed and sat down. She wasn't at all surprised to see Talya perched on the next bed, her lunch tray on her lap.

By means of sign language, she managed to communicate that it was her intention to share her food. Nora nodded gratefully. She was starving. Talya passed over a plate and Nora studied its contents. Unfortunately, lunch closely resembled the stuff the horse had evacuated all over the barn floor. It smelled a lot like manure as well, but she really was famished. She ventured a spoonful. Not bad, she decided. The brown mush did taste a lot better than it looked – or smelled. She downed half of it before returning the plate to Talya. Her friend smiled kindly and refused. She signaled that Nora was to eat it all. So, she did. When she'd cleaned the plate, Talya handed her a glass of greenish liquid. Nora accepted it and was relieved to discover that the lukewarm liquid tasted a little like tea.

When she'd finished everything, she glanced up to see Talya studying her intently. The woman pointed to her chest. "Turk," she stated and pointed at Nora.

"American," Nora responded, "California."

Talya smiled teeth on top, pleased that communication had reached a new level.

Conversation exhausted, Nora lay back down. Within seconds she was fast asleep.

Talya remained in place, watching her only friend, happy to stand guard.

Nora slept through the reappearance of the orderlies, who collected all the trays without ever noticing the new addition.

CHAPTER 18

Al Caribe anxiously paced the floor of his bedroom. He was in a quandary. *What to wear*? The guests he was expecting for dinner were a mix of Europeans and Easterners. He was more comfortable in his Arabian clothes but to make the Europeans more at ease he determined he should probably go with a suit.

He slid open a door in his dressing room and decided on the navy-blue Armani. There were several navy-blue Italian suits, but he hadn't yet worn the Armani and he was in the mood for something new. His thoughts flashed to Nora James and a dark scowl invaded his pocked face. His dark eyes glinted with anger.

She was supposed to have been here for his dinner party but from what he'd been told earlier in the day that was not to be the case. *How could the stupid bastards allow her to escape*? he thought. Oh, they'd be sorry, yes very sorry . . . but that didn't alter the troublesome reality.

He was confident she'd be found. There was, after all, no way off the island and there weren't many places for her to hide. Not that she'd have been presented at his dinner party, but she'd be there waiting in her rooms, available to him whenever he wished to partake. Later on, she'd be allowed to join the table but not until she'd come to accept and appreciate her new place in life. She would be veiled of course. Much as he would have enjoyed showing off his latest acquisition, it wouldn't do to take risks. Hassan hated risk taking – sure things were much more to his liking.

He was so angry that he'd had to re-knot his tie twice before getting it right. He decided on the black velvet slippers, with his crest embroidered on the toes. He slipped them on and checked himself one last time in the full-length mirror. He was satisfied with what he saw. He was quite a striking man; almost handsome he decided –if one didn't look too closely.

He left the suite, closing the door behind him to contain his cats. Some people didn't like cats he'd discovered. It made him wonder about their character. He descended the winding staircase feeling expansive and quite ready for a night of revelry.

He checked his diamond-encrusted Piaget. It was nearly ten. His guests would be arriving soon. Things happened late in Istanbul. Hassan had never understood how his California acquaintances could dine at 8 o'clock. That was the time he usually awoke from his nap.

He paused to glance into the dining room. Everything was perfect. The long table had been set for fourteen and it looked most welcoming. The gold and blue place settings reflected the candlelight beautifully and the gold silverware – he smiled at the oxymoron – gleamed dully, like a Bedouin's weapons.

As he entered the opulent grand salon, he saw a houseman answering the front door. His first guests had arrived. He watched Ansar, a friend and sometime partner, enter followed by his wife Deirdre, a forty-year-old beauty who seemed a little weighed down by her jewelry.

Within a half-hour, the salon was alive with laughter and conversation. Gleaming silver samovars laden with caviar, delivered just that morning from Iran, were passed around by an army of servants. Billecart-Salmon champagne flowed liberally among the women while the men for the most part sipped on the finest scotch. Although Hassan did not drink alcohol, he provided his guests with anything they might desire.

The last guest to arrive was Hassan's neighbor, Ali Sandar who entered the mansion from the water side rather than through the front door. Ali lived no more than fifty yards away and as usual he had arrived by boat. Although there was a gate in the high wall that separated the properties,

Sandar was reluctant to walk the fifty yards. It was the walking home after an evening of revelry that made him opt for the boat. With him was a stunning woman that Hassan had never seen before. She looked very young, he decided, but so beautiful she was probably worth the bother young girls could sometimes be.

Ali crossed to his host, greeted him in the Arab style and introduced his new companion, Nadja. Hassan studied the girl's nervous eyes wondering if Ali had taken her virginity yet. From the dullness of her expression, he decided that she'd already been deflowered. He immediately lost interest.

Behind Ali was a large man in a black suit who moved like a professional fighter. He glanced around the room, wary as a snake. Beneath his left arm was a giveaway bulge.

Sandar and his companion took leave of their host and wandered off to join the other guests in the main salon. They were followed closely by the large man in the black suit who took up his post in the shadows beside two other dark-suited men.

Ali Sandar's vigilant bodyguard was none other than Sofi's fiancée, Mahmet.

Dinner was a sultan's feast. Countless courses were presented to choruses of oohs and aahs. Formally dressed waiters poured priceless wines into jeweled goblets and by the time dessert was served, most of the guests were snookered. Early in the evening, the talk had been light and frivolous but by 1 o'clock the conversation was mired in world politics or sex. A few loud exchanges erupted, but Hassan immediately doused the little frays with either his charm or his caustic wit.

When coffee and liqueurs arrived in the room, the men rose as if on cue and retired to the billiards room, leaving the women to gossip and complain about their arduous lives.

One of the bodyguards stayed in the room with the women. Mahmet and the other guard accompanied the men.

An unusual feature of Hassan's elegant billiards room was the sleek modern fountain that occupied one entire wall. Even if the bodyguards wanted to listen in on the conversation, it would be impossible to understand what was being said.

Four of the men opted for a game while the others lounged around the roaring fire, sipping fine port and Turkish coffee. When Hassan finished his coffee, he handed the almost transparent porcelain cup and saucer across the table to Ali Sandar. Ali took the proffered cup and upended it into the saucer. He placed the cup over the coffee dregs and placed them on his side table to cool.

Conversation continued among the other men. The subject, as was usually the case in this room was terrorism and its growing impact on life in Istanbul. According to one fat man, life in the city was becoming more dangerous with every week that passed. The others concurred that their hedonistic lifestyles were becoming threatened by the new class of fundamentalists who were now wielding power in the worldly and tolerant city. Hassan listened to every word but made no comment.

When the upended coffee cup had cooled sufficiently, Ali lifted it from the table, turned it right side up allowing the dregs to coat the sides. As he performed the ritual, he had Hassan's undivided attention. He held the cup under the table lamp and studied the results for a moment before speaking.

"Well," he began, "things look good, my friend, very good. Your bunions are a bit better, and you will have no sickness over the coming months."

Hassan nodded slowly, hanging on Sandar's every word.

"The Babylon acquisitions are safe. They're on their way and will prove to be even more important than expected." He then coughed nervously as if reluctant to continue.

"Go on," Hassan growled, "what is it?"

"Well, my friend, I see another acquisition that is not going quite so well. It's as if it has been lost in transit. I can't see exactly what it is, but I have the strong sense that this one is very important to you. Is one of your women expecting a child by any chance?"

Hassan shook his head impatiently.

"Has there been a miscarriage then in your house?"

"No damn it," Hassan replied, his ire mounting. "There are no pregnancies allowed in my house. I have no need of some brat arriving on this earth claiming that it has my blood."

Ali placed the cup and saucer back on the table and shrugged. “That’s it then,” he mumbled, “I can see no more. It may come to you what it means. But whatever it is, it’s something very powerful, maybe even dangerous.”

With that, Hassan leapt to his feet. His patience had run out. “I’m suddenly very tired,” he announced to the room. “I’m going to bed. Please stay as long as you wish.”

He strode from the room leaving his guests wordless and staring after him.

“Well, I wonder what is wrong,” said Ali Sandar to no one in particular. “That’s not like him.”

In the safety of his bedroom, Hassan slipped off his clothes and dropped them on the floor. He climbed naked into his huge bed and lay staring at the time, which was projected onto the ceiling in large blue letters. He had a bad feeling. Maybe it was the fish he’d eaten, he decided. He was joined on the bed by his cats, who took up their places like watchful footmen. He fell asleep to a chorus of rhythmic purring and descended into a world of troubled dreams.

CHAPTER 19

Peter was glad he'd worn his warmest clothes. The night was cold and damp. The moon had scuttled behind the gathering clouds leaving the trio in darkness. The ship was silent. Save for the rhythmic creaking as it strained against its anchor chain, there wasn't a sound. They all had flashlights, but Sofi had cautioned against using them at least until they were belowdecks.

Hunched down, they crept towards the bridge figuring that if there was a man posted, he'd most likely be there. They reached the stern without incident and Sofi placed her ear to the door, listening for anything that would indicate the presence of a watchman. There was none. She pulled her Glock from its holster, took hold of the door and slid it aside. Thankfully, its rails had been well oiled, and it opened without a sound.

Inside the wheelhouse, she pulled her flashlight from her pocket and crouched to the floor. At that moment, the moon as if curious, re-emerged and she immediately doused the light. The moon was bright enough to allow a cursory search of the tiny room, but she turned up nothing.

She pointed behind the men, indicating the companionway that led from the bridge belowdecks. They tiptoed down the steps and reached a hallway that smelled sour, as if someone had vomited. There were three doors and they each tried one. None was locked. Peter stepped into the first cabin and shone his light around the space. The cabin was filthy with men's clothes littering the floor and a stained mattress. There were no sheets or blankets or any evidence that a woman had been there.

In the second cabin, Sofi found the same state of disarray. There were two bunks, each covered by a wrinkled blanket of indeterminate color but again, no indication of a woman's presence. She checked all the drawers and the bathroom – nothing.

Demir had no luck either. They met up in the hallway and moved to the end where there was another set of steps heading down. They descended with Sofi in the lead. At the bottom, the air was muggy and smelled of diesel.

At the end of the short corridor was a steel door. Sofi reached it first and tried to pull down on the heavy handle. It wouldn't budge. Demir joined in the effort and together they got the handle to move. The door squealed loudly as Demir pushed it open. They froze in place listening for any sign that they'd been heard. A few seconds passed but no one appeared.

They stepped over the doorsill and entered the engine room. After a quick search, they found nothing of interest and moved on. At the end of the engine room was a door which was a replica of the one they'd just entered. This one opened easily, and Sofi led the way through. They were in a narrow corridor lined with plywood partitions. "The hold," Sofi whispered.

The men nodded and said nothing. Demir hauled open one of the large doors, which rolled up like a garage door. He shone his light into the space. Stacked against the wall were at least a dozen wooden crates. He stepped inside, crossed to the nearest crate and opened the lid. He whistled softly and the others stepped in to join him. Reflecting the beam of his light were the steel barrels of four heavy machine guns, complete with tripods. Peter pried open another box. This one was crammed with boxes of ammunition. They opened several more to discover that they all contained weapons of one kind or another. Two of the boxes held hand grenades, while another contained half-a-dozen small rockets.

"Wheat, huh?" Sofi muttered. "This is the stuff that our terrorists use to kill."

They moved to the next storage pen where they found crates of something Peter didn't recognize.

"Plastique," Sofi answered before the question was asked.

In the corner of the crib were three fifty-gallon drums strapped to the wall. The labels were printed in Italian so none of them knew exactly what the drums contained. The red skulls and crossbones, however, indicated the contents were by no means harmless.

The rest of the compartments were empty, but what they'd uncovered was enough weaponry to start a war.

The narrow passageway ended in a set of steps heading upwards. Sofi again led the way, and they reached a small landing with two small wooden doors. This area was separated from the other living quarters, possibly the captain's cabin. She tried one of the doors, but it was locked. Cautiously, she placed her ear to the door. She heard something, it sounded like someone was inside. She stepped back and looked at Peter whose face was ashen. He was breathing hard, and his brow beaded with sweat. He moved to the door and pressed his ear to the wood. There was a sound, a soft moaning like someone in pain.

"What do you think," he whispered, "should I knock?"

Sofi didn't respond. She glanced at Demir who shrugged, indicating that this was not his area of expertise. Sofi turned back to Peter and shook her head, "I think no," she decided. "We don't know what's in there."

Peter nodded, concluding that she was probably right. After all, she was the professional.

Sofi raised her gun. The men followed suit.

"Kick it in," she whispered, "if there's only one of them, we'll be okay."

Peter and Demir took a step back and in unison kicked the door as hard as they could. The lock held fast, but the door splintered into a half-dozen pieces and fell into the cabin. Sofi raced inside, her flashlight in one hand, her Glock in the other. Peter, his heart in his throat, was right behind her. Demir backed into the cabin, keeping an eye on the stairway behind them in case the crash had alerted someone to their presence. The flashlight beam danced around the cabin walls and floor. There was a small cot, a desk and chair; nothing else. The cabin was empty. A soft moaning sound directed the lights and attention to the source. Peter let out his breath and his shoulders sagged.

The sound was nothing but the wind moaning through the porthole, which had been left slightly ajar. Shaking off his disappointment he watched as Sofi yanked open another door to reveal a small bathroom, which contained a toilet and a small sink. She flashed her light around the space – nothing. She returned to the cabin, joining the men as they explored every nook and cranny looking for any sign that Nora had been there. After a few minutes of searching, they gave up. Peter began to tremble as his adrenalin ran out.

Sofi shrugged and stroked his arm. “Sorry Peter,” she said softly, “I really thought we’d find some clue. If she was here, we’d have found something. Maybe our information was wrong. Maybe she was never here.”

Suddenly Peter’s eyes widened. The shaking stopped. He squeezed between the other two and stepped into the bathroom where he crouched down and carefully studied the toilet paper roll. His hand trembled as he lifted the top sheet and aimed the beam of his flashlight to the spot.

“Yes,” he whispered as tears sprang to his eyes.

Between the top two sheets was a long strand of hair. The hair was red, the exact color of Nora’s. He carefully pulled the hair from the paper and returned to the cabin.

“She was here,” he announced excitedly, “she left this for us.”

“What do you mean?” Demir asked. “What did she leave?”

“This,” Peter replied, holding out the strand of hair for them to see. “It is from a scene in a movie we worked on. I can’t believe she remembered.”

“Very impressive,” said Sofi, smiling, “she’s a clever woman. Maybe she has found a way out of this mess.”

“Oh God,” Peter replied, “oh God I hope so.”

“I think it’s time to go,” Sofi whispered. “We should get out of here before they return. If Nora left you a clue, she’s no longer here.”

Peter and Demir nodded in agreement and followed Sofi out the door. Sofi tried the other small door. It was unlocked. She stepped through and found herself back on deck not far from the bridge. She hurried around the deck to the starboard side and reached the steps that led back down to the dinghy. As she placed her foot onto the steps, she heard something. It wasn't good. She spun around to face Peter and Demir, and from the looks on their faces, they'd heard it too.

It was the sound of a motorboat and it was approaching fast.

"Should we go for it?" Demir asked.

"Too late," Sofi replied, "they'd be on us before we got near our boat. I think we should split up and hide until we find out how many there are. We may be able to surprise them. Chances are they won't think that three people could fit in the dinghy."

Without another word, they headed in different directions, looking for places to conceal themselves. Peter clambered up on top of the bridge and lay in the shadows listening to the motorboat as it came closer. He pulled his gun from his belt and fingered it thoughtfully. A part of him wanted to kill them all. He was sure he could do it without compunction. After all, these animals had manhandled Nora and maybe even worse.

In the next few moments, his rational side won out. He realized that if the bad guys were all dead, he couldn't beat information out of them. He lay still and concentrated on slowing his heart rate.

Demir reached the stern and crouched down behind a hatch cover where he could see the men from the motor craft as they made their way up to the deck.

Sofi climbed into a lifeboat and pulled the canvas over her head, leaving just a crack so she could see out. She heard the engines slow as the launch approached the steps and the cries of surprise and anger as they discovered the inflatable. She listened to the urgent conversation as the men decided how to proceed. Unfortunately, she was unable to make out what they were saying. It took a moment for her to realize that they were speaking Italian.

The stairs started creaking as the men mounted the steps. One by one they reached the deck and crouching low, fanned out around the ship. There were five of them.

"Damn," Peter whispered to himself. He contemplated shooting a couple of them and leaving two to beat to death but before he could move his mind was made up for him.

Two shots rang out from the stern, followed by a cry of pain. The voice was that of Demir. Three seconds later, there was a loud splash as something or someone heavy hit the water.

Sofi lifted the canvas and peeked out. Not 10 feet away stood a man with his back to her. Suddenly her thigh cramped, and she had no choice but to change her position. She moved her leg slowly and carefully but as she did, the lifeboat creaked. The man whipped around to face her and leveled his gun. She took a breath and shot him in the face. He dropped like a stone as his gun skittered across the deck.

As if on cue, gunfire erupted from several locations. More lights flickered on in several of the nearby ships and the sounds of sailors yelling in half-a-dozen languages floated across the water.

Sofi scrambled from her hiding place and headed for the stern and her fallen brother. As she rounded the corner behind the wheelhouse, she ran smack into a man who was hiding in the shadows. She raised her gun to shoot and the man grunted. She recognized him immediately. It was Peter.

"Follow me," she commanded and grabbed his hand. They raced across the stern deck and reached the rail where Demir was crouched, and shots wailed above their heads. She looked knowingly at Peter. Together they hauled Demir up onto the rail and dropped him over. He hit the water with a resounding splash. Sofi leapt up onto the rail and dove in after her brother. Peter realized he had no choice. He slid up onto the rusted railing amidst a shower of bullets, crushing his testicles in the process. Writhing in agony, he fell over the side.

He hit the water and immediately forgot all about the pain in his scrotum. The shock of the icy cold removed every thought except the job of breathing. He struggled to the surface gasping for air and floundered there for a moment until the panic subsided. He spotted Sofi a few yards away, struggling to help Demir, doing her best to keep him afloat. Peter swam over and took hold of Demir's free arm. Sofi was unable to speak but nodded her gratitude. Peter started to swim away from the *Luxor* and the guns but as he started for shore, more than a mile away, Sofi grabbed his shirt and shook her head.

"No," she gasped, "the other way. Stay close to the hull and head for our boat. They can't get at us if we're under the stern."

Peter took hold of Demir's legs. Together they struggled back towards their boat. Sofi was on her back with one arm under Demir's head kicking for all she was worth while Peter did his best to keep the rest of Denir above water. It took forever, but eventually, they reached the stern of the *Luxor* and were relieved to see that their boat was still there, tied to the anchor chain. Fortunately, it was on the port side and hadn't been spotted. The seamen's attention remained focused on the starboard side where Sofi and the men had jumped. They reached their boat without being seen and Sofi hauled herself on board then reached back for her brother. With Peter's help, she managed to get Demir up over the gunwales and into the boat, where he slid to the bottom and lay still. Peter climbed aboard and collapsed beside the wounded man, completely exhausted and gasping for breath.

He watched as Sofi checked her brother for wounds and saw the relief on her face as Demir opened his eyes and smiled up at her. The side of his head was covered with blood, but by the time Sofi had wiped the wound the bleeding had stopped.

"They only grazed him," Sofi announced, sounding very relieved. "He'll be fine."

"Well, thank God," Peter replied. He sat up, "Let's get out of here. We should get him to a hospital."

"No," she answered firmly, "they'll hear us, and they'll come after us. If they do, we're finished. They have weapons that can blow us out of the water. Remember?"

"So, what do you suggest?"

"Well, Demir's okay. He'll have a terrible headache but aside from that he'll be fine. I think you and I should go back onboard the ship. That's the last thing they'll be expecting. By my count we got three of them so there are only two left. First, we'll have the advantage of surprise and two; we may never have another chance to get the information we need."

"I'm going with you," Demir murmured as he struggled to sit up.

"Oh no," said Sofi firmly, "we don't need you slowing us down. You wait for us here. When you hear me call, come to the steps and pick us up. Don't worry about noise. It won't matter by then."

Demir nodded slowly, obviously disappointed

She looked at Peter, "Are you ready? It's now or never. In another few minutes we'll be too cold."

"I'm ready if you are," he replied evenly. He wasn't sure just how ready he was but there was no choice. Nora's life was at stake.

Without another word, Sofi slipped over the side of the launch and back into the icy water. Peter was not far behind. They swam together doing their best not to splash, heading for the steps. They saw the motorboat tied to the platform at the foot of the steps, but their dinghy was nowhere in sight. The crew had either sunk it or cut it loose.

They swam to the far side of the motorboat, where they were hidden from the ship and held onto the side trying to catch their breath.

"We'll stay together this time," she said. "They'll either be in the captain's cabin or on the bridge. My guess is the bridge. They'll be on the radio trying to alert someone."

When she was ready, Sofi nodded and went around to the steps. She pulled herself dripping from the sea and started up the steps. When she reached the top, she pulled out her gun and glanced over her shoulder. Peter followed her closely and did the same. He was sure he was freezing because he could barely feel the gun in his hand.

Peter tapped Sofi on the shoulder and pointed towards the bridge. There was a light on, and he could see the shadows of two men. Keeping low, they crept towards the wheelhouse and the impending showdown.

CHAPTER 20

The day was cloudy, but even on a dull day Hassan's palace was light and airy. He sat in the billiards room listening intently to the news. The pretty girl seated across from him on the blonde leather couch seemed ill at ease. Her voice shook slightly as she explained what she'd learned. She spoke softly in Turkish, and Hassan listened without interruption.

"For three days the Venice Carabinieri were in a flurry," she said. "Two men arrived from California two days after she disappeared. One was some kind of policeman, the other was her representative, either her manager or public relations man; I'm not sure. They spent an entire day with the police, screaming and threatening but in the end, they got nothing. There were no leads. When they reached the conclusion that they were getting nowhere and had succeeded in making enemies everywhere they turned, they left for Rome. They promised that the embassy would become involved and that heads would roll. The Carabinieri were not impressed."

Hassan sighed and smiled. "This is good, Adja, very good. And you met the husband at his hotel after the eh . . . acquisition? I'm curious. How was he?"

"In truth, Pasha, he was terribly upset. I had a drink with him at the Danieli. He seemed like a very different person from the man I saw at the boutique right before we snatched his wife. At the hotel, he got blind drunk. In my opinion, you have nothing to fear from Peter Brandt. He's a typical American. No real capacity for – brutality. I'm sure he'll quickly give up."

Hassan nodded again. "So where did he go when he left Venice?"

"Oh, he took a flight to Rome with the other two. They had no luck at all in Rome, so they returned to America. They stated that they would pull diplomatic strings back in the States. As I said, Brandt has no stomach for the darker things."

"So, you watched him board the plane as instructed?"

"Oh yes, Pasha. All three of them were together."

"And what would you say if I told you that as we speak, he is here in Istanbul, making friends and becoming a real nuisance."

The girl blanched. Like a descending curtain, the blood drained from her face. Her eyes darted nervously around the room. She couldn't decide where to look.

"That will be all for today Adja, Haid will show you out and give you your payment."

The girl stood, and without another word, hurried from the room. Waiting in the corridor was a small man in a black suit.

"Follow me," he said softly.

They left the house through a side door and took the winding path that led through the elaborate formal gardens towards the cliff that barricaded the mansion from the outside world. At the foot of the cliff was a small elevator. The man pushed the button and the glass door slid open without a sound. Adja stepped inside. Haid stepped in behind her. As the elevator ascended the cliff face, Adja gazed out over the palace roof and the dull gray water of the Bosporus. The garrote was slipped around her throat without her even feeling it. Haid spun her towards him so as to see her face. He pulled her body close to his own, savoring the frantic hammering of her heart until it stopped beating. She twitched for a moment or two before the stillness overtook her. Grudgingly, he released the garrote and allowed her to slump to the floor where she lay motionless. Her bulging eyes stared up at her killer. He didn't look back.

The elevator stopped and the street-side door slid open. Two men lifted the body from its resting place and carried it to the open trunk of a waiting car. They deposited Adja into the trunk, closed the lid, climbed into the car and drove away. Haid returned to the elevator. As the door closed, he carefully wiped the blood from the garrote with his handkerchief. When he was done, he slipped the lethal wire and the bloodied cloth back into his pocket.

***

In his private office, Hassan was talking on the phone. He was furious, "You haven't found her yet? Are you as blind as you are stupid? Listen, doctor, I'll give you twenty-four hours. If you are unsuccessful, you will be replaced, and replaced is a powerful word. Do I make myself clear?" He slammed the receiver back into its cradle and glared out the window past the palm trees and the deep blue water of the swimming pool. He watched as Haid crossed the manicured gardens and approached the house. He rose from behind his desk and crossed to a door that opened onto the verandah.

"Haid," he called, "come here."

Haid broke into a run. When he reached the office, Hassan was back behind his desk. "Haid," he announced, "I need you to contact the Syrians. I will require at least two men – the best they have. I need them immediately. It seems there's some cleaning up to be done.

When Haid left the room to make the call, Hassan sat quietly listening to the sounds of the birds singing. He took a deep breath and closed his eyes trying to erase some of the frustration he felt. The loss of Nora was bothersome but hardly cataclysmic. She was nothing more than a diversion and not the reason for his anxiety. His concern was that while others searched for her, they might stumble across information that could hurt him. If the authorities discovered that besides dealing in rare artifacts, he was one of the world's leading arms dealers, they'd shut him down. If they came across the *Luxor*'s true cargo and found out what the barrels contained, he'd end up in jail or worse. Not even he was connected well enough to rise above profiting from terrorism. Arming terrorists in exchange for priceless relics must never be made known. It would be the end of him.

The Americans would make sure he suffered. And the Americans had power, too much power, even in Turkey.

CHAPTER 21

Nora dozed on and off all afternoon. The restful hours were indeed a blessing, providing her body with an opportunity to heal. Every time she opened her eyes, she saw Talya sitting quietly on the next bed. The woman had apparently decided that she was Nora's protector.

By the time the dinner trolleys arrived, she felt better than she had in days. As before, at the sound of the key in the lock, she slipped under the bed and waited for the attendants to leave. Dinner was palatable – slices of roast lamb accompanied by clove-flavored rice and pita bread. Once again Talya refused the food, insisting that Nora eat her meal.

Nora complied but left a little on the plate, indicating that she was full. Talya reluctantly ate the remainder of the meal and nodded her gratitude. She treated Nora like she was her very own princess and was content simply to be in her presence.

After the trays were gathered up, the lights were turned out and the ward descended into darkness. Nora lay staring at the ceiling. Having napped for most of the afternoon, she was not a bit sleepy. A usual, her thoughts turned to Peter. She felt terribly sad for him. Knowing him as she did, she was sure he'd be blaming himself even if it wasn't his fault. She assumed that he would have gone to the police immediately and that he would have called back to the States for advice. She hoped he'd find some comfort from friends. If the situation was reversed, she knew she'd be a complete basket case.

She felt the light tap on her shoulder and peered through the darkness to recognize her lady in waiting. Talya signaled for Nora to follow her as she headed across the room towards the door. When they reached it, Nora was amazed to see Talya pull a key from her shoe and insert it into the lock. She watched in awe as Talya opened the door and moved aside so that Nora could step through. Talya locked the door behind them and beckoned for Nora to stay close behind her. They tiptoed down a long corridor and reached a door identical to the one they'd just left.

Talya pulled a second key from her shoe and inserted the original. She unlocked the door and pushed it open. This room had a bit more light. The moon had risen and cast bright beams across the space; it was much like the ward they'd just left. The walls were lined with cots, but this ward also had floor-to-ceiling shelves filled with books.

Talya made her way down the center aisle until she reached the very last bed, instead of a cot though it was a real double bed. Beside it was a chest of drawers, which held a clock, a reading lamp and a pitcher of water.

Talya reached out and gently shook the person under the covers. With a start, a form turned to face her, pulling the covers down. Nora saw the face of a man staring back at them. It was the handsome face of an older man. He had a shock of silver hair, a perfect elegant nose, inquisitive blue eyes and a neatly trimmed mustache. The man looked very surprised.

"Talya," he said, struggling to sit up. He asked her something in Turkish. She answered and he turned to peer at Nora.

"Well, well," he murmured in perfect English, "can this be true?"

"What?" Nora replied. "What did she say?"

He smiled kindly. "She says she found you hiding behind a tree in the garden a couple of days ago and that you've been hiding in the women's ward ever since. Although she's not quite right, I've always found her to be completely veracious, not to mention resourceful. She's been here for many years and pretty well has the run of the place, without either the knowledge or consent of the administrators of course."

Nora glanced at her friend who was paying rapt attention to the conversation, even though Nora was sure that she didn't understand a word.

"Well, is what she says true? Because if it is, it would be the first time anyone ever broke into this place." He smiled again and Nora felt better than she had in a long while.

"Yes, it's true," she replied. "I actually didn't know what this place was. If I had, I would probably have made a different choice."

He nodded knowingly and leaned in to get a better look at his visitor. "Well, well," he whispered, "you are a very beautiful woman. Do you know that?"

Nora felt herself blushing. It was a question she'd never been asked before and she wasn't sure how to respond. Thankfully, a response wasn't expected because the man went right on talking. "My name is Simon Weathers," he offered, extending his hand.

"Nice to meet you," Nora replied, shaking his hand. "I'm Nora Jam . . . eh Brandt."

"Pleasure," he said warmly. "Now, please allow me to make myself presentable and I'll be curious to hear your story. I'm sure it must be a beaut."

He climbed out of bed, opened a small closet and pulled out an elegant silk robe. Donning the robe, he ran his fingers through his hair and sat back down. He patted the bed beside him, inviting Nora to join him. She did. Talya settled onto the floor and sat with her legs crossed, gazing up at them.

"Talya tells me you're a Yank," Simon continued. "I'm a Brit myself. I'm confined here due to some unfortunate drug trafficking activities. Such a crime can result in a death sentence in this country, but the authorities assumed that for a man of my age to be involved in such larceny, he must surely be bonkers. Perhaps they were right . . . oh well. As a result, I've been here for nearly three years. I must say the sojourn has provided me ample time to debate the issue with myself."

Nora was having trouble finding words – Simon Weathers – the drug smuggler. It was hard to fathom.

"I'm sure you'd like to ask questions, to hear details, to try to understand. If we have time, I'll be happy to attempt to justify my choices. I don't have much occasion to converse in English in this place and I'd very much enjoy the opportunity. But first, I think I should hear your story. It must be fascinating."

She started from the beginning. Simon listened to her tale, offering no commentary. Occasionally, he nodded and once or twice, his eyes opened wider. The description of her hymen reconstruction caused his mouth to fall open before he regained control.

"My, my, my," he muttered when she'd finished, "never heard of such a thing. Sounds like a movie, don't you think? Damn good one too."

"Actually, I'm in the movies. I've made quite a few. Let me tell you, none of them was as frightening as this."

During the entire telling, Talya had remained frozen in place, listening intently as if she understood every word.

"So, we must get you away from this place. I'm afraid that if you presented your case to the staff, they'd assume you belonged here. They don't have much imagination – or compassion. No, we must get you out of this bedlam."

"And how can we possibly do that?" Nora asked. "As you said, breaking out of here is much more difficult than breaking in."

"I don't know yet," Simon replied softly. "But allow me to think about it. Let's meet again tomorrow. Join the women when they go outside for exercise, and I'll meet you there. I guarantee you won't be noticed. The keepers pay no attention and half of them are morons. Our hour in the garden is the highlight of our day, you know. However, there are others in here that never get to see the sky. They're locked away in darkness; prisoners in this place until the day they die. If the poor souls weren't violent when they entered these walls, let me tell you, they became monsters soon thereafter. Unfortunately, the staff undergoes a parallel transformation."

***

Nora was unable to sleep. The meeting with Simon Weathers had provided a glimmer of hope. She hadn't felt hope in ages. As usual er thoughts turned to Peter. She tried to imagine what he might be doing at that moment, but his face wouldn't come into focus. It was ironic really. They'd travelled all the way to Venice in an effort to sort out some bumps in their marriage. The things upsetting her had been at the forefront of her mind when they'd arrived. Marriage had become a constant irritation, perhaps the inevitable result of too many years and too much time together.

His need to correct her, to disagree for no reason at all, had driven her mad. Some days it had seemed like he couldn't agree that the sky was blue. The slightest thing would have set either of them off and their arguments sometimes led to threats. The '*D*' word had been tossed into the mix on more than one occasion. She'd learned that when two passionate people collide the wreck can be absolute. It all seemed so silly now. She now realized that what had been a stupid power struggle could be fixed. She knew that now that she could articulate the problem, it had been replaced by this abyss she'd been dropped into. She'd loved that man with all her heart for fifteen years and adored him still. He was kind and smart and funny and irritating as hell. And oh, how she needed him now.

She fell asleep shortly before sunrise but was awakened by Talya urgently shaking her shoulder. As Nora dragged her brain into wakefulness, she saw her friend pointing anxiously at the door. Nora started to slip from her bed to the floor, but she was too late. As she pulled the cover off, the door opened, and two men entered the ward. Nora's first thought was that Simon had betrayed her, but the men, one of whom had a stethoscope around his neck, marched right past without paying her any attention. Simon certainly was right about the staff's powers of observation, she concluded.

She peered out from beneath her covers and watched as they stopped five beds down from hers. The one with the stethoscope bent down and placed the instrument on the occupant's chest. A moment later, he straightened, shaking his head. The men had a brief conversation and then headed back for the door. Nora ducked back under her covers until she heard the door close. When she reemerged, Talya sat on the adjacent bed wringing her hands in anguish and huge tears ran down her face.

Nora reached for her friend and drew her into her arms. For a minute or two, Nora rocked her like a baby until she felt Talya's sobs gradually subside. Talya pulled away and pointed, using excited, animated sign language, she managed to impart the reason for her grief. Nora understood her immediately. The woman five beds away had died during the night.

CHAPTER 22

Sofi reached the door to the bridge first. She glanced through the glass and without waiting, grabbed the handle and slid the door open. She stepped through, gun drawn and smiled at the shocked faces of the two men. She pointed her Glock directly at the face of the tall one and barked orders in Turkish. In unison, the men raised their hands and dropped to their knees. Behind her, Peter watched them intently; aware that a part of him hoped one of them would do something stupid. He had no doubt he could happily empty his gun into either one of them. He didn't have long to wait.

As the taller man removed his gun from his belt and slid it across the floor toward Sofi's feet, the fat one made a fatal mistake. He slowly withdrew his weapon from his pocket as directed and made to slide it to Sofi. For a second, she took her eyes off the man, anticipating the sliding gun. But instead of releasing it, he grasped the handle and pointed the pistol at

Sofi. Without blinking, she shot him through the eye. Before Peter could even begin to react to the threat, the fat man was face down on the wheelhouse floor, a pool of dark viscous liquid spreading from underneath him.

Sofi immediately spun and took aim at the tall man's face again.

"Please," he whispered, this time in English, "don't shoot."

"Is there anyone else onboard?" she demanded. "If you lie to me, you're a dead man."

He shook his head allowing his eyes to dart around the room, settling for a second on Peter.

Peter had the impression that the man had recovered from his initial shock and was now trying to decide on a course of action. Obviously, given his line of work, this was not the first time he'd been in a precarious position. He was a paid killer and not someone to underestimate.

"Peter," Sofi said firmly, "find a rope or something. We need to tie this man up before we have a conversation."

Peter scouted around the wheelhouse and found a coil of tight rope stashed in one of the lockers. As Sofi kept her gun trained on the man, Peter hauled him roughly to his feet and lashed him to the huge wooden wheel with his arms and legs outstretched. He then stepped back to evaluate his work.

"Looks like Da Vinci's Vitruvian man," said Sofi grinning, "very artistic, Peter. I'm impressed. Now just in case our friend here is not being truthful, why don't you watch the door while I have a little chat with him?"

Peter moved to the doorway where he had a full view of the deck as Sofi moved as close to the prisoner as she could without retching. The man, aided by the sweat that now soaked his shirt, smelled like a septic tank. "What is your rank on this sorry rust pail," she asked in Turkish.

The man shook his head and responded in Italian.

"I see," she continued, switching to English. "So, apparently your Turkish is selective, and I don't speak your language. Let's use English, okay?"

The man nodded unenthusiastically.

"So, your rank, are you the cabin boy? The steward?"

The man's eyes glittered with defiance. "I am the captain," he snarled.

"Oh, very good," Sofi said evenly, "just the man we want to talk to – the man with all the answers."

He glared at her.

"We discovered during our search of your eh . . . ship that you've recently had a female passenger onboard. Am I right so far?"

The captain stared at her and said nothing.

Without warning, she took a step forward and smashed him across the face with her gun. Immediately, blood began dripping from a deep gouge on his cheek.

"Let's try that again, captain," she said softly. "We know she was here. We uncovered evidence of her presence in one of your cabins. What's more important is the identity of those who took her from the ship or if you transported her yourself, we'd very much like to know where you delivered her."

The man glowered at her and said nothing.

She again raised her pistol and stepped closer.

He flinched. "This will do you no good," he growled "You can't kill me because you want information that only I have. If I gave it to you, the man who commissioned my services will kill me. You see my dilemma – or is the dilemma yours?"

Sofi stepped back and quietly studied the man's face. "Okay" she said calmly, "you leave me no choice then. I'd really like to see you walk the plank, but that seems a bit dramatic and won't get us the information we need. I do, however, have a better idea. The bodies of your crew that are now floating under the boat are attracting quite lot of interest. At last count, we spotted about a dozen sharks nosing around. By now there are probably fifty. Interested?"

She saw the spark of fear in the man's eyes as the defiance was replaced with something quite different. She knew that most seamen had an almost irrational fear of sharks; that in their minds the monsters of the deep had been elevated to almost mythic status. "So, here's my idea," she glanced over her shoulder at Peter, who was paying rapt attention. "What if we lower you over the side and submerge just your legs into the water? It will look like small fish to the sharks, something delectable and not at all threatening. After they take your legs off at the knees, we can haul you back onboard and watch as you bleed out while we witness your agonizing death.

I recognize that you're a strong man, but I'll bet that before you die, you'll give us some useful information. Once you do, we will of course transport you to the nearest hospital where they may be able to save your miserable life. Since you're already dripping blood, it won't take long for the beasts to discover you. Now how does that sound?"

The captain was panicked. She'd guessed right. His face was white, and his lips trembled.

When finally he spoke, his voice trembled too. "Alright," he croaked, "I'll tell you. You're probably sick enough to carry out your threat. I'll tell you what you want to know."

As Peter kept careful watch, Sofi slipped her pistol back into its holster. "Shoot," she said, grinning.

A few minutes later, they had what they needed and were left with a decision. Sofi stepped outside to join Peter and closed the cabin door behind her. "So, what do we do with him?" Peter asked. "We can't set him free. He'll be on the 'ship to shore' before we're ten yards away, but if we leave him locked up here, we're taking a gamble that no one finds him."

"Personally, I'm tempted to toss him overboard," she replied. "We can leave his feet untied of course to give him a fighting chance. Problem with that is that if he's given us bad information, we have no recourse. Maybe we should take him with us. Then again I don't know if I can stand the stench."

"I vote we leave him here," said Peter. "I have an idea that might work. We tie him up in his own motorboat, disable its engine and anchor it a good distance away. Even if he gets loose, he'll be reluctant to get in the water. Then we cut a small hole in the boat just big enough to let the water in slowly – allowing say twelve hours before the boat sinks. If he's told us the truth, we'll be back in time to save his sorry ass. If he lied, well it's his fault when he becomes shark bait."

Sofi looked at him, looking both surprised and impressed, "That's very good. You're catching on – you're a quick study."

. When Peter released the captain's legs, he aimed a vicious kick at Peter's knees. Peter managed to sidestep the blow and delivered a solid punch to the man's ear. The man folded like an ironing board and hit the floor hard.

"Oh yes," Sofi said grinning, "you definitely have potential."

Together, they hauled the captain to his feet and shoved him out the door in the direction of the steps. A few minutes later, the motorboat was anchored about a hundred yards from the *Luxor.* The furious captain was tightly gagged and strapped to the steel stern bench. Peter had removed the distributor cap from the engine and tossed it overboard.

"What about water?" Peter asked. "He's got nothing to drink."

"Aw, isn't that too bad." Sofi replied scornfully. "Let's hope his information is correct so that we can get back here in time to save him."

Demir had followed them from the ship and idled alongside as his sister and Peter made the captain as uncomfortable as possible. Once satisfied that the man was well secured, they joined Demir aboard the launch and headed for the island of Büyükada, where, according to the captain, he'd delivered Nora two days before.

"So where are all the sharks you mentioned?" Peter asked as they sped across the flat water. I didn't see a single one."

"Oh, there aren't any sharks around here," Sofi responded and chuckled. "They hang around the docks where the fishing fleets come in. Come to think of it, I've never seen one out here."

Peter shook his head, "You amaze me," he laughed.

CHAPTER 23

Nora climbed out of bed and followed Talya from the ward. Nora wore slacks, a cotton shirt and running shoes, all of which Talya had filched from the orderly changing room. They tiptoed down the darkened corridor and Nora waited nervously as Talya unlocked the men's ward. Simon was waiting for them as arranged.

Earlier that day, Nora, as instructed, had joined the women when they were taken outside to exercise. As Simon had promised, her presence had gone unheeded. She'd found him sitting alone on an iron bench beside a dried-up fountain and had listened intently as he outlined his plan for her escape. Horrifying! The scheme was absolutely horrifying.

Even now as they silently descended the main staircase like some bizarre incarnation of *Wynken, Blynken, and Nod*, she wasn't sure she could go through with it.

By the time Nora had found Simon in the garden earlier, he'd already heard about the death in the women's ward. The unfortunate event had become the basis for his scheme. He'd explained that since the dead woman was Jewish, she'd be transported to the mainland to be buried within twenty-four hours, probably the next morning. When Nora heard what he had in mind, she'd shuddered. "Oh no," she'd gasped, "there's no way I could do that."

"I'm afraid that if you can't, you'll be the next candidate for burial. I know what I'm suggesting is terrifying, but I'm afraid it's your only chance. Try to think of it as an opportunity; providential if you will. If you can do this, you'll get to Istanbul. Getting out of the undertaker's shouldn't be too difficult. It's not the kind of place where they lock people in." He'd then pulled a slip of paper and a roll of money from his pocket and handed them to her. "This is the address of an associate of mine in Old Istanbul. If you can make your way to him, he'll help you. I've also written him a brief message. You must show it to him. It will assure him that I sent you."

"I'll try," Nora had said softly. She'd sat for a moment, her eyes downcast, her breathing was shallow, and all of the color had left her face. She'd returned with the others to the ward and lay on her cot trying to summon the courage she'd require. When it was time to go, she was ready. She knew it was her only chance.

The two women and Simon reached the main floor, crossed the vestibule and entered a narrow cool hallway. At the end of the corridor, Talya pulled yet another key from her mouth and inserted it into the lock of a heavy steel door. The security door opened with an angry squeal and the trio froze in place, listening for any sign they'd been discovered. The silence continued – they were safe.

They descended a set of steel steps and reached yet another corridor. This one was wide, with a concrete floor. Ahead a couple of fluorescent lights lit the way. Slowly, Nora became aware of the smell. It was a musky, acrid aroma she'd smelled somewhere before. It took her a second to remember where.

"The zoo," she murmured, "it smells like the LA Zoo." It was then that she noticed the row of cells lining the long corridor and the poor animals that inhabited them.

"Don't look inside," Simon whispered, "it's a sight you'll never forget. The memory will haunt you forever."

As if she'd been dared, she looked and immediately regretted her decision. Beside her was a dark cell where an emaciated creature stared back at her from behind steel bars. The thing – she had no idea if it was a man or a woman – was dressed in filthy rags. The hair was shoulder length and gray, the eyes yellow and hollow. The thing stretched a grimy claw through the bars, pleading. In her heart, Nora knew that the creature was begging for death.

In one of the cells, its occupant was naked and chained by the neck to the wall. He was crouched on the floor, and snarled at them as they passed, now more animal than man. Some of the cells were occupied by people in filthy straitjackets. It was without a doubt the most horrific tableau Nora had ever seen. If she hadn't been so afraid, she'd have been in tears.

Simon pointed to an empty cell, "If you don't get away, I'm afraid you could end up in there. You can't hide forever and when you're discovered they'll want you safely out of sight."

As they neared another large steel door, Nora heard the sound. It began as a low moan coming from one of the cages Within moments, others had joined into the chorus until the corridor was filled with demonic wailing. Nora was forced to cover her ears to blot out the terrible noise. She knew that hell could be no worse than this dreadful place.

Talya hauled open the door, ushered the others past her, stepped in behind them and slammed the door shut. Immediately, the clamor ended. Compared to the room they'd just left, this one was ice cold. Talya found the light switch and flicked it on. A single light bulb hung from a frayed wire, swaying slightly from the concussion of the slammed door, casting fingers of light and shadows across their faces, turning them into bizarre masks. The room was mostly bare. A few cardboard boxes were stacked in one corner. A pile of burlap sacks filled another. In the center of the room was a large steel table on top of which was a long canvas bag with a zipper running from end to end.

"Here she is," said Simon, sounding almost reverent. "The reason this can work is that she's a very small woman. The men who will remove her are not on the same shift as those who brought her here, so they won't notice the difference." He glanced at his watch, "The sun will be up soon and it's my guess they'll want to get her on the first ferry. I suggest that you get in while we're here to help you. I know how utterly disgusting it will be in there with her, but I believe you can do it. You must employ all the strength that has sustained you thus far. You must shut your mind off and overcome your fear. The pill I gave you will help you cope, and we'll stay as long as we can. And until they come, you can leave the zipper partially open."

Nora felt her legs going first. As she slumped to the floor the room went dark.

A sudden movement woke her from her faint. At first, she thought that the small cold body she was nestled against had moved. She nearly screamed. She then realized that the bag was being lifted. The men grunted and complained as they hoisted the bag onto something she assumed was a trolley. She felt herself being wheeled along the corridor. The smell of the place was instantly recognizable and was marginally better than the effluvium emanating from her bag mate.

Ironically, the clip-clop of hooves indicated that she was once again being transported by a horse-drawn carriage. She wondered if it was the same one she'd come to know so well. She realized then that she'd gone completely mad.

CHAPTER 24

By the time they pulled into Büyükada's tiny harbor, the sun was up. They tied up at the quay and climbed the slippery seaweed-covered stone steps to the pier. On the other side of the roadway, a small ferryboat had disgorged its passengers and was now in process of being loaded for the return trip to Istanbul. Shabbily dressed locals trooped aboard, seeking out any available bench. At the stern two men wrestled with a long canvas bag, trying to drag it up the rickety ramp. Halfway up, the bag had become wedged in the side rail and the men were trying to dislodge it.

Ever the Good Samaritan, Peter Brandt moved in to help. He stepped onto the ramp, grabbed the other end of the bag and helped them heave it aboard the ferry. Mission accomplished, he hurried to rejoin the others who were now halfway to the street.

"Damn," he panted when he caught up, "poor guys. That thing was heavy. I wonder what was in it."

Demir studied him for a moment before answering. “Actually Peter, that was a body bag. It must be on the way to the undertaker. There is no graveyard on the island

“Wow,” Peter said, grimacing, “you’re kidding. The guy must have been enormous. The thing weighed a ton.”

Sofi entered the harbormaster’s office and emerged a few moments later with directions to the house they needed to locate. “Now,” she began, “it’s time to formulate a plan. We can’t just barge into the place with guns drawn. We have no idea what we’ll be facing and from all indications, these people are more than willing to kill. I suggest we go to that little coffee shop,” she pointed across the picturesque little square, “and grab a cup of coffee and something to eat.”

As Peter started to protest, she raised her hand to stop him.

“I know you’re desperate to keep going Peter, but you must trust me. We’ve been running on adrenalin since yesterday and we need to regroup and replenish. we’ll have to be at our best if we’re going to succeed. We can’t go off half-cocked. Come on let’s refuel.”

Much as he wanted to, Peter decided against arguing and followed obediently as the other two headed for the coffee shop.

When the sweet roll was placed in front of him along with a steaming mug of black coffee, Peter realized that he was famished. He'd been running on empty; a sure formula for mistakes. Sofi was right – as usual.

As if on cue, she started to lay out the plan. "First, we need a horse and carriage. We'll scout out the property; to see if there's a way in. A lot of the homes here are very old. Some have security some don't. This island is mostly summer homes for Istanbul's elite – it's both a place of refuge and exile. Leon Trotsky was one of its more infamous residents for a time. There are powerful people here; people who are used to getting their own way.

"I wish I'd had the opportunity to find out who owns the house but maybe we still can. A well-placed bribe might help. Maybe we should try before going there."

They finished their meal. Peter had consumed three pastries and two cups of coffee. He felt much better.

They left the coffee shop and headed for the line of horse-drawn surreys parked just off the square. The third negotiation brought the desired result. Sofi managed to hire a vehicle that they could use and even better, she'd gotten the name of the owner of the house.

Peter and Sofi climbed into the dilapidated, covered carriage while Demir clambered up onto the driver's seat and took the reins. The horse, a sorry-looking black and white specimen who'd seen better days, turned to see who the stranger was that was about to interrupt his nap.

Responding to the rap on his skinny rump, the beast broke into a walk and pulled out of line. Demir guided the horse across the square, turned left and proceeded up a steep hill which paralleled the water.

Peter stared in amazement at the houses they passed. Set well back from the street in their own leafy glades, the shingled Victorian mansions exuded wealth and, for the most part, very good taste. They passed a rambling four-story hotel called the Splendid, and Peter felt like he was living in a scene from *The Great Gatsby*. On the wide, sun-dappled verandah, well-dressed patrons sat beneath colorful umbrellas sipping tea and nibbling on finger sandwiches. He was convinced he was about to awaken from a dream.

They turned a corner and found themselves facing the sea. On the horizon, the towers of Istanbul rose, shining, from a gulf of blue. Half-a-dozen ferryboats plied the expanse of water and Peter couldn't help but wonder which of them carried the corpse he'd helped load. The thought gave him the creeps.

A half-mile later, they reached the house they were looking for. The elegant Ottoman Victorian structure was very much in keeping with its neighbors. A wrought iron fence and high gate fronted the property. A brick path led from the street to the front door.

As they crawled past the house, Peter's heart raced. *Was Nora inside*, he wondered, hardly able to contain himself. Once they'd passed, Sofi reached for his arm.

"From what I could see, the fence surrounds the entire property," she said. "We should try to get a look at the rear, just to be sure, but there's no chance of getting in without being noticed, particularly in broad daylight."

Peter nodded, disappointment clouding his eyes. "So do we wait for dark, or what?"

"Well, I'm wondering if a bold approach might work. The guy at the dock told me the owner's a doctor so the idea of simply knocking on the front door and asking for his help is not entirely crazy. I think it may be worth a try."

About a hundred yards past the house, they found a narrow lane, which led to the backs of all the houses on the block. Demir turned the carriage and they continued down the alleyway beneath a canopy of blossoming trees. At the end, they turned right again, until they finally reached the doctor's house. Demir pulled the horse to a stop, and they sat for a moment studying the target. From where they waited, the house was partially obscured by a stand of leafy trees. Peter could just make out a couple of large windows on the upper floor.

Just then, the form of a woman crossed in front of one of the windows. Peter's heart skipped a beat, but the excitement soon faded. The woman returned to the window and stopped and ran a brush through her long dark hair. It wasn't Nora. Peter sighed.

As Sofi suspected, the high fence continued along the back of the house enclosing the entire property. To compound the problem a pair of Rottweilers approached out of nowhere, rushing at the fence barking at the interlopers.

"So, breaking in is going to be impossible," Sofi said softly. "Let's get out of here before the dogs give us away."

Demir turned the horse around and they made their way back the way they'd come. When they reached the street, his sister directed him to pull over.

"Well Peter," she said, "I think my first idea was the best. I'll just go the door and see what I can find out. Do you agree?"

"Yes," he replied breathlessly. "Should I go with you?"

"I don't think so. I pose no threat. My chances are probably better alone." She glanced at Demir who nodded his assent.

"Wait here. I'll be right back." Sofi hopped down from the surrey without looking back and headed for the house. Peter stared after her, listening to the pounding of his heart. Demir stretched out his legs, rested his head on the seatback, and closed his eyes. Although his wound was already on the mend, a headache lingered on.

Sofi reached the gate and searched for a bell. There was none. She tried the handle and discovered that the gate was unlocked. It swung open soundlessly. She shrugged, stepped through and made her way up the path to the front door keeping her eyes peeled for the dogs. At that moment, she heard them barking in the distance and breathed a sigh of relief. It sounded like they were still focused on the back fence.

There was a bell at the front door. She pushed the button and waited patiently. She heard approaching footsteps and smiled innocently as a peep hole opened. A wary eye appeared, framed by a gleaming mahogany face.

"Yes, what is it?" the black man asked in Turkish.

"Is this the house of doctor Shamir?" Sofi asked, trying to sound anxious. It wasn't much of a stretch.

"Who is asking?" the man was none to friendly.

"Well, there's been an accident with a carriage just around the corner. I was sent to see if the doctor's home. A boy has been hurt and he needs the doctor's help."

"Doctor not home," the man grunted and started to close the little door.

Sofi then heard a woman's voice coming from somewhere behind the man.

"Who is it?" the voice asked.

Sofi listened to the man explain and heard the woman's response. Immediately, the lock turned, and the door swung open.

"Please come in," the man muttered.

Sofi stepped into the cool vestibule past the man and was met by a young woman who was holding a small child by the hand.

"What has happened," the woman asked, "someone has been hurt?"

The black man disappeared down a hallway.

Sofi repeated her story and saw the woman's eyes fill with concern. "I'm so sorry," she said softly. "I do wish we could be of help but unfortunately, my husband is not at home."

As she listened, Sofi studied what she could see of the house, looking for any indication of something out of the ordinary. There was nothing. "So where is your husband?" she asked gently. "Is he expected home soon?"

That's when she saw the flicker of something different in the woman's eyes. It looked like concern, maybe even fear.

"What's your name?" Sofi asked, trying to make the woman feel at ease.

"My name is Beyaz," she replied. "This is Turik, my son."

"Hello, I'm Sofi. Hi Turik and how old are you?"

The little boy didn't reply and instead he held up four fingers.

"Well, you're a big boy for four, aren't you?" This elicited a verbal response. "You're pretty," he offered shyly.

"Thank you, Turik." Sofi replied smiling down at the tot, "I'm flattered."

She looked back at the woman and could tell somcthing was amiss. She seemed nervous, preoccupied. Sofi decided to keep her talking. "So where is your husband? Is he on the island?"

"No," Beyaz replied. "He's not. The truth is, I'm a bit worried about him. He went to the city yesterday for a meeting. He was supposed to return last night but I haven't heard from him. We have an apartment in the Adalar Towers. I was there myself until two days ago. We only use this house on weekends. I've been calling my husband every hour but there has been no response. It's not like him."

It was then that Sofi had the feeling she was being watched. She looked quickly to her left and caught a flash of a dark-skinned face disappearing behind a crack in the nearby door.

"Are you here alone then," Sofi asked innocently, "except for the houseman of course?"

"Yes, I am, quite alone. I think I should call the police. I'm getting very worried."

"Well, I do have a friend in the police department. I'd be happy to call her if you'd like."

"Oh yes please. Would you? I'd be so grateful. Please, come with me, there's a phone here in the library," she pointed behind her to the doorway where Sofi had caught the houseman eavesdropping.

Together they entered the library and Sofi gave it a quick, professional once-over. Although the furnishings were of fine quality and the art was quite good, she wasn't sure it was the house of a man powerful and wealthy enough to arrange the abduction of an international celebrity from the streets of Venice.

As Beyaz led Sofi towards the desk and the telephone she suddenly stopped in her tracks.

"Wait, what about the child – the one who is hurt? I completely forgot; how selfish of me."

Sofi reached out and stroked the woman's arm. "Don't you worry about him," she replied. "The police were already on their way when I came here on the chance your husband would be home. I'm sure the boy's fine. It wasn't a terribly severe injury."

Sofi picked up the telephone receiver, called her office and had a brief one-way conversation with her answering machine. When she was finished, she explained that her friend was not in the office but that she'd left a message.

She then headed back towards the front door. Before leaving she wrote down a name and phone number for Beyaz. "If you don't hear from your husband soon, call this number. She's a very good policewoman and I'm sure will do all she can."

As they shook hands, Sofi stole another quick glance to her left. Again, a face disappeared from the opening in the doorway.

As she made her way back to the waiting men, she thought about what she'd learned. She was sure that Nora wasn't there and if she had been, it was without Beyaz's knowledge. She had a momentary pang of concern for the doctor's whereabouts. If by chance he was somehow in league with the perpetrators and had performed them a service, there might well be a reason for worry.

Now her concern was that the captain of the *Luxor* had sent them on a wild goose chase. She prayed he was suffering as much as he deserved to.

As she approached the waiting carriage, Peter stepped forward to meet her. His face was a mask of anguish as he searched her eyes. He didn't bother to ask.

"I'm sorry Peter," she said softly, "she's not here. I'm not sure she ever was. The houseman was acting very strangely. Then again, maybe it's his job to be suspicious."

She watched Peter's shoulders sag and knew she had to do something. What that was, however, was proving very elusive.

CHAPTER 25

Hassan sat in the shade beneath the palm trees in his garden, sipping a tall glass of dark liquid. Standing in front of him were Haid, his chief bodyguard and two other men dressed in khakis. Both men sported closely trimmed beards and military-style boots. Each of the men had deep-set eyes; eyes that suggested danger.

"So, you know what is required of you," Hassan was saying. "I don't care who has to get hurt, but you've got to find the woman. We know where she was last seen. I've spoken with the doctor who treated her, and he was the last person to see her. He's had no success in tracking her down even though she's stranded on a small island with few places to hide – idiot." He shook his head and sipped from his glass of iced tea.

"I've discovered that the doctor has an apartment here in the city and that he is there now. Haid has the address. I think it might be advisable to have a chat with him before you head out to the island. He may know more than he's telling me. If you are successful, you'll be well rewarded. If you fail, you'll have to deal with your superiors, with whom I have some influence. I wish you well." With a wave of his hand, he dismissed the Syrians and watched as Haid led them through the gardens towards the elevator. He knew that these men could do the job. If they couldn't, no one could. The Syrians had their very own brand of coercion; methods for extracting information that had been perfected over thousands of years.

A few minutes later, he watched the elevator doors open, signaling the return of Haid and was surprised to see that he was accompanied by Ali Sandar and his bodyguard, Mahmet.

"Good morning, my friend," Sandar said solemnly, as he reached Hassan. "I'm sorry to arrive unannounced but there's something I must discuss with you." He glanced over his shoulder to make sure no one was within earshot. He noted the three guards patrolling the grounds, and Mahmet standing a discreet distance away.

"May I sit?"

"Certainly, my brother – do sit. Will you take some iced tea?"

"Please yes."

Hassan reached for a small brass bell and rang it. A second later a young, uniformed man emerged from the house and hurried towards the men.

"More iced tea," Hassan growled without ever looking at the young man.

"So, how's the new, eh . . . companion?" he grinned knowingly at his neighbor.

"Oh, Nadya's gone I'm afraid. Seems I demanded too much of her and the jewels were not adequate compensation. As a matter of fact, that's what I wanted to talk to you about. The filthy slattern managed to slip out of the house while I was sleeping. She must have had a boat waiting. It's the only way she could have gotten past my men. That she left is not my concern. The fact that she left with the jewelry I'd given her is totally unacceptable. I've had my men searching for her for two days, but they've had no success. She has not returned to her apartment. She's disappeared."

"That's too bad, Ali," Hassan said, nodding in sympathy. "So, you were not able to please her. Maybe it's time for you to try one of these new American drugs; the ones that turn you into a lion. Would you like for me to get you some?"

Ali was not amused. He looked away and inhaled deeply.

"Don't tell me you fell for her, Ali. Oh no – such a terrible mistake. You realize that for you to retrieve your jewels, you may have to hurt her. Are you willing to do that?"

Ali faced his friend. "I don't know if I can hurt her, Hassan, but I really need to find her. Will you help me? I know you have sources that no one else has."

"Yes, my friend, of course I'll help. Unless she's left the country, which is unlikely in so short a time, my people should be able to track her. I'll need all the information you have on her, including where she came from. Where did you find her?"

For the next few minutes, Hassan listened patiently as Ali related what he knew about his missing courtesan. The irony was not lost on him. Here he was, about to get involved in tracking a missing girl for his neighbor, while his own priceless acquisition had apparently disappeared from the face of the earth.

As he spoke, Ali wrote down the pertinent information, including her address, phone number and the names of friends she'd talked about. When he was done, he handed the paper to Hassan, and then drained his glass and rose to leave.

"By the way, who were the two men I saw leaving your elevator as I arrived? They looked very serious."

"Oh, they're serious alright. They're helping me with something of my own that's gone missing. You don't want to get involved with them, though. We'll find some other way."

"By the way, thank you for the party. It was a spectacular evening. I'm sorry you left so early. There was some pretty good fun after you'd gone to bed."

"You're welcome, Ali. I'm glad you had a good time."

As Hassan watched his neighbor cross the gardens towards the elevator that would take him up the cliff to his waiting car, he thought about the men he'd just hired. Part of him missed the action but the days of doing his own dirty work were long gone. He'd made his first kill as a thirteen-year-old in Bahrain. He'd been lured into a fancy car one warm summer evening by a Saudi pig that had made the mistake of assuming Hassan was a prostitute. When the man refused to let him go, despite his protests, Hassan had been forced to stick him. He was proud of his curved blade, a gift from his father, and kept it razor sharp. The Saudi had bled like a butchered bull although it took him a long time to die. When the fat man finally expired, Hassan had popped out his eyes, just for fun. He was surprised that he'd been able to kill with so little emotion. He was also surprised at how much he'd enjoyed the experience. From that day on, he'd been willing to kill at the drop of a hat.

Killing women had proved even more stimulating. He'd lost count of the number he'd dispatched over the years. He fooled himself into believing that the killings were purely pragmatic; the cleanest way to eliminate the possibility of his castoffs talking. The truth was Hassan killed for sport. He wondered if he'd kill Nora James once he'd tired of her. The thought excited him. As he thought of her, the idea that she may have somehow escaped the island occurred to him. What if she'd managed to reach Istanbul? Ever careful, always prepared to deal with any contingency, he reached for the telephone.

He placed two calls to friends, one to the police station, the other to a man at the American Consulate; a man who was in his debt.

CHAPTER 26

The foul-smelling burka had been a piece of cake compared to the horror in which Nora was now imprisoned. The rocking of the ferry and the sickly-sweet smell emanating from her decaying companion was making her nauseous, but she knew that the sound of her retching would be fatal. Although the canvas allowed a little air to penetrate the bag, the stifling claustrophobia combined with the reality of what she was lying beside, forced her to take a chance. She pulled open the zipper a little.

She gratefully inhaled the salt smell of the sea, trying not to think about her gruesome circumstance. She focused on Peter and what life would be like when she was released from this hell. The thought that her freedom was imminent kept her from totally losing her mind.

She would never have believed that her experience as an actress would help her survive this. It was during the filming of a mediocre horror piece called *Dead Even*, that she'd trained herself in the practice of mind over matter. In the movie, she had to be buried alive. Until this past week, it had been the single-most horrible experience of her life. The first time, they'd closed the coffin lid on her, she'd freaked out. Her screams of panic had caused the director the let her out of the box. He was not happy – her claustrophobia had cost a whole day of filming.

That evening, she'd had a long session with a hypnotist who'd helped Peter and her to quit smoking. She'd returned to the set the next day determined to film the coffin scene and managed to get through it, but never again agreed to a part that involved confinement in small spaces.

She heard the engines slowing and soon thereafter, she felt the telltale bump as the ferry reached the dock. She closed the zipper and again concentrated on remaining still.

It seemed to take forever but eventually, she felt the bag being lifted. Again, the carriers grunted under its weight. She heard them gasping for breath and by the time the bag was deposited, the men were grouching loudly.

She listened to the sound of the vehicle starting and pulled the zipper open again. This time, her nostrils were flooded with the sweet stench of the city. It was a warm, humid day and the combination of aromas was fetid. She closed her eyes and prayed. "Only a few minutes more," she intoned. "Oh, please let me hold it together. Oh God please."

Her prayers were answered. The funeral home was apparently not far from the dock. The van slowed to a stop, and she heard a door slam. She quickly re-zipped the bag. As she lay whispering to herself in the cloying darkness, she listened to the metallic grinding, as what she assumed was a metal gate sliding open. The van started moving again but stopped almost immediately and the engine was shut off. Her heart leapt with joy. It was almost over.

The same two voices muttered angrily again as the bag was hoisted from the back of the vehicle. She started to count. She figured occupying her mind might prevent her from going mad. She'd reached 300 by the time they reached the resting place, accompanied by a few more angry words that she assumed were swear words even though they were in Turkish.

She landed hard, banging her arm against something that gave out a loud metallic clang. Then they were gone.

She couldn't take it anymore. She had to get out. She pinched the zipper slide and started to pull it open when suddenly she heard voices, different voices. This time the voices were those of women. They certainly weren't wasting any time. She knew that she was about to be prepared for burial. She lay perfectly still, listening to the footsteps. She felt a pair of hands on the canvas and a moment later, the bag was ripped wide open. Nora blinked in the sudden light and started to sit up. Staring at her were the horrified faces of two women.

One screamed, while the other turned and fled. Her screaming co-worker wasn't far behind her.

Nora realized that it was now or never. She scrambled from her prison and fell to the floor like a sack of potatoes. She'd probably hurt herself, but she felt no pain. The door stood wide open. She scrambled to her feet and raced from the room. She entered a long corridor and didn't slow. She just kept running.

Somewhere behind her she heard the maniacal screaming of the terrified woman. The poor creatures would probably never be the same..

She rounded a corner, almost losing her footing on the slippery floor. She spotted a door, a double glass door. Beyond the door was the blessed light of day.

"Almost," she muttered.

She was ten paces away, reaching out her arms to throw the doors open, nearly there. That's when the man appeared out of nowhere right in front of her. He was big, wearing a uniform. When he saw Nora bearing down on him like a mad woman, he reached for his belt. He popped open a leather holster withdrew his gun and leveled it. "*Durdurmak*!" he barked.

CHAPTER 27

By the time they arrived back in the city, all three of them were sweating. The day was very warm and unusually muggy. The men dropped Sofi off far enough away from the police headquarters so that she wouldn't be seen and headed for a much-needed bite to eat.

Demir led his friend to a dingy little waterfront place that served excellent kabobs. Demir had certainly been right about everything else he'd touted, but it wouldn't have mattered. Both men were starving.

The hot, greasy food was like manna. Both men put away two helpings before ordering one to go for Sofi.

It took Sofi a few minutes to reach headquarters and when she entered the ugly post-modern building office, she hurried down the hall and up a flight of stairs, avoiding the elevator and the chance of running into any co-workers. Explaining her wet clothes would be awkward, especially since there had been no rain in days. She reached her office without incident and stepped inside. She closed the door behind her and squeezed in behind her desk. She turned on her computer and started typing.

Within three minutes she had the doctor's address. She hit print and waited. The good doctor would be their next stop.

At that moment, she heard the door open and spun in her chair to see Mahmet towering over her. He didn't look happy.

"Hi," she ventured, trying to sound casual, "how are you?"

"That's my question," he muttered angrily, "or more importantly, where the hell have you been? I thought you'd gone missing. I was about to call the police."

Although, it sounded like an attempt at humor, it wasn't. Mahmet's face remained a mask and his eyes smoldered.

Sofi took a deep breath. "Well actually I've been working on a case. It's a bit out of the ordinary and has been taking a lot of my time I'm afraid. I'm sorry Mahmet. I know I should have called, but the case has been overwhelming."

"Does it have anything to do with that American you met the other night, the one with the missing wife?"

She thought about lying but decided that it would serve no purpose. Mahmet would see through her, and it was not her habit to lie. Besides, he was the man she was to marry. She could not be dishonest. She dropped her eyes, "Yes," she said softly. "It has something to do with him. It's just that I felt so sorry for him. He is so terribly – lost. He has no chance in this city without help. By the way my investigation is unofficial, so I'd be most grateful if you didn't mention it to anyone. My supervisor thinks I'm following some drug leads and has given me a couple of days to tie up the case. As we both know, Lieutenant Nalis is less than a dedicated policeman. He doesn't really pay much attention unless his payoffs are late."

"I don't want you to see the American again. Cut off all contact, now."

It was Sofi's turn to be angry. After the day she'd had, she was in no mood for this. "Is this an order Mahmet, because if it is you're obviously living in the wrong century. You know me well enough by now to understand that I don't respond well to men ordering me around."

His eyes flared and he clenched his fists. She watched him bite his lip as he struggled to maintain control. He let out a long breath. Apparently, he'd decided that it was time to change tack. "It's just that I worry for you Sofi. I know you're strong-willed and sometimes hotheaded. I don't want the woman I'm to marry getting hurt or worse. You don't know what you're dealing with here. If what the American told us is true, he's up against the most dangerous people in Istanbul. I don't want you in that kind of danger," he attempted a smile, which failed.

"Please understand, Sofi, I love you. I only want what's best for you. I know these people. I know them very well. They will not tolerate interference. Do you not understand?"

"I do understand Mahmet," she replied, softening, "but I'm afraid I have no choice. If I don't help this man, Peter, I will never be able to live with myself."

"Peter, is it?" Mahmet was angry again. "Is there more to this than just your sense of justice? Do you have feelings for this man?"

"Yes, I do have feelings for him," she flashed back defiantly, "but it's not what you think."

"Fine," he growled. He turned on his heel and headed for the door. When he reached it, he glanced back over his shoulder. "Drop it," he ordered, "I'm warning you, Sofi."

"Or what?" she yelled at the slamming door. She then sat staring at the door, steaming and shell-shocked. Never had she seen Mahmet so angry. And that wasn't all. Equally disconcerting was that his last words had been delivered in English. He almost never spoke English.

By the time Demir and Peter returned to the spot where they'd dropped Sofi off, she was waiting for them. She hopped aboard and shook a piece of paper at them. "Got it," she said.

When Peter handed her the food, she nodded. "Thanks," she said, "now let's try to stay dry for the rest of the day."

Peter laughed. "Good idea," he agreed. Sofi unwrapped the sandwich, took a bite and chewed in silence, staring out over the water.

"Is there something wrong, Sof?" Demir asked.

She shook her head and continued to stare. "We need to return the boat," she said, "then we're going to pay a visit to doctor Shamir." She pointed Demir towards the marina where they'd rented the boat. It took them nearly half an hour to reach their destination and during the trip, Sofi was strangely silent.

At the marina, Demir and Peter headed for the office while Soifi made for the lady's room.

"Do you think she's okay?" Peter asked as they walked.

"I really don't know," Demir replied, "this is not like her. Maybe something happened at her office. But she's a strong woman and determined. She won't talk about it unless she wants to."

Fifteen minutes later, they were sitting at a little cafe enjoying a quick cup of coffee. When they were done, they hit the street, looking for a taxi. Luck was with them, within five minutes Demir had flagged down a surly looking driver who scowled at them like they smelled bad. They were not the problem.

Demir gave the man the address and settled back into the seat. "I know we're going out of our way," he said, "but with the traffic at this time of day, it'll be quicker in the long run."

The traffic was terrible, and it took them twenty minutes to reach their destination. They climbed out of the taxi at a car park close to Sofi and Demir's house, where they picked up Demir's car. Peter and Sofi shoehorned themselves into the cramped space, trying to leave Demir enough room to drive.

They eventually escaped the clogged city center and headed towards New Town and its towering glass towers. Demir drove along the shoreline for a while until Aldar Towers loomed in front of them. Adalar Towers were fashionably garish, built of blue glass set into golden frames. Peter thought he could have been in Vegas. Demir found the right building and a place to park that would not have accommodated any other motorized vehicle, except maybe a motor scooter.

They climbed the pink marble steps and entered the gaudy lobby where an officious-looking doorman glared at them from behind a fake gold desk. He addressed them in Turkish. Although Peter didn't understand a word, there was no doubt the man was treating them like street urchins. When Peter glanced at the wrinkled and stained clothes of his companions, he could see why the man was less than impressed.

For the first time since he'd met her, Sofi pulled her badge from her pocket and shoved it into the imperious man's face. He folded like a wet suit.

As Sofi glared at him, he called the doctor's apartment and when there was no answer, he led them to the elevator. Peter was amused to see that the car was lined with mirrors. He took a quick peek at himself and grinned.

Thirty floors in thirty seconds and in complete silence. The doors slid open, and they stepped out into a thick-carpeted hall. The doorman rang the bell, waited a minute or two, and when there was no answer, unlocked the door.

He stepped aside allowing the visitors to precede him.

The apartment was airy and modern, carpeted entirely in white shag. The floor to ceiling windows boasted a view of the Bosporus all the way to the Suleiman Bridge.

They found the doctor in the bedroom. He was naked, lying flat on his back on the bed with a towel draped discreetly across his manhood. A bloodless bullet hole created a third eye, evidence that the doctor was dead before he was shot. The first indication that he'd suffered unspeakable pain was the fact that the skin had been peeled from the soles of his feet. The removed skin lay curled on the floor next to the bed. There was little doubt that whatever information the doctor possessed, he'd given it all up.

Sofi crossed to the body, touched the man's face and looked up at the others. "He's still warm," she said, "he's most likely been dead less than an hour."

She turned to the bedroom door where the doorman waited, holding onto the jamb, pale as a ghost, unable to tear his eyes from the corpse.

"Who visited him in the last two hours?" she asked in Turkish.

When the man didn't respond she grabbed him firmly by the arm and shook him out of his stupor. "Who came looking for him?" she demanded. "I warn you, I don't have time for any crap."

He dragged his eyes away from the body and attempted to focus on Sofi. He sighed deeply and dropped his eyes. "There were two of them, Syrians, maybe, but in Western clothes. They must have known the apartment number because they didn't come to the desk. I thought about stopping them but decided against it. They looked like the kind of men who would not appreciate being stopped."

"How long were they up here?"

"Half-an-hour maybe – they left about an hour ago."

When Sofi had gathered all the information from the doorman, which wasn't much, she performed a quick search of the apartment just in case the killers had left any clues. She wasn't hopeful, because from the condition of the body, she could see that these guys were professionals.

As they descended in the elevator, she filled the men in on what little she'd learned.

"So, who were the killers and why the doctor? How is this related to Nora?" Peter asked.

"I don't know for certain, but I have a feeling there's a connection. Maybe she was hurt during her journey from Venice and needed a doctor, one who would keep his mouth shut. Then again, maybe she tried to escape and was injured in the process. The other possibility, which I think may be more realistic, is that she did manage to escape and they're looking for her. The men who visited the doctor needed information from him. It's my guess Nora is loose somewhere in the city. If so, she's running for her life."

Sofi's theory terrified Peter. At the same time, it gave him a sliver of hope.

"But she has no idea I'm here. Do you think she would go to the embassy, or the police?"

"I would certainly hope not, although that is probably what she'd do, but the gamble would be great. Everyone in this city owes someone a favor. More than likely she'd be given away."

CHAPTER 28

Nora lowered her shoulder and caught the uniformed man right in his solar plexus before he could level his weapon. The pistol clattered to the floor as the man collided with the wall. With a groan, he slid down the wall to a sitting position, shaking his head, trying to clear the cobwebs.

She bolted through the door and took the steps three at a time, reached the driveway and headed for the gate. From inside the bag, she had heard the sliding gate. She now saw that it provided a real obstacle. Without breaking stride, she scanned the entry for a walk-in opening. There was none. She was left with no choice and headed straight for the gate. It was going to be tough, but she was determined to find a way over.

As if in answer to a prayer, at that very moment, the gate started to open. By the time the gap was two feet wide she was through it. Just outside was a car awaiting entry. She turned right and fled, without looking back. She was flush with exhilaration – the taste of freedom was intoxicating.

She reached a corner that fronted onto a busy thoroughfare, slowed and glanced over her shoulder. There was no pursuit, she'd made it.

Trembling from the excitement and feeling terribly thirsty, she entered a small coffee shop, sat at the bar and ordered a Coke. When it arrived, she upended the glass, pouring the fiery liquid down her throat. It was the best Coke she'd ever tasted. Her thirst sated, she paid the woman behind the counter and headed for the street. It took her almost ten minutes to flag down a taxi. Grateful, she climbed in, and requested the American Consulate. The driver apparently understood her and nodded, punched the meter and nosed into the impossibly snarled traffic.

Twenty minutes later, the cab pulled up in front of an imposing building that was flying the Stars and Stripes in conjunction with the Turkish flag. She fanned the bills Simon Weathers had given her, allowing the taxi driver to extract the amount of the fare. When he pocketed several denominations of whatever the currency was Nora had a feeling she might have been ripped off.

She approached a high security gate, behind which were two uniformed men. She was disappointed that they looked Turkish rather than American. She beckoned to one of them, who sauntered over to her.

"Yes," he asked, "what is it?"

Thankfully, he spoke English.

"I need to see someone," she urged. "It's very important. I'm an American citizen. Please, let me in. I was abducted a week or so ago, in Venice. Please let me talk to an American official."

"Show me some identification," the guard smirked.

Apparently, the man didn't believe her.

"Listen," she answered, sounding a little testy, "I don't have any ID, but I'm Nora James. I'm a very famous actress. They took all my things when I was kidnapped. I've spent the last few days in an asylum on Büyükada and I'm sick and tired of being treated like a dog. Now open the damn gate and let me in."

The guard grunted, spun on his heel and walked across to the other guard, who'd been watching with some interest. The men had a brief conversation during which the one who'd been dealing with Nora pointed at her repeatedly. She waited impatiently as they continued to discuss her future. The second guard nodded, stepped away from his partner and entered the guard house. He picked up a telephone receiver and punched a button.

Outside the gate, Nora's good graces were wearing thin. She tapped her foot and glowered at the guard who'd refused her entry. She glanced at the residence and noticed a man watching her from the second-floor window. He was speaking on the telephone. She assumed he was speaking with the guy in the guard shack, but when she looked back, she saw that the guard was no longer on the phone. She then checked out the window above and saw that the man realized he'd been spotted. He immediately disappeared behind a curtain.

Something was not right. She felt a sudden chill up her spine. What was taking so long? Why hadn't they let her in? Wasn't it obvious she was American? Didn't she have rights?

The phone rang in the guard shack and the guard picked it up. He looked over immediately at Nora. She looked up at the second-story window. There were now two men watching her. One was on the telephone; the other had something in his hand he kept looking at. He was comparing her with a photograph.

The guard exited the shack, signaled to his partner, and headed towards Nora. That *was it. Something felt very wrong.* She turned and ran. She had no idea what had happened, but she was now convinced that she'd been the subject of conversation with someone who meant her no good. It struck her that she wasn't in America and that she'd need to be careful about automatically trusting anyone.

She looked back in time to see the embassy gate slide open. Without waiting to see what was about to happen, she picked up speed. She made a right at the first corner she came to. She was in a residential area and there weren't many people on the street. She realized that if they were after her she'd be easy to spot. She ran towards a hedge two houses away, crouched down behind it and stared at the corner. A black

Mercedes raced through the intersection with two men inside, and they were in a very big hurry. She exhaled, grateful she'd trusted her instincts.

She continued down the street until she reached a main thoroughfare. She managed to flag a taxi quickly and read the address from the slip of paper she'd pulled from her pocket.

The traffic was more reasonable than earlier and before she knew it the taxi pulled over. She climbed out, surprised to discover that instead of being at a house, she was at the entry to a huge market that looked like an old European railway station. She headed inside wondering how she'd ever find the address she sought.

At the first shop with a window crammed with silver trinkets, the barker accosted her in English. She had an idea. Smiling, she accepted his invitation to enter and before she knew it , she'd bought a bracelet. Her new friend happily directed her to the shop she was looking for.

She headed down the main street of the market, trying to ignore the cats that scurried between the legs of the seemingly oblivious pedestrians. As she went, she occasionally glanced back looking for any evidence that she was being watched. Maybe she was being paranoid but accepted that she had a very good reason.

She turned down a side alley and walked past a carpet shop, where a short fat man with a row of gold teeth watched her curiously. He started towards her, but she picked up her pace and inserted herself into the moving sea of shoppers, leaving *Golden Tooth* far behind.

She kept circling back to be sure she wasn't being followed. A few minutes later, she concluded that her efforts were useless. If someone was watching her in this busy place with its hundreds of shops and countless narrow lanes and dark alleys, she'd never know it.

She managed to find her way back to the main thoroughfare, a street marginally wider than the others and turned right looking for the shop address. She passed dozens of shops selling everything from the mundane to the exotic. There were electronics stores side by side with spice merchants and tea vendors.

Eventually, she arrived at a corner with four little cafés and turned left into a small alleyway. Halfway down, she found what she was looking for. The shop window was filled with leather goods of all descriptions, although purses seemed to be the shop's specialty. She was surprised to see Louis Vuitton and Gucci and Prada bags all displayed together. Then it dawned on her that the place dealt in very good knockoffs.

She rapped on the closed door and immediately heard urgent voices. A moment later, the door was opened by a handsome, middle-aged man who sported a full moustache, steel gray eyes and a jauntily arranged fez. She was reminded of some Humphrey Bogart movie. The man was not tall but seemed somehow regal.

"Good afternoon, madam," he said in passable English, "my name is Farris. How may I help you?"

"Can I come in?" she asked. "I have a message for you."

The man was instantly wary. He nervously glanced over his shoulder and then peered up and down the alleyway. Seeing nothing out of the ordinary, he returned his attention to Nora. "From whom is this message?" he asked.

"It's from Simon Weathers," she announced and was surprised to see Farris smile. He looked at her as if she was mocking him and slowly shook his head.

"I'm afraid that's impossible, madam. I haven't seen Simon for years." He then lowered his voice, "The last I heard from him, he was being deported from Turkey as the result of some transaction that went badly. I'm sure he returned home to England and I'm positive he would not set foot again on Turkish soil. He wouldn't take the chance. Simon was a very careful man. The only reason he got into trouble was because he was betrayed by someone he trusted; someone who was jealous of his success."

Nora reached into her pocket and presented Farris with the piece of paper Simon had given her.

The shopkeeper opened it and glanced at the words and his eyes widened. "Please," he said," his demeanor changing completely, "please come inside. You must tell me where you got this." He opened the door and stood aside allowing Nora to enter. He followed her inside and closed and locked the door. The shop was small and appeared to consist of just one room. Every surface was piled with handbags and wallets of all descriptions. Half of the floor was covered with pieces of luggage, all of which were knockoffs of the very best designers. The air in the little shop was rich with the smell of good leather.

The man unceremoniously dumped a load of evening bags onto the floor revealing a chair. "Please," he insisted, "please sit."

Nora glanced around, surprised that they were alone. She would have sworn she'd heard more than one voice when she knocked on the door.

As soon as she was seated, he began asking her questions. "So where did you say you got this paper?" he queried in apparent disbelief. "It couldn't possibly have come from Simon Weathers."

"Are we alone?" she asked.

"Oh yes please," Farris replied, "quite alone."

She told him the whole story, starting at the present and going backwards. He listened in silent astonishment. Her description of her escape from the asylum resulted in a couple of gasps but apart from that Farris was dumbstruck. She finished her tale with her abduction from the Venice boutique, although she couldn't remember much about it.

"So, Simon told me to be very careful. He said to avoid the police and to be very wary of the Consulate. I had the impression he knew what he was talking about. That's why I'm here. He said you would help me."

Farris nodded slowly. "Of course, I'll help you," he said softly. "I owe Simon a great deal. Now what can I do?"

"Well, I need somewhere safe to stay. Also, I need access to a telephone. I must call home. My husband probably thinks I'm dead."

"Well, I do have a cell phone here," he said, "but it will not call to the United States. You must come with me to my house. My wife will be very pleased to have you stay with us. You will eat and rest and use the telephone as much as you'd like. You'll be safe there." With that, he rose from behind his little desk and went about shutting off lights, locking the safe and making sure everything was in order. When he was done, he showed Nora to the door.

She waited as he locked up, glancing occasionally over her shoulder, very aware of her newfound paranoia. She was suspicious of everything and everyone. She was a very different Nora James from the guileless one that had gone missing in Venice.

As they left the grand market, a sedan pulled up beside them. The driver leapt from his seat and hurried to open the back door. Farris indicated to Nora that she should get in. She climbed in, slid across the seat and Farris got in beside her. He muttered something to the driver and smiled at Nora. "Everything will be fine now. You will see."

After wrestling his way through traffic for nearly an hour, Farris' driver pulled up in front of a middle-class house, which looked exactly like all its neighbors. He waited for the driver to open their door and without a word marched to the front door of the house with Nora close behind him.

Using his key, he unlocked the door, pushed it open and gestured for Nora to step inside. He called out, announcing that he was home and directed Nora to a small sitting room that was nicely appointed in very expensive-looking leather furniture. She couldn't help wondering which designer had been ripped off.

Shortly, they were joined by a pretty woman who looked to be at least twenty years Farris' junior.

"Ah ah," he greeted her, looking very proud, "this is my wife Kafta." He then spoke in Turkish to the woman who immediately stuck out her hand and smiled warmly.

Nora took the proffered hand and smiled back.

"She doesn't speak much English," Farris announced, "but she's a fine cook and she'll provide you with good food." He turned back to his wife and explained what he'd just said. "Now I'm sure the priority is letting people know you're safe," he said switching back to English. "There's a phone right here. If you give me the number, I will be happy place the call for you. It's a bit complicated, I'm afraid."

Nora recited her home number in the States and waited trembling with excitement as Farris dialed. Kafta left the room, murmuring something to Nora that she didn't understand. Nora was beside herself as she watched her host dial a long list of numbers. She could tell by his face that there was something wrong.

"Damn," he muttered, replacing the receiver. "No international calls for two more hours. This happens sometimes; it's one of the benefits of having a state-run telephone system." He sighed and shook his head. "Come. In the meantime, we'll have something to eat, maybe a nice shower and some fresh clothes, too."

Nora rose and followed him from the room. The kitchen was small but airy and modern. Kafta was already busy at the stove and whatever she was doing smelled wonderful.

"Why don't I show you where to shower," Farris suggested, "Kafta will lay out some clothes for you. By the time you're done, the meal will be ready. What do you think?"

Nora smiled and nodded. "Good idea," she agreed, "I could use a wash. Be better for everyone."

If he picked up on her attempt at humor, he gave no indication. He led her down a narrow hall to a flight of stairs and proceeded up. She followed.

Upstairs there were three doorways. He opened one, which led into what Nora assumed was the master bedroom. He pointed out the bathroom and left her to herself. She walked into the bathroom, turned on the shower and gratefully peeled off her clothes. She avoided checking herself in the mirror, deciding that it might be best to wait.

The shower was deliciously hot and strong. She leaned her head back and allowed the torrent to splash across her forehead. It was like a great massage. She was pleased to see that her incision was on the mend. There was no sign of bleeding. She was disappointed that she couldn't call home but resigned herself to the wait, thankful that she was out of danger and would hopefully soon be out of Istanbul. As she luxuriated in the warm force of the shower, she decided that it would be a long time before she took another European vacation. Home now sounded like paradise.

By the time she'd finished showering, there were fresh clothes laid out on the bed. She slipped them on, towel dried her hair and risked a peek in the mirror. The face staring back at her looked a bit thin and a little tired but otherwise it wasn't bad. Her eyes looked as determined as ever.

She skipped down the stairs wearing her borrowed clothes; jeans and a sweatshirt and headed for the kitchen. She could hear Farris and his wife were in the middle of a discussion but as she stepped into the room, the conversation broke off. Farris attempted a smile, but he seemed uncomfortable. She glanced at Kafta, but the woman had her back to her, busy with something on the counter.

"Please," said Farris, "have a seat. Our meal is almost ready."

Unsure as to how to feel, Nora took a chair. Her thoughts started spinning. She'd been sent to Farris by someone who trusted him, but something didn't seem right. Her instincts were once again on high alert. She understood, however, that she could give no indication of her worry. She needed to play along until an opportunity arose.

As Kafta placed the steaming food on the table, Nora noticed that her hands were shaking, and she was having trouble meeting Nora's eyes. Farris passed a bowl of rice across the table followed by a plate of stew that smelled wonderful. Nora smiled and spooned a good amount of onto her plate.

"This smells great," she said and started to eat although her appetite was not what it was before her uncertainty kicked in.

They ate in silence. Kafta never once looked at her husband. She remained completely focused on her food. Despite her nervousness, Nora ate every bite but refused seconds. She did agree to a cup of coffee and thanked her hostess for the delicious meal.

"Maybe we should try the phone again," said Farris as they sipped their coffee. "We never know when service will be resumed."

Nora nodded, "Oh yes please. Let's try."

She followed him to the sitting room and paced nervously as she waited.

"We're in luck," he said triumphantly. "I can call the States now. What number should I call?"

Nora breathlessly recited her home number again, praying Peter would be there. Nodding, Farris handed over the receiver. "It's ringing," he said.

After four rings, the phone was answered, and she nearly fainted from excitement. She was listening to her husband's voice. But as quickly as the joy filled her it faded away. She was listening to the answering machine. She left a message complete with a return phone number and Farris' address as he recited it to her. Burning with disappointment she handed back the receiver and sagged onto the couch.

"Is there another number we should try?"

"Of course," she whooped feeling a bit foolish, "there are lots of people I can try." First, they tried her parent's house in Santa Barbara. There was even a chance Peter could be there. He was close to her folks and in his time of grief they very well might be together.

When she heard her father's booming voice, the tears came. Choking them back, she told him the news he'd been praying for. A second later, her mother, also in tears was on the other line. She gave them a brief synopsis of her days of horror and asked about Peter.

"Peter's not here," said her father. "He hasn't returned yet. He's in Istanbul with a couple of friends he made. They're looking for you. Somehow, he figured out where you'd been taken. He called last night. I must say he sounded depressed. They've been having no luck at all."

"Oh my God," she breathed, "poor Peter. But I can find him now. Where is he? Give me his number."

Farris left the room and returned a moment later with a notepad and pen. She scribbled down the number.

"I've gotta go," she said breathlessly. "I'm going to try Peter. I'll call you later, okay?"

She paused listening.

"Oh yes, I love you too, more than ever. Bye for now."

She hung up and handed the receiver and the phone number to Farris.

"It's a hotel," she explained. "Oh God, please let him be there."

Farris dialed and when the phone was answered, he asked for Peter's room. After what seemed like an eternity, he sighed and asked for the address of the hotel. Shaking his head, he hung up. "They say they haven't seen your husband all day. But I'll take you there if you like. You can wait for him."

"Oh yes," she grinned, "please. That'd be great."

As she prepared to leave, Kafta collected Nora's clothes, put them in a plastic bag and handed them to her. At the door, she mumbled something in Turkish, still unable to meet Nora's eyes.

As they stepped outside, Farris' car pulled up in front of the house. The driver remained behind the wheel as Farris opened the back door and handed Nora in. He climbed in beside her. Nora should have felt excited but instead, she felt something else. She had a strong sense of foreboding.

After a while, they crossed a high suspension bridge. Beneath them sprawled the old city, crowding the shores of the Bosporus. Farris had apparently run out of conversation. He hadn't said a word for at least fifteen minutes.

Once across the bridge they turned off the main road and entered a neighborhood of impressive mansions set behind high walls and gates. She had a feeling they were nowhere close to Peter's hotel. She glanced surreptitiously at Farris. He stared straight ahead.

"So where are you taking me?" she asked softly. "How much did they pay you?"

He didn't look at her. "There was no payment involved," he replied. "A man like me needs powerful friends in order to be successful. It is my duty and my honor to be of service. It's good for business. It's essential for my family."

As the car slowed for a tight corner, Nora grabbed the door handle and wrenched it as hard as she could. Nothing happened. The door remained closed.

"Child safety locks," Farris said calmly, "prevents accidents."

That was it. The man's smugness was the last straw. She was on him before he knew it, clawing at his face like a mad cat. After a pretty good struggle, he managed to fend her off enough to reach for his belt. A gleaming blade appeared in his hand, the tip directed towards Nora's face.

"Enough," he demanded, "for your sake I don't want to have to mark you. The Emir will not look kindly on damaged goods."

Minutes later, the car rolled to a stop before a huge set of metal gates. Immediately, the gates started to swing open. The car drove slowly through, and Nora got her first glimpse of her new prison. Farris leaned in close to her.

"There are many worse things in life than what you're about to experience. The streets of our city are filled with young beautiful women who'd gladly trade places with you. And, since I won't be seeing you again, I feel it's only fair to tell you – I'm the one who betrayed poor Simon. I do hope you understand. It was nothing personal. It was strictly a business decision. I'm surprised he hasn't figured out that it was me."

CHAPTER 29

Peter had made all the calls he'd been postponing. He'd postponed speaking to Nora's parents and although he always tried to sound hopeful, he knew they guessed the truth. He'd called his office and one or two of his best friends. He'd had to dissuade them from hopping on the next plane, explaining that they would merely complicate the search, which he wasn't feeling too optimistic about.

He stared out the window of his hotel room, feeling lonelier than he'd ever thought possible. He tried in vain to eradicate the sense of doom that had descended upon him. The truth of the matter was that they'd hit a wall. There were no leads and no reason for hope.

He stretched out on the bed and stared at the ceiling. He tried to picture Nora's face but for some reason, it wouldn't come. The harder he tried the more her image faded. He shuddered and closed his eyes.

He slipped into a sleep so deep he never heard the telephone ringing. He was locked into a dream so horrible, he prayed to wake up. He couldn't. In the dream, Nora was being transported down a path lined with leafless trees. The moonless sky was black as ink. She was stretched out in a horse-drawn hearse with no driver. She was as beautiful as ever, wearing a long white robe, and looked as though she was blissfully asleep.

Ahead of her, a freshly dug grave was waiting. Two gravediggers, wearing baseball caps stood leaning on their shovels, smoking cigarettes and watching the slowly approaching carriage. Peter recognized the men but couldn't remember how he knew them.

The hearse pulled to a stop beside the grave. Inside, Nora, lay perfectly still staring up into darkness. A solitary tear ran down her cheek and splashed onto the canvas floor of the hearse. The image was truly awful. Nora was being conveyed to her own funeral – alive!

Suddenly, the scene changed. He was sitting at a table in a ship's cabin playing cards with an assortment of characters. The captain of the *Luxor* was there. Beside him was Omar, the carpet salesman. Sofi's fiancé, Mahmet, was there too with his gun lying on the table in front of him. The man dealing the cards was a fat man dressed in a gleaming white caftan smoking a thin cigar. Peter didn't know the man but assumed his presence was significant. Apparently, they were playing for a woman who was gagged and roped to the wall. At first the woman was Nora but as he looked closer, she became Sofi.

He awoke exhausted, feeling worse than before the nap. He looked at his watch and was surprised to see that he'd been sleeping for hours. How could he still be tired? He struggled to his feet and wandered into the bathroom. He turned on the shower and brushed his teeth to get rid of the terrible taste in his mouth. He felt like he'd smoked an entire pack of cigarettes. In fact, he had.

He stood under the stinging hot water trying to remember his dream. He couldn't. In the bedroom the phone rang a dozen times. He never heard it.

He dressed slowly, left the room and headed down the stairs. He was hungry but needed a drink before getting something to eat. As he crossed the lobby, heading for the bar, the front desk clerk called out to him.

"Mr. Brandt, I just had a call for you. I put it through to your room, but you didn't answer."

The young man reached behind him and handed Peter a message slip. On it was a name he didn't recognize and a phone number."

"The man said he needed to speak with you right away. He said he knew about the location of your wife."

Peter stopped like he'd been struck.

"He said what?"

The clerk repeated what he'd said.

Peter reached for his phone in his pocket and began to make the call.

"Damn," he muttered angrily. His phone was dead again. It didn't work very well in Istanbul anyway, and now it was losing its charge quicker and quicker. He turned to the receptionist, "A phone, quick!"

The young man handed over a telephone from behind the desk. Peter grabbed it and dialed feverishly. He was so excited his finger slipped off the sixth number. He started over, this time dialing very carefully.

The phone was answered by a man who spoke no English, so Peter handed the phone to the receptionist instructing him to ask whose name was written on the message. It took all the strength he had to control himself as he listened to one side of the conversation being conducted in Turkish.

From the clerk's response, Peter could tell that the news wasn't good.

"There's no one of that name at this number," the young man said apologetically. "It's a dry-cleaning shop in the Kadikoy district."

Peter just stared at the guy for a moment. He had no words. Was the message a cruel joke or something even more sinister? He backed away from the desk and wandered blindly into the bar where he took the closest stool and ordered a double.

CHAPTER 30

In the servant's wing of Hassan's palace, Haid changed his clothes preparing to go look for Sandar's missing girlfriend. His master had received a tip just an hour before and Haid had been tasked with the mission. He slipped on a dark windbreaker and his favorite baseball cap, checked his image in the mirror and headed out. Halfway down the hall, he knocked on a door and waited. The door opened and he was joined by another man.

"Ready?" the smaller man asked, smiling.

"Oh yes, Riza my boy," Haid replied. "This'll be fun. We may even be able to get a drink."

They crossed the Sultan Mehmet Bridge and entered Old Town, heading for Esentepe and its clubs. His employer had told him that Ali Sandar had met the girl in one of the clubs. He couldn't remember exactly which one, but Haid figured it was a good place to start.

Haid found a parking spot and together the men entered the Havana Club. It was a boisterous spot where the rich young Turks hung out, getting drunk early with the hopes of getting laid later. By 10 o'clock, the place was packed. Firm young bodies packed the dance floor, grinding against each other with abandon.

Haid and Riza squeezed their way to the bar and managed to order. When the two double Johnny Walker Blacks were placed in front of them, they clinked glasses and hungrily downed the contents. After another round, they were ready to circulate. They moved through the crowd selecting likely prospects and taking them aside for questioning. Not one partier put up any protest. It was apparent that men like Haid and Riza were able to conduct their inquiries with impunity. Private police were a part of life in the city and people had learned that it was best to tolerate the intrusion.

After an hour of questioning, they came up empty. They left the Havana and crossed the street to Switch. Inside was a slightly less well-heeled clientele, just as inebriated as their wealthier counterparts. After half-an-hour of questioning, Haid found a promising contact – the girl was extremely pretty, no more than twenty years old and drunk enough to share what she knew about the missing young woman.

She said that Nadja had been romanced by a wealthy man, who had a palace on the Bosporus and that she'd gone to live there. She insisted she hadn't seen her friend since. Haid was not so sure. Despite her protests, he forcibly steered her to a back door that opened onto a deserted alley. He left Riza inside to watch the door and the crowd. The club's employees knew better than to interfere, but some drunken kid might take it upon himself be a hero.

When the door closed behind him, Haid breathed deeply, enjoying the respite from the din. Haid pushed the girl against the wall and held her in place with a hand to her throat. "Where is your friend Nadja," he asked softly, almost intimately. The girl shook her head and said nothing. "I see," Haid said, smiling as he reached his other hand up under her skirt. "I will hurt you. Now tell me what I want to know before I disfigure you for life." He leaned in closer and squeezed tighter with both hands. The girl's eyes flew wide open and filled with terror. Haid leaned in closer. "Now I think it's time you came clean," he said softly, "it's your last chance."

The girl whispered hoarsely. "She's on her boyfriend's boat, the *Tahal*, Quay Number 13, the old docks."

Haid let go and watched impassively as the girl slid slowly down the wall to the ground where she sat staring up at him with wide sightless eyes. He shrugged unapologetically and headed back inside to find Riza and share the information.

He found Riza at the bar, berating two young girls and interrupted his fun. He imparted his news and they each had one more double scotch before heading for the docks.

The traffic was impossible as usual. It took nearly forty minutes to reach their destination. Riza had spent a few years as a stevedore and knew his way around the waterfront and had no trouble finding Quay 13. The *Tahal*, a broken-down retired deep- sea fishing boat was berthed in the second to last slip. The two men stepped onto the boat and waited in the shadows listening for evidence that somcone was onboard.

The moans of pleasure coming from the aft cabin indicated that indeed there was someone there. Haid smiled at his companion and headed towards the noise. As they went, he pulled a slender wire from his pocket. Riza clutched his gun. Without pausing, Riza kicked in the door.

Bathed in candlelight a young couple sat bolt upright staring at the shattered door in panic. The girl, a stunning blonde that Haid had last seen as Ali Sandar's companion did her best to cover her bountiful breasts. The young man leapt from the rumpled bed, intent on dispatching the strangers. It was a very bad mistake. Seconds later, he lay quite still in a pool of blood as Haid removed the garrote from around his throat.

The girl's screams jogged Riza into action. He walked across to the bed and hit her with his gun. The screams stopped as she collapsed to the sheets, unconscious. He and Haid both took a moment to appraise the girl's beauty. Riza eyed her hungrily and looked beseechingly at Haid, who wordlessly shook his head, refusing permission.

Disappointed, the smaller man wrapped the girl in one of the sheets and effortlessly hoisted her onto his shoulder. Two minutes later, they were back in the car, heading for a nicer part of town.

CHAPTER 31

Mahmet Batur sat smoking an American Marlboro, watching the boats jockeying for position. Although it was one of his favorite spots in the city, he'd never brought Sofi to the little outdoor restaurant on the water that served the best *manti* in Istanbul. It was a place reserved for the meetings; a place where no one knew him; a place that had to remain secret.

As he waited, his thoughts turned to his beautiful fiancé and the muscles in his face tightened perceptively. It was a monumental screwup and he was in it up to his neck. What kind of bad fortune would allow Sofi to be caught up in a situation he'd spent years cultivating. Even she was unaware of his real identity. He'd spent many a night pondering how she'd react when the truth came out – and out it was bound to come. He did love her, although not at first, but he'd come to adore her. He fully intended to marry her and take her far away from the hotbed Istanbul had become. She'd been the prefect entree into an element of the city he could never reach on his own. He'd been too many years away. Sofi's father had been deeply involved in the city's underbelly and Mahmet had been assured that Kalum could supply both the introductions and the paperwork to get him where he needed to be.

The fact that the old man was killed on the job was unfortunate, but Mahmet was already dating his daughter and saw no reason to stop. Her decision to become a cop came as a big surprise, however, Mahmet never argued with her decision. He knew that having a cop in the family could only help in the grand scheme.

He needed to find a way into the world on the far side of the straits where all the wealth and power resided, and he had come up with a plan to do just that. From his research, he'd decided that Ali Sandar would be his target. Ali was a man of great wealth and influence and from all accounts, was not the most ruthless of the club members.

The club, as Mahmet called it was a group of men who lived in an impenetrable enclave on the Asian side of the Bosporus. Most of them had inherited their wealth and position but one or two had wrestled it away from men too weakened by their lifestyles to stand up against men so brutal they'd stop at nothing to become part of the rarified clique that dwelt there. They were not men to be trifled with. Their life mission was absolute power and veneration, even though they were venomous as wasps.

Mahmet was twelve when his parents left Turkey to join his dad's brother in Hackensack, New Jersey. He remembered how his mother had cried as the plane lifted from Ataturk Airport, bound for a new and frightening world. Mahmet, on the other hand was thrilled. The thought of a life in America with its beautiful cars and women, like he'd seen on TV, stimulated his young imagination beyond his dreams.

It was after his stint in the U.S. Army's ROTC program at the University of Texas that he'd been recruited to join the USS. The agency, although a branch of the CIA, was highly specialized and not well known. Terrorism, specifically arms dealing, was the unit's mandate.

His Middle Eastern looks combined with his ability to speak Turkish as well as some Arabic had made him a very desirable candidate. The fact that his military record was exemplary and that he'd graduated near the top of his class guaranteed his appeal.

Now he was back in the city of his birth and right at the epicenter of an impending disaster. As far as he could see, there was no satisfactory outcome. Either the mission would be blown, or Sofi would get killed – or both.

The shadow falling across his table snapped him back to the present. He looked up, squinting into the sun and recognized the man he'd been waiting for.

"Serge," he said, offering his hand.

The other man sat down with his back to the water and extended his own. "Mahmet," he rejoined without a smile, "it's good to see you. It's been a while. I must say you don't look any worse for the wear. Istanbul seems to be agreeing with you. How long has it been now, three years?"

"Four," Mahmet replied.

"And this must be our tenth time meeting here if my memory serves me right."

"Eleventh," said Mahmet smiling. "Let's order some food and I'll fill you in."

"Sounds good," Serge nodded enthusiastically, "I'm starving. The food on the plane was unrecognizable."

Mahmet summoned a waiter and ordered for both of them. There was no point in asking his superior. He always had the same thing.

"So, something is not right?" Serge began in English, as soon as the waiter was out of hearing. In Serge's line of work, one could never be too sure. That's why he always preferred to meet close to running water. It had a very negative effect on eavesdropping. Although Serge spoke with a slight accent, his English was perfect. He'd been an agent in the East Med region for almost eleven years; station chief for six. Although his personality left a bit to be desired, he was a brilliant operative and a top-notch commander.

In that regard, the two men had a lot in common. Mahmet's personality was also a bit lacking, but he was a resourceful, loyal soldier, who would risk his life without question. These two had saved each other on more than one occasion over the four years of their association.

Serge Volitz had been recruited out of the NYPD at the age of twenty-six. Now, at thirty- eight, five years older than Mahmet, he was tiring of the life. The son of a Russian father and a Lebanese mother, he'd grown up in Moscow before spending two years in Beirut after his father had been killed in a drug deal gone bad. He'd immigrated to the United States at the age of fourteen and by nineteen was a cop on the streets. By twenty-five, he was assistant captain of detectives for the Bronx. His language skills and his street smarts had brought him to the attention of those who were constantly on the lookout for new talent, and after six months of intense training, he'd been sent to a part of the world he understood and could blend into.

With some flourish, the young waiter deposited two steaming bowls of *manti* on the table and conversation took a backseat for several minutes. When the bowls were clean, Serge leaned in and for a moment held his friend's troubled eyes with his own.

"So, what's up?" he asked. "It's bad, huh?"

"Yes, it's bad alright. It's also unbelievable. The coincidences: the chances of this happening I figure are a million to one." Mahmet took a long swallow from his water glass and stared past his companion towards the Bosporus. Serge watched him and waited patiently for him to resume.

"I think I've found the source, the top guy in the region. He's a major dealer in art and artifacts, not much of it on the up and up. He's a nasty piece of work, well protected and well connected. It just so happens I'm employed by one of his neighbors. As luck would have it, I've spent some time in the company of this man. His name is Mohammed Hassan al Caribe. He's a Bahrainian ex-patriot and a stone-cold killer. He's ensconced in a palace on the Bosporus that sits at the foot of a two-hundred-foot cliff. It would take a team of Berets to penetrate the place, which makes him tough to get to without pissing off the Turkish government. As you well know, they're already skittish."

Serge listened without interruption or change of expression.

"A ship reached port a few days ago from Venice. I was given some information about the ship's cargo. It's the real stuff; grenade launchers, lots of guns, regular gear but also several vats of bio-chemical stuff. I wasn't told exactly what it is, but it's enough for a major statement; enough to depopulate a major city. I was ready to call in an intercept when – and you won't believe this – my fiancé Sofi gets involved in a kidnapping case, trying to help some American film maker whose wife was abducted in Venice and shipped here. And here's the best part, the bio-weapons and the woman arrived here on the same ship, at the behest of Mohammed Hassan al Caribe."

Serge nearly jumped in but stopped himself.

"You think that's weird? Listen to this. This al Caribe guy who's trading arms for art is more than just a collector of statues. He's a collector of people too; young, females of the gorgeous variety. The guy's a real sick bastard. He comes off gay as a butterfly, but the word is he's a real lothario; a lady-killer – literally. And he's a very high stakes player. The woman he abducted is Nora James for Pete's sake. He had her shipped here along with his weapons. So now I find out that Sofi, clever little cop that she is, is closing in on this guy; the guy it's taken me four years to uncover. And now, she's gonna march right into the middle of this and blow the whole damn thing. Do you see the irony in all this, my friend?"

"Oh yes," Serge replied, unable to mask the twinkle in his eyes, "you've got yourself into a good one. So how do you propose getting out?"

"Well, I've already tried to knock her train off the tracks. I've tried to talk her out of her mission. I've tried to warn her about the danger. Hell, I've thought about threatening to call off the wedding, but she's a stubborn one. That's one of the things I love about her, and I do love her, Serge. I've never felt this way in my life. She's gonna be the mother of my kids and she could get killed here. Also, I've got a job to do; a job I can't do because of her. Do you understand?"

"I do understand, my friend," said Serge, "but we've got to intercept that shipment and put al Caribe out of business. We've no idea where the goods are headed or who the intended target is. You have no choice. You must continue. You know you must."

Mahmet looked away again, focusing intently on the boat traffic. He knew there was no time for him to be replaced. Even if someone could take his place, the shipment would be long gone, and Sofi would still be in jeopardy. A total *lose-lose* situation. "She doesn't even know I'm American," Mahmet said softly as if talking to the sea. "She's never heard me speak English, really. My story is all a lie. When she finds out the truth, she'll probably leave me anyway. I mean hell; would you want to spend your life with someone who's lied to you for four years?"

"So, you've got to stay with it. I hate to do this to you my friend, but there are huge stakes here. You have an obligation to your mission, to your country. Any other obligation must take second place. You knew that when you signed up."

"I know. That's why I was gonna get out. This was to be my last mission. Sofi's everything I want. With her I can have a real life, safe in some little backwater town where I can teach, and she can teach me, and together we could teach our kids." Mahmet had never cried in front of another person. This was as close as he'd come.

CHAPTER 32

Sofi was exhausted. She climbed the three flights of stairs to her tiny apartment just three streets away from her mother's place. Inside, she opened a can of condensed soup, added water and placed a saucepan on the stove.

She and Demir had dropped Peter off at his hotel and had paid a visit to their mother. They'd reached a consensus that they needed to take a few hours to rest and clean up. They'd been running on nerves and Sofi had insisted on the break, explaining that in their condition, they were likely to make a mistake, possibly a fatal one.

`She sat on the couch sipping the hot soup from a mug. She tasted nothing. She'd flipped on the television to catch up on the news – big mistake. Nowadays, all the news was so depressing. The local channel was reporting on the murder of doctor Ishmael Shamir. Unfortunately, it was one of five killings in the city that day. She thought about the poor woman on the island, the one with the sweet little boy. She wondered if she had yet heard about her husband's death or if she was still waiting for him to arrive home.

Feeling depressed, Sofi stretched out on the couch, changed the channel to a travel program and closed her eyes.

The ringing of the telephone woke her. She was surprised to see that it was dark outside. She must have slept for hours. In a stupor, she reached for the offending instrument and lifted the receiver to her ear. She shouldn't have answered. It was Mahmet and he sounded just as cold as he had during their last conversation.

"Have you thought about what I said?" he demanded. "I hope you've had a chance to come to your senses, Sofi. You've become involved in something you know nothing about. You could get hurt if you continue with this. You're being a foolish woman."

She started to fight back but didn't have the energy. "Sorry, Mahmet," she said quietly, "I'm sorry to be such a disappointment to you." Then, without another word, she dropped the receiver back onto its cradle.

Within seconds she was back asleep, back in a world she'd been so rudely dragged from. She was fourteen again, playing on the beach at Buyukada with Demir and her father and Peter Brandt when he was a boy.

Again, the phone wakened her, but this time the voice was kindly. It was her brother "Hi," he said, "did I wake you?"

"Of course not," she lied, wondering why she felt the need to.

"Listen," Demir continued, "I just got a call from Omar. He told me that according to his people, a couple of goons were searching the clubs tonight, looking for a missing woman. The woman apparently belonged to one of the untouchables. He thought it might have been Nora. Also, he told me he saw a woman fitting Nora's description in the bazaar this afternoon. He tried to approach her, but she got spooked and disappeared into the crowd. The bad news is that one of the girls these guys questioned at Switch has turned up dead."

"Wow," Sofi breathed, "maybe Mahmet is right. Maybe he knows more than he's telling us. He's with these people all the time. Maybe he heard something."

Suddenly, she remembered the captain of the Luxor. He'd been floating on the Sea of Marmara for hours. Surely, he would have been spotted by now. She said a quick goodbye to her brother and called police headquarters. She identified herself to the desk sergeant and asked for the supervisor on duty. A moment later, Lieutenant Rhad was on the line. Sofi knew him to be an honest cop. Without telling him how she knew, she told him about the *Luxor* and its cargo of weapons. She also informed him about the motorboat anchored a hundred yards off the ship's starboard bow and the captain waiting to be arrested.

She was now wide awake. She stood and wandered into her cubbyhole kitchen where she put the kettle on. She was in desperate need of coffee and no wonder. According to the kitchen clock, it was five-thirty in the morning. As she waited for the water to boil, she thought about all that had happened since meeting Peter Brandt. Although only a few days had passed, she felt like she'd been involved for weeks.

She poured the steaming water over the ground coffee and watched the dark brew dripping into the carafe, thinking about how she'd pass the next few hours. She was eager to get back to the search but realized there was nothing to be done until morning. There were no new leads, but she had faith that something would turn up. Maybe a visit to Switch, where the girl had been killed would yield some information.

She needn't have worried. The ringing phone snapped her out of her reverie. She hurried back into the living room, wondering who could possibly be calling her now. The voice on the line was not one she recognized. Without preamble, the man told her to go to the Sunken Cistern in one hour, and enter through the Eye of the Needle. Inside, the voice said, she'd find her brother, Demir, who would be meeting with someone who had information about her father's death and how it might be linked to the disappearance of Nora James. With that, the caller hung up. Sofi shuddered. She was suddenly filled with a strong sense of foreboding.

The cistern was part of a vast underground labyrinth, filled with enough water to sustain the city through any siege. It had performed its function since the reign of Constantine in the fourth century. The Eye of the Needle was the name for a small portal at the rear of the structure. It was an entrance whose existence was known to very few.

She called her brother but got no answer. She was surprised. She called Peter, woke him and told him about the strange phone call. Explaining that she hadn't been able to find Demir and arranged to meet Peter at the cistern.

She changed quickly, washed her face, brushed her teeth and her hair and headed out. For once, there was no traffic in the streets. She easily secured a taxi and within a few minutes was standing in a tiny cobbled poorly lit street awaiting Peter's arrival. Two minutes later, a taxi pulled to a stop and Peter climbed out.

"Still no luck with Demir?" he asked.

She shook her head. "I'm worried about him," she said. "This makes no sense." She led the way to a small doorway that was barely large enough for a man to squeeze through. "It's called the *Eye of the Needle*," she explained. "It's named after a Jerusalem gate that was too small to allow camels through unless they were on their knees. She turned the steel ring handle and the heavy old door swung open. She entered first and Peter followed.

What he saw inside took his breath away. It was like they'd entered the realm of the Phantom of the Opera. They were standing on a narrow catwalk looking down on a vast lake crisscrossed by dozens of walkways. The cathedral-sized, dimly lit space looked like a giant checkerboard. Rising from the lagoon were soaring marble columns that supported an intricately carved vaulted ceiling. The place was beyond eerie. To add to the atmosphere, classical music echoed from the damp walls. As they slowly descended a narrow flight of worn stone steps towards the pools, they were surrounded by the sound of dripping water.

Sofi pulled her gun out and led the way across a walkway that bisected one large pool and took them to a grid work of similar paths that went off in all directions into the shadows. Peter gasped as a soft splash emanated from somewhere off to their right. It was followed by a series of similar splashes. They rounded a corner, crept past a column and saw the source. In front of them was a pool whose surface was covered with ripples. It didn't take long to determine that the pool was home to dozens of rats that were now swimming away from them. Peter shuddered and glanced over at Sofi who continued, searching as she went. It was the spookiest place Peter had ever seen but the young woman beside him seemed completely unimpressed.

"I'm sure glad we scared them off," he whispered, indicating the fast-moving rodents

"They're not afraid," she whispered, "they're after something. There must be a new food source somewhere nearby."

They found the food source in the fifth basin. He was floating face down in the water with his arms and legs outstretched. Sofi froze in place, staring down into the death pool. A moment later, she started moaning, increasing in volume until she was wailing like she'd been stabbed. Her anguished cry resounded throughout the Basilica of death like the keening of a hundred mourners. She didn't have to see the face to know that the dead man was her brother.

Peter held her tightly, in order to prevent her from leaping into the icy water. After a brief struggle, she collapsed against his chest and allowed two or three deep sobs. As she pulled away from him, he glanced over her head and saw a shadow move. He thought he'd been looking at a single dark column when suddenly a form beside it crouched low and began to scamper away.

"Stop," Peter yelled, "stop or I'll shoot!"

He watched the figure race across the walkway as it disappeared into the darkness. It then reappeared for a moment as he passed under one of the downlights. Peter thought the man looked familiar, but it was impossible to be sure. The man was large and resembled Mahmet.

He turned to see if she too had seen the man, but she was paying no attention. Rather she was staring into the pool, mesmerized by the floating corpse of her brother.

"I think it's time to call for help," Peter said softly and placed his arm around her and walked her away from the scene. "You need to report this. Call someone you trust. You don't want him to stay there, do you? And someone needs to come for him."

Biting her lip, she pushed past him and headed for the door through which they'd entered the catacomb. By the time he stepped through after her, she was on her phone. She rang off and faced Peter, her eyes afire. "They won't get away with this you know. They took my father and now my brother. It's my turn now, and they'll be sorry."

When the two police cars arrived, Sofi had a quick word with one of the officers and then headed in the other direction. Peter followed along but remained a pace or two behind in case she didn't want company or in case she did.

She reached a main street and hailed a taxi. When she secured one, she slid into the backseat, leaving the door open. Peter climbed in beside her as she directed the driver.

They arrived at her place a few minutes later. Peter handed the taxi driver a few notes and climbed out. Sofi was already through the front door. He could hear her footsteps as she hurried up the stairs. He locked the door behind him and followed her.

She stood across the room beside the window looking out over a puzzle of rooftops that led to the straits. He knew she was not ready, so he found his way to the kitchen, discovered the light switch, and began the search. The strongest thing he found was a bottle of red wine, but he went about popping the cork, grateful there was anything remotely alcoholic.

He unearthed a pair of water glasses, returned to the small living room, filled both glasses to the rim and handed one to Sofi. She took it without acknowledging him and took a long swallow. He chose the armchair in the corner and sat there, glass in one hand, bottle in the other. It didn't take long until his services were again required. On Sofi's third swallow, she emptied her tumbler and extended it in his direction. He rose to comply. She didn't look at him or the refill.

"There are cigarettes in the kitchen, top drawer by the fridge. Would you . . .?"

Peter placed the bottle beside her on the windowsill and went in search of the cigarettes. He returned a minute later triumphant. He held two ashtrays, one for her, one for him.

He lit her cigarette and his own and retired to his chair. Halfway through her second cigarette, she spoke. All the time, Peter had sat quietly watching her, noticing that she looked like Ava Gardner in *Night of the Iguana* staring out at the evil world with a halo of blue smoke ascending slowly above her. For the first time in his life, in this circumstance, he could say he knew how she felt. Such a loss could only be understood by those who'd suffered one.

"They killed my father the same way, you know. It was three years ago yesterday. He'd gotten too close, just like

Demir." She took a long drag and released a tight stream of smoke and controlled anger. We found him in the Marble Sea after a telephone tip. He'd been in the water for days. That's why I wasn't concerned about sharks in the Marmara."

She stubbed out her smoke and crossed the room where she refilled her glass, emptying the bottle. Noticing what she'd done, she shrugged, and headed a little untidily for the kitchen. Peter listened to the slamming of cupboard doors and the unmistakable crackle of an ice tray being upended. She returned bearing a bottle of dark red liquid that Peter recognized immediately. In her other hand she had an ice cube tray. She waited impatiently as he upended his glass, offered him the ice cubes and refilled his glass with a debilitating pour of Sour Cherry Vodka. She teetered back to the couch, settled in and half-filled her own glass.

"My father was not just a florist you see," she stated matter-of-factly. "I knew nothing at all about his other life until the time of his death. I was twenty-three. I'll never forget. It was the week before my birthday." She sighed, took a swallow from her glass and leaned back against the cushion. "I should have suspected that there was something different or should I say special about him and his business. He was the only merchant that I knew who never paid protection fees. It had never occurred to me, but he was treated with something more than respect. People were eh . . . aware of him. He'd been missing for two days when my mother sat me down along with Demir and told us the real story of my father. It seems that he'd risen through the ranks of the army and found himself in a special unit that was involved in secret operations. This part of his career prepared him for a comfortable position within the government's Secret Police. An unfortunate encounter with a cabal of fundamentalist gunrunners resulted in him being wounded and forced to retire from the force. It was at a time when our country was being pressured by the fascists. The muezzins no longer called the faithful in Turkish; Arabic had become the language of the mosques. The battle has not subsided, Peter, it's just begun. There are dark forces afoot in my country. It's the bridge to the West and the pathway to Western thought. If Istanbul was to become a haven for fundamentalism, the bad guys would have a foothold in Europe. Can you imagine, a radical Islamic capital right in their midst?"

Peter was surprised to discover he'd reached the bottom of his glass. Just as well, he figured. He knew he'd had plenty. But it was not to be. She crossed the floor on her knees and splashed a fist-sized shot into his glass; mostly.

As she retreated, crawling backwards, she continued with her narrative.

"My mother's grief was so intense that it was easy for Demir and me to get information she'd never have told us ordinarily. It seems that, although my father had officially retired, he remained a consultant for the *blackshirts*. He became an integral part of the underground war; a war to preserve the openness and universality of our culture, a culture that has stood at the world's center for three thousand years.

"I have no illusions about my father; I came to understand that he moved in the city's underbelly, he consorted with truly bad men in order to accomplish his mission. I'm told he was clever, cruel at times and that he would hesitate at nothing in pursuit of his quarry. He'd killed many times and had played the game with the criminals and the corrupt from Syrians to Iranians. But despite the darkness of the roads he travelled, the man's integrity was beyond question. He was ultimately an honest cop. We were told that he was killed because he would not look the other way. But he couldn't do that. Do you understand?"

Peter nodded. "Yes," he said quietly, "so, what makes you think there's a connection?"

"Well, for one thing they were both garroted, not drowned. It was the smell of Demir's blood that excited the rats. It must have happened just before we got there. It was a message for us. Somebody wants us to stop what we're doing. And these people will kill us if we continue."

"Well, we'd better get going," Peter slurred. He felt the booze doing some of his talking, but he was telling the truth. The fact remained he had no intention of giving up. He had the feeling Sofi wouldn't be far behind. "You know, I got a look at that guy in the cistern," he said, "I've seen him before."

"Where?" Sofi sat bolt upright, immediately professional. "Where did you see him?"

Peter averted his gaze, unsure as to what to tell her. "I'm not sure," he fibbed, "but I'd certainly recognize him again."

"Don't lie to me, Peter," she said, sounding suddenly sober. "This is important. People are getting killed, damn it. I can't see you very well but I'm a professional and I can smell a lie."

Peter said nothing.

"Well?" she sounded impatient.

"Sofi, I'm pretty sure I met him at your mother's flat. I think it might have been your fiancé, Mahmet – same build; same hair."

The silence in the room was suddenly deafening.

"Impossible," she growled, "I've known Mahmet since before my father died. He was of great help to us at the time. Although we'd never met Mahmet, he was a friend of my father's. He's been nothing but supportive of my family. I know he seems a bit fierce at times but underneath he's truly a sweet, loving man." She took a long, slow breath, "Besides, he loved Demir. He would have no part in hurting my brother or my family."

"Well," Peter replied, happy to retreat, "there were a lot of shadows and not much light. I could have been mistaken. The guy was moving pretty fast."

She didn't say anything. Instead, she reached for a cigarette. A blue flame sparked the dimness and lit Sofi's face. Peter could see it was wet with tears.

"So," he asked, "do you have any ideas about who's responsible?"

"Yes, I have, but it's going to take more than that. The people involved in these activities; arms dealing, drug smuggling and kidnapping are a powerful group. They are surrounded by layers of protection, both literally and figuratively. Armed guards and dogs patrol their palace grounds night and day. At the same time, they're very well connected, having cultivated, meaning *paid for* relationships over the years, sometimes over generations. I understand that we need help, but the official circles are already compromised. We'll have to find a different way."

CHAPTER 33

Nora awoke in what was without a doubt the most sumptuous bed she'd ever slept in. She felt like she was floating on air. The image of a magic carpet came to mind, but she chased the specter away.

A knock on her door was followed by the appearance of a trolley being pushed into the room by a young man wearing a white robe with blue stripes and a crimson turban. Behind him was an older woman also in a robe – although hers was all white.

There was no greeting. Instead, the young man went about setting covered dishes on an ornate table by the window. Once he'd finished, he crossed to the door, bowed deeply and disappeared, still without a word.

The woman approached the bed and in passable English, explained that she was there to inspect Nora's vagina. Nora studied the woman's face, half expecting her to break into a smile, to announce that she was joking. No such luck.

"I must have a look at your healing," the woman continued. "The Pasha is most concerned about your comfort and wishes to pay his respects but first requires a report regarding your progress."

Nora now understood the meaning of the word *dumbstruck* – that was exactly how she felt. She forced her eyes to look away from the woman and stared for a moment through the floor to ceiling windows that looked out over the sparkling sea.

A moment or two later, she recovered enough composure to look back at the woman and form some words. "What day is it?" she managed.

"It is Thursday madam. Tonight, the Pasha plans to dine with you. So please allow me to do as he has requested."

"Three days," Nora murmured, "I've been here for three days. Have I been asleep all that time?"

"Oh yes," the woman replied, "the Pasha's doctors said that complete rest would be your quickest road to recovery, and he agreed. He is not a patient man."

For some reason, Nora found herself allowing the woman to turn back the covers and open the silk nightgown she was wearing. She proceeded to remove Nora's panties, and everything was exposed.

As the woman started to pull Nora's legs apart, Nora clenched tight and held up her hand, palm facing the woman.

"I'm sorry," she said firmly, "but before this goes any further, I must insist on one thing."

A look of worry crossed the woman's face.

"Before we become BFFs, I really need to know your name."

The woman's mouth fell open and then a flicker of a smile entered her eyes. "Adara," she answered, "my name is Adara. It means virgin."

"Oh, does it now? And is it true?"

The woman flushed bright red and nodded vigorously.

"Very well Adara, you may proceed but be gentle."

Adara studied Nora's face for a second to see if she was serious then pulled on a pair of latex gloves in preparation for inspection.

There was no change in Nora's expression, but the leg clench relaxed a little.

Then, Nora felt a finger being inserted and a subsequent very personal exploration. "What, no stirrups?" she ventured, but received no response.

Seemingly satisfied, Adara removed her finger, pulled off the gloves and offered a wry smile. "All seems good," she announced, "you are healing very well. Soon you will be ready to go."

Nora was unsure as to what exactly the woman meant but chose to just let it pass.

Without another word, Adara pulled Nora's panties up, arranged the bedcovers and bowed politely before turning away. A moment later, the door clicked shut and the lock was engaged.

Nora lay perfectly still, trying to process what had just happened. She felt like a brood mare being prepped for impregnation. Some of her wanted to cry but she was too much in shock to let that happen.

CHAPTER 34

Sofi and another officer by the name of Hakam arrived at the murder scene well after midnight. The station had received a report of shots fired and she and Hakan had been assigned the call. It had been years since she'd been down to the old docks and things had certainly not gotten any better in her absence. It was a part of Istanbul so horrible that even the rats were nervous.

She'd managed to catch a few hours of sleep after leaving the cistern. She'd been unable to speak to her mother because she couldn't explain her involvement. For some reason, she hadn't called Mahmet either. She wasn't sure why not but didn't have time to think about it. She had not had time to deal with her brother's death, let alone begin the grieving process. Sofi was tired, tired and hurting. Most jobs would have offered a day or two off to deal with the horror and the grief, but such was not the case when one was employed by the Istanbul Police Department.

As a result, she was now driving through the hell that was the old docks, looking for the crime scene. They found the right quay and parked the car. How they were supposed to find the vessel was another question entirely.

She and Hakan began walking slowly down the pier, lighting their way with their flashlights, looking for any sign of a shooting. There was none.

Then as they neared the end of the pier, having passed twenty or so boats, most of which looked abandoned, they spotted a rusty old scow that appeared to have a light on.

"Must be the place," she muttered to her partner, "men first." She pointed to the boat rail and watched as Hakan climbed over and headed belowdecks.

She sighed deeply, shuddered and climbed aboard. She found Hakan standing in the cabin with his hands on his hips quietly surveying the mess. A naked man was stretched across the bed, which was soaked in blood. The gas lantern that hung from the ceiling swayed to and fro as the cops moved about the cabin causing their shadows to float around like ghosts.

After a thorough search, they found no evidence of gunfire. They did, however, determine that the young man had been garroted and had bled profusely. The fact that he was wearing a condom was unusual. The motive was anybody's guess.

They headed back up top to the welcome fresh air and waited for the ambulance and the medical squad to arrive.

Hakan started to ask Sofi about finding Demir's body in the cistern but the look on her face quickly changed his mind. They sat on the cold pier smoking in silence as they waited for the medical team to arrive.

It was mid-morning before Sofi was back in her bed, completely exhausted and trying to fight off her dreams. She knew she'd have to see her mother as soon as she woke. She wasn't sure what to do about Mahmet. The fact that they'd had a row was a blessing, she acknowledged. Maybe she'd have some time to decide how to deal with him. Although Peter's suggestion that he'd seen Mahmet in the cistern was ridiculous, for some reason she was troubled by the idea.

***

The sun poured in through the huge open windows of the palace. The pure white mousseline curtains fluttered in the afternoon breeze and the caged birds sang like they were free.

Hassan was pleased. His man Haid had found Ali's missing plaything and had returned her to the palace mostly unharmed and sexy as hell. He'd had a chance to have a good look at her and could see why old Ali was smitten. She was wearing nothing but a sheet when she was delivered, but Hassan had her bathed and dressed in such a way as to make her appear respectable.

Looks, of course can be deceiving, he mused. He sat on the verandah outside his bedroom watching the ships, yachts and dhows jockeying for position. It was a view he never tired of. It was commerce at work and commerce was everything. It made his world go round.

His reverie was interrupted by one of his houseboys announcing the arrival of his guest. He could never remember any of the boys' names, hell he couldn't even tell them apart.

He placed his cigar in the ashtray and rose, indicating to the boy that he should dispose of the thing. He strolled into his bedroom, checked his appearance in one of the half-dozen mirrors and headed down the corridor towards the staircase.

He nodded to Ali Sandar who was waiting at the bottom of the stairs, so exited he could hardly form a greeting. Not far behind him, standing in the shadows was his ever-present bodyguard, Mahmet. Hassan remembered Mahmet's name because he had at one time approached Sandar about hiring the man for his own use. Sandar had not responded well, so he'd let it go. Hassan already had a top-notch team but whenever he saw something he liked he had an overwhelming need to possess it.

"She's right down here," Hassan murmured, leading the way down one of the galleries towards the back of the house.

Hassan was not a man to accept loose ends and this girl had proven herself to be just such an inconvenience. But he was not an entirely heartless man and thought it best to let his friend down easy.

They reached a door where one of Hassan's men was standing guard. Hassan nodded to the man who unlocked and opened the door and stepped through to make sure everything was in order. He nodded and moved aside allowing al Caribe and Ali Sandar to enter.

Nadja was sitting on a bed staring at the men as they entered. Her eyes were red from crying and a bandage covered the left side of her face. As soon as she saw Sandar, she leapt from the bed, ran to him and threw herself into his arms. "Oh, thank God," she whispered through her tears, "I thought you'd never come."

Ali couldn't help himself. He hugged the girl tightly and gently patted her back. He whispered something in her ear, which elicited a damp smile.

"Well," al Caribe announced, "I think I have seen all of this that I need to. Ali, I'm glad you are pleased. Now why don't we leave her for now and she will join you again this evening at dinner."

Sandar looked like he was about to protest but one look at his friend's face and he decided against it.

"Thank you, Hassan," he offered instead, "I very much appreciate your finding her." He gently pulled away from the girl and turned towards the door. "I shall see you this evening, my dear," he murmured to the girl. "I look forward to it. Welcome home."

With that, he exited the room with al Caribe close behind him. The girl offered a pathetic little wave as her patron disappeared.

Sandar headed back down the corridor smiling, delighted with the way things had gone. Behind him, al Caribe nodded to the guard and turned to follow his guest.

The guard pushed the door open and stepped through. As he did, he pulled a long knife from his belt.

The sound of the earsplitting scream never escaped the walls.

***

The bedside clock read 9:30 when there was a soft knock on Nora's door. Before she could respond, the door opened. A large man with a swarthy complexion and strange light-colored eyes stepped in and stood gazing at her. He wore a white robe and keffiyeh secured by a gold agal. The man looked very rich and very dangerous.

She rose from her chair by the windows where she'd been passing the time watching the boats. She had been fantasizing about an escape plan but had not yet managed to hit on anything feasible. She'd managed an escape in several of her movies but none of the strategies fit the scenario she was in now.

The man continued to gaze at her without saying a word.

Her initial reaction was that she'd seen the man somewhere before, but she dismissed the thought. That would be a coincidence for the books. She'd been bathed and dressed by a pair of young women who spoke not a word of English, so conversation had been very limited. She now wore a flowing, white Dior dress with gold shoes, a stunning necklace and earrings to match, as well as a heavy bangle bracelet with a huge blue-green stone at its center. The girls had left her hair long and it tumbled to her bare shoulders, radiant as fire. She had been allowed a look at herself in the dressing room mirror and no matter the circumstance she had no quarrel with her appearance. The girls were good at their job.

She stood very still, watching her captor watching her. Her insides were in knots. She was sure he could hear her heart hammering in her chest, but she refused to give any indication that she was terrified.

He spoke no words as he took a few steps towards her, inspecting his acquisition both for its beauty and for its essence. Seemingly pleased with what he was seeing, he moved closer. He stopped within a few feet of her and bowed ever so slightly.

She managed a breath.

“I am Mohammed Hassan al Caribe,” he said softly, “I will be your host for the foreseeable future, and I bid you welcome to my humble home.”

Nora’s inclination was to snort but she managed to suppress it.

The man’s presentation was even actually worse than she’d imagined. He spoke with a refined English accent, but it did nothing to dispel her worst fears. Despite his splendid clothes and his elegant manners, Hassan was one of the ugliest men she’d ever laid eyes on. It wasn’t so much his dark, pock-marked skin or the bulbous nose or even the reptilian lips partially hidden in the goatee. It was his eyes – his pupils were pale brown and undefined, almost ragged. They were the eyes of a predator, a creature that held cruelty in high regard. In a word he was hideous.

Nora remained silent. Even in her world of imagination she’d never rehearsed her lines for this moment.

“I see you are uncomfortable,” he offered, “it is to be expected. After all you are not here by your choosing but still, there is a choice to be made. This can be a short-lived hell for you or as they say in your country, you can make the most of it. It is my intention this evening to present you to my guests. Some are my friends, and some are my enemies. Unbeknown to them, I do know which is which. You will be seated on my right and you will wear this,” he extracted what looked like a veil from his pocket. It was fashioned of fine gold mesh with a diamond-studded chain. "It wouldn't do, of course, for you to be recognized while half the world is searching for you. In time it won't be necessary but for now, I must insist. There will be other women wearing veils, so you won't feel singled out. I also strongly advise that you engage in very little conversation. The man that will be seated beside you speaks no English whatsoever and is, at the same time, as deaf as a stone One can never be too careful," he chuckled, revealing a glint of gold coming from inside his mouth.

"Yuk," was the first thought that came to Nora's mind.

"Do you understand?"

Nora nodded without speaking.

"Now," he continued, "just to be sure we have no misunderstandings, I want you to dispel from your mind any thought of making a scene. It's probably best if you don't go ripping the veil away to reveal who you are and screaming for the police. First of all, there are no police nearby and many of them work for me anyway."

Nora felt herself deflate. The monster had been reading her mind.

"In an effort to assure us that there will be no drama, although we all know it's something you're very good at, I would like to show you something." From another pocket, he pulled out a photo and handed it to her.

She took it from him, looked at it and gasped. It was the first sound she'd uttered since Hassan had entered the room.

"I understand you know this man," he said, his cruel streak now on full display.

She nodded, "That's my husband," she breathed as a tear spilled down her face.

"Well, it might interest you to know that he is in fact in Istanbul and he's doing his best to find you. Truth is, he's doing a damn good job, considering. But, if there are any shenanigans from you, Peter Brandt will die – tonight."

Nora looked at him, her eyes glittering, no longer with fear but with fury.

"Are we agreed?" Hassan asked.

"We are," she spat.

"By the way, this is not the first time we have met. I had the pleasure, brief as it was some months ago at a Hollywood affair. I met your husband that evening as well."

She knew she'd seen that face before. It was not one that was easily forgotten. She offered no response.

"So, in a few minutes I will send someone to escort you downstairs. Please do remember the things we discussed as it will be better for everyone," and with that he turned and left the room.

She remembered him now. She remembered flashing to him on the journey from Venice. And she remembered how repulsed she'd been when he'd cornered her at the party in Beverly Hills. And now she was his, to do with as he pleased.

***

When Hassan reached the bottom of the stairs, he saw that the grand salon had filled up a bit. It was to be a small, intimate affair with only thirty guests but already there was chatter and laughter. He smiled to himself. He did enjoy entertaining. He was proud of what he had and who he was and didn't mind sharing. He was a generous man, in some ways.

As he headed into the room, Ali Sandar hurried to meet him. "She's not here Hassan. You told me she would be here."

Hassan took his friend by the arm and steered him away from the guests down a wide gallery until they reached a fountain, with a couple of chairs nearby. Hassan indicated a chair and waited for Ali to sit before sitting himself.

Ali stared at him eager and excited, "Where is she, my friend? I cannot wait another minute."

Hassan looked at his neighbor for a moment before answering.

"I'm afraid you won't be seeing Nadja again, Ali. I was informed by my men that they found her in a very compromising situation. She was in the company of a most undesirable man, one who could bring the very worst kind of attention to us should she tell him about things she may have heard."

Ali's mouth was moving but he made no sound. Eventually, he managed to stammer, "But I loved her, Hassan.

She was the first one since Halla died who understood me. She loved me and wanted nothing but my love in return."

Hassan was about to say something cruel but controlled himself. "It was too dangerous, Ali. It is a very perilous time for us. Any unwanted attention could ruin us both or worse. The shipment that arrived from Italy last week was almost discovered. The Luxor *was* stranded here in the Sea of Marmara for two days due to personnel issues and she was boarded by the police. It's a good thing they were searching for a missing person and had no interest in the cargo. You well know that if the authorities had discovered what we are shipping, we'd be dead in the water, literally. This is why we need to be overly cautious. Thankfully, by this time tomorrow the ship will be somewhere in the Black Sea, safe from prying eyes."

"But Nadja had no knowledge of our business dealings. As a matter of fact, she expressed no interest."

"She was getting too close to you, Ali. I saw that you were very enamored. I was hoping the situation would cool, but unfortunately, I got the impression that you were in over your head."

Ali looked like he was about to cry, like he was being scolded by a parent, but he managed to hold back the tears. Grown men could not cry. Such a display of emotion would be his shame forever. He coughed, waiting for his mind to settle. "So, what have you done with her?" he asked fearfully, his eyes shining.

"She has been sent far enough away so that she cannot hurt us. Maybe after the next couple of shipments we can return our attentions to the art trade. It's not nearly as lucrative but it is much less dangerous. If what I expect does happen when our buyer receives his goods we will be living in a much-changed world. It will be best to reduce our exposure. When things settle, I will let you know where Nadja has been taken. But, until such time, I'm sorry my friend but there's simply too much to lose."

Sandar didn't know what to believe but he knew better than to question Hassan al Caribe. He'd seen other men try and watched those men die. He finally nodded without speaking, rose to his feet and started back towards the festivities. As he slowly walked down the corridor with his head bowed, Mahmet stepped from the shadows and moved in behind him.

As he followed his Pasha at a discreet distance, Mahmet reached up and removed his earpiece.

***

Dan O'Henry was the first in the office as usual. Although the embassy in Ankara dealt with the bulk of the official business, there was still plenty of busy work at the Consulate in Istanbul. No sooner had he poured himself a cup of coffee and sat down at his desk than the phone rang. He let it ring a couple of times before picking up the receiver.

"Hello," he said then waited.

"Yes," he replied nodding.

His eyes widened as he listened.

"You're sure?" he asked in a hoarse whisper. "Right away," he said, nodding again and hung up. He sat back in his chair for a moment, staring out the window at the waterway, lost in thought. He then reached for the receiver again and dialed.

"It's O'Henry," he said when his call was answered. "We've got her."

He listened and nodded.

"It's up to you guys now. She's docked in the Marmara, but we don't know for how long."

CHAPTER 35

The sea was calm as the *Luxor's* anchor rose from the dark water. The low humming of the engines was the only other sound. Once the anchor was safely stowed, the ship turned away from the city lights and steamed into the darkness. Her heading was north-by-northeast. In three hours, the Sea of Marmara would be behind her, she'd be through the Bosporus and safe in the dark waters of the Black Sea.

Next stop Sevastopol for the first of the deliveries then onto the *Odessa* where the bio-chemicals would be off-loaded. There was enough destructive force in what she was carrying to alter the course of the war with Russia. Then watch out world. But what did he care? He knew the places to hide.

They were running without lights just to be on the safe side. It had been arranged that no port police would be in the vicinity, but they were supposed to have departed Marmara two nights before. Captain Arim still didn't know what had hit them, but it had been a real disaster. Thank God he'd gotten the woman off the ship and safely ashore before all hell broke loose. Messing that up would surely have cost him his job, maybe even his life. Al Caribe was not a man to be trifled with.

It was a good thing the Pasha had friends in the police department. Otherwise, he might not have been rescued from the launch. He'd been provided with half-a-dozen new crew-men and instructions to leave Istanbul as quickly as possible. It was baffling though, that despite all the safeguards, the *Luxor* had been boarded and searched. Such a screw up should never have been allowed to happen. Good thing the raiders were in search of something else and had no idea of what they were looking at.

There was enough chemical weaponry in the hold to eliminate every living soul in the city they were departing. It was enough to start a war or to finish one. Thankfully, it wasn't intended for Istanbul, because in the wrong hands, it could wipe the great city from the face of the earth.

***

Peter stood staring into the sea. The ships moored in the darkness were nothing more than shadows rising and falling in unison, lifted by the meager swells. He'd been pretty much left to his own devices while Sofi and her family attended to the details of Demir's funeral. He'd thought it best to give them some breathing space. Although they were fond of him, for the most part, tragedy such as this was for family and close friends. He'd eaten alone and had made his way down to the water, trying his best harness his thoughts. He'd run out of ideas but had never been very good about accepting defeat. There had to be something he was missing. He gazed into the water and began entertaining a most bizarre thought. He wondered if the same water he was looking at had carried Nora away. When he found himself beginning to resent the water, he thought it best to redirect he thoughts. If the craziness and hopelessness he felt creeping in was the onset of depression, he would have none of it. There was no time.

Who? – was the question of the day. Who, out of all the millions of people who knew his wife, had the audacity and the resources to execute such a plot? Infatuation was one thing. This blatant theft of a human being, and a world-famous one at that, was beyond anything Peter's mind could grasp. How desperately insane was her captor? Did he really believe he could keep her hidden from the world? Would he want to?

Peter thought not. It would be like stealing a priceless painting and then hiding it from everyone. Such behavior made no sense. What would be the point of possessing a masterpiece if it couldn't be displayed? Wouldn't flaunting it be essential?

If nothing else, Peter Brandt was good at stories. His imagination had stood him in good stead throughout his career. It was the reason for his success. He could grab an idea out of thin air and turn it into reality. He would hire writers to expand on his ideas, directors to mount the thing and actors to bring it to life. And this was the time for him to find that one thing. He needed to set his mind free and allow the muses in.

The abduction in Venice was masterful, of that there was no doubt. But that was not where the story started. Nora's captor had to be someone she had met before, not just a fan who worshiped her from afar. She was just so available. There were countless events and openings and personal appearances where she spoke with hundreds of people in one night. But this thief was not just anyone. He wouldn't have met her at some crowded event. No, this would have been an intimate affair where someone held her attention for more than a moment.

Nora was alluring at a distance and entrancing but for someone to fall so hard as to covet her, would require time with her. And it had to be someone with great power, great wealth and an ego that was satanic.

Istanbul was the destination. That much he knew. The Luxor had been moored here in this Sea of Marmara and Nora had been on it. And she'd been removed from the ship right here in Istanbul.

The more he thought about it, the more the cluster of palaces on the western shore of the Bosporus seemed to make sense. The inhabitants were untouchables, he'd been told. They were wealthy beyond imagination and powerful enough to have whatever they desired. The enclave of the cosseted fit the bill perfectly. This was something he needed to know more about. Some research was required, and research was part of his job description.

He turned his back on the sea and headed for the comfort of his hotel. He had a feeling he might sleep that night. He had the beginnings of a plan. It sure beat the hell out of helplessness. He'd been warned about wandering the streets alone at night, but his personal safety was the last thing on his mind.

What's the worst they could do? Kill him? Then again, they had killed Demir. He resolved to try to be less flippant. It was not the time for his favorite deflection ploy.

CHAPTER 36

Sofi ended up in charge of the funeral arrangements. It was not a job, she relished but neither was it one she resented. It made sense really. If the circumstances had been the other way around, Demir would be fulfilling the role.

Others in her family were not capable in such situations. Sofi and Demir were the emergency *go-to*s always – so here she was. Mahmet would have helped had his job not been so demanding. Not only was his presence required every day except every second Saturday, some nights he was required to remain at the palace. It seemed that his master was more than a little distrustful.

Sofi had tried on many occasions to get her fiancé to open up about his job and his employer, the renowned Ali Sandar but she'd gotten nowhere. Sometimes she had her doubts about committing to a man who was a complete secret. But she did love him and prayed that in time, she'd be allowed into more of his life. Other times, she was ready to throw in the towel. Her mind would ask a million questions, the most common one being, could she really be with someone she couldn't know.

They'd retrieved the body from the medical examiner in just one day, which was a blessing because of Islamic law. The only exception was for war or foul play and Demir's body certainly qualified. She and her mother had washed his body in warm water three times and dressed him in a simple white tunic. The undertaker had collected Demir and transported him to the family plot where he would be buried simply, beneath a small mound of earth, turned towards Mecca.

The days of paid mourners and wailing processions were long gone and the whole ceremony was conducted with honor and restraint. There were only a few family members and friends at the graveside. There were tears but Sofi shed none. Tears would have to wait until her job was done.

Mahmet had managed to make an appearance at the cemetery but had been unable to stay for the reception. He'd explained that his presence was required at the palace because his master was visiting the home of his neighbor and friend. It was to be an especially grand affair and Ali Sandar was always very careful when visiting the home of Al Caribe, one of the most powerful men in Istanbul. As Mahmet had explained the situation to Sofi. She'd had a strange feeling, but it evaporated before she could grab hold of it.

The reception at her mother's house was muted and heartfelt. Demir was much loved and would be missed terribly. Sofi was the consummate hostess but in truth a part of her was missing. Her thoughts kept turning to Peter and his quest. She wondered what he was up to and wished she could be helping him. She thought about Mahmet and his gala in the netherworld. She thought about the absolute power of these demi-gods and just how much they could get away with. The strange feeling about Mahmet picked at her again, but again she dismissed it.

CHAPTER 37

The knock on the door again roused Nora from her reverie. She waited for it to open but it didn't. She crossed the room and opened the door to find a young man dressed in a black tuxedo standing there. She couldn't remember if she'd seen the young man before, but he gave no indication.

"The Pasha is waiting you," he said shyly.

"I'll be right there," she replied.

She made her way to the bathroom and put on the veil. She took a quick look at herself, and her breath caught. "Wow," she whispered, "I'm a princess, a princess in a gilded cage." Then the darkness returned to her. She forbade the tears as she'd learned to do over the years. Tears destroyed makeup and makeup was everything. She grabbed the gold evening bag and made for the door.

Halfway down the stairs, she heard the unmistakable sounds of a party. Some of her felt like she was making a grand entry. That was it, she decided. She was a capable actress, and this evening would require the very best of her skill. She could do it just like she'd done it hundreds of times before.

She entered the grand salon and by the grace of God, there was no major reaction. It took her a moment to recognize that she was not the only veiled woman. Most of the other women, maybe twenty or so wore veils as well. It was like a costume party so no one would know who she was. Of course, it made perfect sense. Al Caribe could have her there at his party but only he would know – brilliant.

As if he'd heard his name called, he turned to her and smiled that horrible, loathsome gash of a thing. He then strode towards her, gathered her elbow in his meaty hand and directed her into the midst of the revelers. A young man approached with a tray of pink champagne, and Nora nearly knocked the tray from his hand in her eagerness to get a hold of some alcohol. She slid the glass behind the veil and downed the pink stuff in one swallow. She placed the empty glass back on the tray and grabbed another.

She became aware that by now she was being watched but she didn't really care. What could they do? Kill her? She smirked inwardly. It was an expression she'd heard Peter use countless times. The irony had not eluded her.

She took a quick survey of the room. The women, whether slender or not so much, were all beautifully dressed and dripping in jewels. The men reflected the women perfectly. Some were arrayed in Arab finery, others wore tuxedos. All were polished to a high gloss. It was the *Great Gatsby* of Istanbul.

She detected a slight curiosity but that was to be expected. After all, she was the host's date. The fact that her identity was concealed was empowering in a way. There was something about it she liked.

As she prepared to be introduced and wondered how that was going to go, a gong sounded, apparently the indication that dinner was served.

As they made their way to the dining room through a long glass gallery where birds in actual gilded cages sang for the guests, Hassan introduced her to several people. She understood not a word and felt no requirement to either smile or acknowledge. She simply carried on, reminding herself that she was playing a role and acting her ass off. The thought nearly elicited a giggle, but she managed to stifle it.

The dining room was decorated like a Bedouin tent. Glittering chandeliers hung from the soaring ceiling and an array of fine carpets covered the floor. The tables were set in a T-shape and al Caribe, still clutching her elbow steered her through the guests toward the top of the T, like she was some kind of show pony.

She found her mind pulling away, disassociating from the scene. It was a technique she'd used sometimes to get through a sequence with scores of extras that felt like it would never end.

Al Caribe placed her in a seat and slid in beside her. Soon there was someone seated on here other side. She made no effort to acknowledge his arrival. She was trapped and caged and blissfully past caring.

Having watched other women manage the inconvenience of their veils, she went about eating what was placed before her. Although every plate was a piece of art, she tasted nothing. She did however manage to consume a few more glasses of wine before her captor noticed and cut her off.

When the meal was finished, al Caribe spoke a few words. A couple of guests offered responses. Nora understood none of it. Never in her life had she been so ignored. It made her feel sad.

Throughout the room there was laughter and nodding and slapping of backs. And music was coming from a corner of the tent where half-a-dozen musicians sat cross-legged on the carpeted floor playing instruments she'd never seen before. She was a *stranger in a strange land.*

From her daze she was aware of someone approaching and extending his arm as if inviting her to stand. She did so and followed along obediently as the young man in the tuxedo, the same young man who'd escorted her to the party steered her toward the staircase.

She arrived back at her room to find the girls waiting dutifully. Without a word, they undressed her, gave her a nightgown and removed her makeup.

She climbed into bed unaware of the girls leaving or the lights being dimmed.

She lay in the near dark with her eyes open. That's when she began to shake.

The shaking didn't stop until she was safely asleep.

CHAPTER 38

Peter slept through the night and awakened to a cloudy day. It was one of the few he'd seen since leaving the States. He showered and dressed quickly. He wanted to make sure he kept his thoughts in order. He stopped in the lobby bar for a quick coffee. He had a large pastry as well, not knowing when he'd have another chance to eat.

He used the back door, walked quickly to the corner and was lucky finding a cab. He directed the driver and sat back watching as Istanbul raced by. He realized that every person he saw had a story, but he doubted that any was as twisted as his.

The cab pulled to a stop in front of an ornate building that looked like it had been there for a thousand years. It had in fact been there for two thousand. He paid the driver, got out and climbed the wide steps to the very grand front door and stepped inside.

The sign was in several languages and mercifully one was English. He was pleased to see that he was in the right place. The day was going well so far. He hoped his good fortune would continue.

He'd decided that he needed to find out more about the Bosporus mansions and thought that the library would be a good start. He thought wrong.

The young man at the Information desk informed him that the library contained no such records. Rather, he would have to try the Hall of Records that was miles away on the far side of the bridge. Peter took a deep breath, doing his best to remain positive, offered a tight smile of thanks and headed for the door.

This time it took a few minutes to hail a cab. He was in a very busy part of the city. Eventually, one pulled over to the curb and he settled in for what was to be a long ride.

He thought about Sofi and how she was doing. Burying her brother had to be a terrible experience. He wondered if it would be insensitive to call and decided that if he merely offered his good wishes, it might be okay.

She answered on the first ring and didn't sound the least bit glum, instead, she seemed energized and ready for action.

"So how is the family?" he asked.

"Oh, you know," she replied, "it's a very difficult life moment but life can be difficult. I don't have to tell you."

"True enough," he replied, refusing to allow the sadness.

"What are you doing?" she asked. "Have you come up with anything?"

"Well, no, but I had an idea. I have this strong feeling, a hunch maybe but I wanted to find out more about the palaces on the far side of the strait. I don't know why, but my instinct is telling me to do some research. I just left the library. There was nothing there, but they sent me to the Hall of Records and I'm on my way there now."

There was a pause, and then she asked, "The Hall of Records?"

"Yup."

"Unfortunately, Peter, even if they have what you're looking for, they'll never give you any information. For one thing, you're a foreigner and we are a city that loves her secrets."

There was another pause.

"So, you're saying I'm wasting my time?"

"I'm afraid so," she responded.

"Well, I'm sorry to hear that. I guess there's no point in me going all the way over there if it's a total waste of time."

"Wait a minute," Sofi said, "I have an idea. I'm not doing much this afternoon. I'll meet you there. There might be a chance that they will let me look at the records, what with my official-ness and all."

Peter felt himself smiling. Sofi had that effect on him quite often. Her effort at American slang was cute.

It took nearly forty minutes in traffic that made Manhattan look mannerly, but miraculously Peter arrived at the Hall of Records without a scratch.

Sofi drove up in a police car shortly after. She parked right in front of the building, directly under a *No Parking* sign and jumped out of her car. The sign was in Turkish, but the universal tow-truck graphic left no doubt.

She spotted Peter immediately, hurried over to him, offered a perfunctory hug and bade him to follow her.

At the registration desk she presented her credentials and was directed to the second floor where computers filled with everything one could possibly want to know about Istanbul since it had been Constantinople sat side by side on long tables.

They picked a quiet corner, powered up and started asking questions. There were over fifty mansions in the Beşiktaş District, but they managed to narrow their search to a dozen. An hour later, they'd narrowed the search even more. There weren't many that fit the description Peter was looking for.

There were famous historic palaces like the Zarif Mustafa Pasha Mansion and the Nuri Pasha Mansion, but they were too well known, too exposed. The house Peter was looking for would be more private, more hidden away.

Finally, they were down to a handful of homes that might fit the bill. They began a search for ownership, but the quest turned up nothing. Ownership on these homes was not listed. There was no record of any sales since 1913. These were homes that were passed down through generations. Any sales would be very private and very secret. Each of the homes was valued between $100 and $300 million. The inhabitants were serious players and were not to be trifled with.

There were a few pictures or descriptions of the houses, but no addresses were listed. There was, however, one detail that was interesting. Apparently, a few of the mansions were protected by a high cliff and required an elevator to gain access to the property.

Sofi sat studying the list trying to pinpoint exactly where these hidden gems were located. "Wait a second," she whispered in conjunction with a low whistle, "I know this house." She pointed to a picture, "I've never been there but Mahmet has. This is the house where he works. He told me that he has to take an elevator to get down to the place."

"You're kidding," Peter blurted. Had they been in a library he would most certainly been shushed, strongly.

"No, I'm not kidding. That house belongs to Ali Sandar. He's Mahmet's Pasha, his master. That house has been in the Sandar family for over 300 years and Ali is a fixture in Istanbul society. His wife died a few years ago and since then he has been host to a succession of young beauties, opportunistic girls with dreams of becoming the next Missus Sandar – as if. That's as much as I know, and Mahmet will not give up any details about Sandar's business or his house. I think he's in shipping; container ships and ports maybe but I'm not sure."

"So, can you try Mahmet? See if he will help us?"

"Not a chance. As I told you, I can't get any details out of him. He's been sworn to secrecy and a man like Mahmet would die before breaking his word."

Peter nodded and sighed. For a long time neither of them spoke.

"This is amazing, though" Peter whispered. "I've got a feeling about this. As you were talking, I felt this creeping chill across my scalp. I've only had that happen a few times in my life, but every time it led to something major."

"I can't imagine that a man of Ali Sandar's standing would be one to kidnap a Hollywood movie star, but he might well know the person who did," Sofi said thoughtfully.

CHAPTER 39

The sun melted slowly across the Black Sea before slipping out of sight. The *Luxor* steamed on into the gathering darkness at a steady eight knots heading for Sevastopol. Captain Arim was feeling better than he had in days. It was a blessing that all the drama of Istanbul was comfortably behind him.

Suddenly, the sea began to shift and slide away. Soon, the dark water started bubbling and continued until it was boiling. The crew rushed up from below decks, yelling and wailing in terror, watching from the railing as the entire sea around the ship erupted.

In slow motion, not 50 feet away, a great monster appeared from out of the blackness and began to take shape. Within seconds it all became clear as 300 feet of gray steel surfaced right alongside them. The conning tower of the nuclear submarine was still spilling water when the top burst open and two men appeared pointing very serious weapons directly at the crew of the *Luxor.*

A voice came on over a loudspeaker, sounding like the voice of God as it dispatched the orders. "Engines full stop," it barked, "and prepare to be boarded."

As Captain Arim and his crew watched in horror, a small inflatable appeared on the sub's deck along with three sailors. The craft was pushed into the sea and the men climbed aboard. A minute later, it was bobbing alongside the *Luxor.*

The voice continued, "Engage your ladder now."

Amazingly, a couple of the crew found their legs and their courage, and a rope ladder dropped over the side.

Two uniformed sailors climbed aboard the freighter as the third paddled back to the submarine.

One of the sailors guarded the crew as the other climbed up to the bridge, his weapon at the ready. He stepped through the door to find the captain standing by the wheel, his hands raised.

"Captain Arim," the sailor announced, "you are hereby under arrest. We will be returning to Istanbul where your cargo will be off-loaded."

"But how can the U.S. Navy be here in the Black Sea?" the captain stammered, his voice shaking.

"What are you talking about, captain?" the seaman asked as the great bulk of sub sunk back into the sea and disappeared like it had never been there.

"It seems like you've been seeing things."

The captain started to speak but apparently thought better of it.

"So, back the way you came, huh?" the sailor said. "Better get moving."

CHAPTER 40

Peter had spent the morning wandering and wondering. He'd walked beside the Bosporus again staring across at the palaces. The more he looked, the more convinced he was that one of them was holding Nora captive. He had an idea. He now knew the area where the most likely mansions were located and decided he had to get a better look.

He headed for the main thoroughfare where he'd discovered that taxis were easier to find and within minutes managed to flag one down.

"Beşiktaş," he announced to the driver as he slipped into the backseat.

"You sure?" the man managed in semi-English.

"Yes, I am," Peter replied firmly.

"Street?"

"I will show you," Peter announced and waved the man on.

With some reluctance the driver acceded.

Midday traffic was hell as always but after about half an hour, the driver managed to negotiate the Bosporus Bridge and entered a neighborhood of stately trees, high walls and impressive gates.

"This is it," he whispered to himself. He just knew.

The driver, however, was showing a bit of impatience. He pulled the car over to the side of the road and stopped, turned to face Peter and shrugged. "Where we go?" he asked, sounding testy.

Suddenly remembering a name from his visit to the Hall of Records, Peter blurted, "The Hasip Pasha Mansion."

The man looked at him like he'd lost his mind. "No go there," he replied firmly.

"Yes go," Peter urged, reaching into his pocket to show an impressive amount of cash.

"Maybe okay go," the driver said, sighing. "I show you, okay?"

"*Çok iyi*," Peter replied feeling proud of himself.

The driver glanced at him in the mirror. His expression indicated that he'd decided his passenger was nuts.

A few moments later, they arrived at the end of the road. Well, it wasn't in fact the end of the road, but it was as far as they were going. A barricade and a guard house stood in front of them. Two well-armed men in uniforms watched the taxi approach. Looking bored, one held his hand up as the other swung his weapon into position.

"You see?" said the driver impatiently.

"Yes, yes, I do see," Peter replied.

With a sigh, the driver turned the taxi around and headed back towards the bridge and the traffic hell that was waiting on the other side.

***

Peter climbed the stairs to his room, kicked off his shoes and stretched out on the bed. He lay staring at the ceiling willing the tears away. A dark wave of hopelessness began to break over him but before it took him completely, he was saved by the blessing of sleep.

Within minutes he was in a dream that was so real he could smell the room he found himself in.

He and Nora were at a party, a formal affair. The room was filled with people dressed to the nines. Some he recognized, some he didn't. There was drinking and laughter and music. And the room was filled with smoke – everybody was smoking cigarettes. Some of the women held long glittering cigarette holders. That's how he knew he was dreaming.

Nora was playing piano, a Steinway. And she was singing. Suddenly the music stopped. From where he was standing on the other side of the room, Peter watched as a tall heavy-set man dressed in a kaftan grabbed her from behind and began dragging her from the room towards a terrace that overlooked a six-lane boulevard filled with cars creeping along, honking their horns.

Peter fought with all his might to get to her, but it was impossible. The crowd kept closing in on him until finally he lost sight of her.

Suddenly, the man in the kaftan turned and looked directly at him and laughed.

Peter tried to scream but he choked on the cigarette he was smoking.

With a whimper, he came awake. He was trembling with fear and soaked with sweat and tears. The room was dark now. He lay still catching his breath and his mind.

He knew at once that what had just happened to him was no dream.

He'd remembered the night. He'd seen the man. He knew he was on the right track.

***

Nora sat by the window watching the boat traffic. Today the sky was cloudy, and the water was dark and ominous. She allowed her mind to wander, anything to escape the reality of her prison.

A soft knock on the door interrupted her daydreams. She turned to see the woman who'd examined her before.

"Good afternoon, ma'am," she said softly. "I have been sent to see to you again I'm sorry, but it will take just a minute. May I?"

Nora thought about it for a moment. She considered refusing the request but could find no advantage in being uncooperative. "Very well," she replied without enthusiasm. "Where do you want me?"

"On the bed would be fine. Thank you."

Nora crossed to the bed and lay down as the woman put on a pair of latex gloves and approached the bed.

As she removed Nora's panties and began to probe, Nora again felt violated and angry and fought hard to maintain control. She closed her eyes tight trying to ignore the ignominy, but it didn't work. Rather she began to picture what was going to happen. The horror she'd been dreading was near and there was nothing she could do to stop it. Soon, the beast was going to walk through her door and do with her as he wished. It was all she could do not to weep or vomit or both.

"You are doing very well," the woman stripped off the gloves and calmly wiped her hands on a towel. "The Pasha will be pleased." With that she turned and headed for the door.

Nora reached for her panties and pulled them on as her body convulsed. A wave of nausea followed, and she was suddenly soaked in sweat. It was at that moment a thought entered her mind. Never had she had such a thought. She tried to push the image away, but her mind refused to co-operate.

The list of methods available to her was not long but it was graphic. There were no weapons and no drugs. The alternative was unthinkable – or was it? She flashed to the final scene in *The Last Tree*, the only Western she'd ever done. The imagery of the hanging was truly gruesome.

Suddenly she was cold. She pulled back the covers and slipped underneath. Her body involuntarily curled into the fetal position and the tears came. She waited and waited to get warm, but warmth didn't come.

***

Peter stood under the scalding hot shower washing the sweat from his body and hopefully the nightmare from his mind. When he'd endured all the pain he could, he climbed out and started drying himself. As he did, he had a thought. When he was done with the towel, he pulled on the hotel robe and returned to his bedroom. He grabbed his phone from the bedside table and sat in a chair by the window. He searched his contact list until he found what he was looking for and tapped the screen.

The person that answered did not sound happy. "Hello," the voice croaked.

Peter glanced at the clock by the bed and groaned inwardly.

"Sorry, Jack," he muttered. "Sorry to wake you. I forgot how early it is there. It's Peter Brandt. I'm calling from Istanbul."

He listened for a moment and responded.

"Yeah, Jack. Thanks. It is a total nightmare. Listen, I need to ask you something. Remember the dinner party at your house a couple of months ago? Nora and I were there."

He listened.

"Yes, that one. Well, there was a guy there, an Arab guy. He got a bit inappropriate with Nora and I had to get involved. I don't know . . ."

Listening.

"Oh, you do. Great. Who was the guy? Do you know?

He listened again, nearly crushing his phone in his urgency.

"Caribe – did you say Caribe?"

He listened again, alternately panting and holding his breath.

"Oh, I don't know, it may be a lead. I'm getting desperate. At this stage I'll try anything. It was just a thought. So, you don't think Istanbul?

Pushing against the wave of disappointment, he listened again. Ready now to get off the phone.

"I would really appreciate that, Jack. Anything you can find out. Yeah. Thanks again. Sorry about the time."

He listened nodding, said goodbye, put the phone on the table beside him and stared out at the water. His fists curled tighter and tighter until he broke the skin on his hand. He let out his breath and went on staring, feeling empty. There was nothing left to feel.

Suddenly, his phone rang, and he jumped a foot. He grabbed wildly for it thinking that maybe Jack had found something.

It was Sofi.

He agreed to meet her in his hotel bar in half an hour. The last thing he needed was futile conversation, but he knew that staring out at the Bosporus for the rest of the day would yield nothing.

He dressed slowly, aware that he was beginning to accept defeat. It was a terrible feeling – the worst ever.

The bar was quiet, but it was early. He secured a private table and ordered a double scotch on the rocks. He was not in the mood for anything frivolous like sour cherry vodka.

He'd just taken his first sip when Sofi appeared at the table. She'd crossed the entire room without him noticing. He considered that maybe he was a tad distracted.

She offered her typical stunning smile and collapsed into the chair across from him.

"You look wasted," he mumbled.

"That's because I am," she replied. "A copper's work is never done, you know."

He tried to smile in response but missed the mark. "I guess there's a lot of crime going on, then?"

"Like it's going out of style," she smiled ruefully.

The waitress arrived and Sofi ordered a glass of Sauvignon-Blanc and sat back. She looked at him for a long moment and said nothing.

Instead of looking back at her he lifted his glass to his lips and took a very long swallow.

"So, what's going on, Peter?" she asked. "You seem down. I haven't seen you like this before."

Just then, Sofi's wine arrived. She didn't bother to clink or salute. She just drank.

They sat for a few minutes, each trying to find the right thing to say and coming up empty.

Eventually, Peter spoke, "I'm about done, Sofi. It is more than I can handle. I think I've reached my limit."

"Oh no, Peter," she began, and then stopped herself. It was not the time for platitudes. She was aware of the horror the man was living. She knew loss and she knew the pain he was in.

"I'm gonna book a flight home," he continued, "I've exhausted all my leads and all my friends." He suddenly realized what he'd said, how insensitive it was. His breath caught. "If it wasn't for me, Demir would . . ."

She reached across the table, placing her hand on his arm and shook her head. "Don't, Peter," she whispered, shaking her head, "it was not you. You are not the bad guy here. I'm so, so sorry we couldn't do more but Istanbul is a tight ship and I'm afraid I don't have the power to peel away the layers."

He looked at her and saw in her dark eyes that he was not alone with his pain.

"Maybe it wasn't Istanbul after all," he mumbled. "I had this idea; a fantasy really about who took her, but now I think I was wrong or crazy, I'm not sure which."

Sofi just looked at him waiting for him to finish.

"I called a producer friend in LA thinking he might help me track someone that I thought might be involved," Peter let out a long breath that was almost a shudder. "He told me I was wrong, that the man I had in mind was not even a Turk."

"And what was this man's name?" Sofi asked, thinking that keeping Peter talking might help to loosen the tightness around his heart.

"Caribe," Peter said, looking away, "something like that. He wasn't sure. He's going to get back to me if he finds any info but I'm not real hopeful."

Peter didn't notice that as he was speaking, Sofi had sat bolt upright. She was now staring at him like she'd been slapped. She struggled to find a response to what he'd just said and eventually found one. "Have you eaten, Peter?" she asked. "I think maybe you need some food. Your energy's down and it's depressing you. I think we need to order you something to eat. Unfortunately, I cannot stay with you, but you must eat something. There's somewhere I need to be. I forgot all about it. It's official business and I'm already late."

Peter simply looked at her not knowing what the hell had just happened. The kind, gentle soul who was doing her very best to quiet his pain was suddenly a storm cloud about to burst. As he began to babble some response, she stood up, turned and literally ran from the bar.

As soon as she was in the car, she grabbed her phone. "Meet me at my house," she said tersely, "there's something I need to say, and it has to be in person."

CHAPTER 41

There was a soft knock-on Nora's door. The door swung open, and a young man stepped into the room. Standing at attention, dressed this time in a pure white kaftan was the young man who had escorted her to and from the party.

"Good afternoon miss," he began, "the Pasha has requested you to the gardens by the sea. You will meet for him in one hour. I will be here for show you." With that, he turned away and disappeared out the door.

She stared after him and it took a moment to realize that she hadn't heard the lock. She stepped towards the door, reached for the handle and turned it. The door opened. The messenger had forgotten to make sure she was locked in.

She knew that it was now or never. The boy had made a mistake, more than likely a fatal one for him. She ran to the dressing room, threw on a pair of slacks and a sweater, slipped into some comfortable shoes and ran back to the door.

She stepped out of her room and started down the corridor in the opposite direction from which the boy had gone. At the end of the hall, she had a choice. She guessed that turning right would take her in the direction of the water where she could maybe flag down a passing boat. Her decision was made when she heard sounds of activity coming from the left. As she listened, she made out pots clanging and conversation and deduced that it was the kitchen down on the main floor.

She took one last glance down the corridor and could hardly see the end. She'd visited some imposing houses in her travels but this one was beyond. Formidable was the word that came to mind. She'd gotten a glimpse of the formal rooms on the evening of the party. They were without a doubt, in a class of their own.

She heard a pot clatter again in the distance and made her decision. She turned right. A minute later, the corridor turned into a gallery with walls of glass. Off to the left no more than fifty yards away she could see another house. It was very large and built of pale limestone, but it appeared to be half the size of the one she was in. She wondered how she could get to the neighboring house and resolved to give it a try. It took forever to reach the end of the gallery. Through a large window she had an unobstructed view of the Straits. From her room, she'd been able to see just a small stretch of the water. Here she could see a lot more of it. There were ships and boats of all sizes and descriptions, all in a mad scramble to get somewhere. The fact that there were no collisions was as big a miracle as swimming across the Straits would be.

She sighed and crept silently down a set of stairs that looked like they might lead to the gardens she'd seen from her room in front of the house. She assumed that these gardens were the intended meeting place where the Pasha would be waiting for her. She knew that time was of the essence. Soon they would be looking for her and the chances of hiding seemed remote.

She reached the ground floor and found a door that led outside. She pushed it open and stepped out into the blessed sunshine for the first time in days. Just steps away, she noticed a thick hedge that she thought would protect her from being seen by anyone on the front verandah. Unfortunately, she'd have to get across the lawn and if anyone was watching she'd be spotted.

"Desperate times," she muttered and went for it. A skip and a jump and a mad dash and she made it. She crouched down holding her breath waiting to see if she'd been spotted. A minute passed and no alarm was raised or any sounds of a pursuit. She gathered her courage and peeked around the corner of the hedge.

Lying before her was the full expanse of the palace. It seemed to stretch out for half a mile or more. There were windows and balconies and soaring columns. There were pools and fountains and beds resplendent with flowers. It was better than any movie set she'd ever seen. Cecil B. DeMille would have approved.

She noticed some activity on one of the verandahs. A white-clad servant was placing a glass on a table where a man sat gazing out at the waterway. She studied the man for a moment and gasped – it was him – al Caribe!

She turned and ran half crouched behind hedge and heard someone call out. She raced across an open space and slid behind a large tree up against the wall that separated her prison from the house next door.

Mercifully, no one appeared from the front of the palace. She crept from the safety of her hiding space and staying close to the wall which towered at least twenty feet above her. She searched the entire length and spotted a heavy metal door no more than thirty feet away. She assumed it provided access to the neighboring property. Her heart in her throat, she ran for the door and discovered that there was no handle, no knob. She pushed hard on the thing, but it didn't budge. She sighed, bent into the crouch again and ran on. A minute later she reached the end of the wall where it met with a high cliff. She was cornered, there was no doubt about it. She ducked behind a large cypress and scoped out the area.

She'd come a long way, but it seemed like she'd reached the end of the road. There was no way out without going back through the house and trying another exit. She knew the chances of that were remote at best.

Then out of the corner of her eye she saw movement. She then made out a guard standing fifty feet away across the clearing. Sitting beside him was a dog. She hadn't seen him at first because he'd apparently been standing in the shadows. If he hadn't moved, she would not have spotted him and would probably have been caught.

She recognized that the dog was no amateur. It was a Belgian Malinois, the very best guard dog on the planet. It was a dog that would attack on command and kill without hesitation. She'd worked with one in *Dog of Flanders,* and they'd never become friends. She slipped back behind the tree and tried to formulate a plan.

A minute later, she peeked out and was nervous when she saw that the man and the dog were on the move, probably a scheduled patrol.

It was then she noticed that further down the cliff wall was a contraption that took her a moment to recognize. She studied the thing and realized that it was an elevator car. She could see the track ascending the cliff. The front of the elevator was made of glass and the doors were wide open.

"Oh God, is this it?" she whispered, "is this my way out?"

She considered the situation, trying to gauge her chances. How long would it take to cross the clearing? How long would the guard and dog be gone?

It would be a sprint of fifty yards or more across a wide gravel path and she'd be out in the open all the way. She was surprised that there wasn't more activity in and around the house. Surely her absence had been discovered by now.

She'd escaped like this before, but she'd been accompanied by a camera and a director, a co-star and an entire film crew. This time, on the other hand, was a solo performance.

"It's now or never," she murmured and bolted.

As she ran, she listened for sounds of pursuit. There were none. She started wondering if the lift was working, if it required a key. "Hush," she admonished herself, "this is not the time."

She was over halfway there when she heard it. It was the rhythmic beat of a pursuer, and he was coming fast. She could hear the deep breathing and the pounding of feet on the gravel.

She fought to not look over her shoulder, but she lost. She took a quick glance and her stomach cramped in horror. Thirty yards away but closing fast was the Malinois. His eyes glittered with the zeal of the chase and his tongue lolled from his jaws dripping great streams of saliva. As he galloped toward her, great clouds of pebbles flew up in his wake.

She was nearly there, no more than ten yards from the doors when she thought she was done for. She could almost feel the dog's hot breath as he closed in.

Something made her turn. She needed to face her end.

The dog had leapt into the air and was on her. His mouth was open, his teeth flashing in anticipation. She could smell his breath and she could feel his purpose.

Suddenly, a shot rang out. The beast that had just reached her throat collapsed from view and lay gasping and twitching at her feet. The horror hit her like a wave. Her hands went to her mouth, and she managed to stifle the scream that was rising from her soul.

She looked towards the house and saw the guard lower his weapon. Then she saw that there was another man standing beside him; a man dressed in a pure white kaftan.

Without notice her stomach erupted and she vomited all over her would-be assassin.

CHAPTER 42

Sofi opened the door to find Mahmet smiling down at her or at least trying to. He bent to kiss her, and she acquiesced without enthusiasm.

"What's wrong?" he asked as he headed for the fridge and a cold beer. Sofi didn't drink beer, but she always had some on hand for Mahmet. As a matter of fact, Sofi hardly drank at all but in the past week, she'd drunk more than she had in years.

She had never acquired the taste for alcohol. Occasionally she would sip on a sour cherry cocktail to be polite, but she didn't really like it. The evening she'd spent getting drunk with Peter had been a one-time thing and the situation had demanded it. Although with the crazy plot she was involved in might lead to a lot of drinking if she wasn't careful.

"I'm just a little surprised you were able to make time for me on such short notice," she said.

Mahmet deposited his large frame on the couch, leaned back and sighed deeply.

"I usually have to make an appointment and count my blessings when I get to have you to myself."

"I know," he replied, "I know it's been tough, but things are going to get better. Pasha is in Crimea for a few days to manage some shipment. So, I don't need to be back at the house until Saturday."

"Wow, things are already better. That's the most information you've shared in a year."

He smiled and took a swig of his beer. "It sounds like he's getting out of the import–export business for a spell. He's part owner of the port at Sevastopol and figures he can do without the hassle of trading and shipping for a while."

"And that's good, right?" Sofi asked. She'd established her position at the opposite end of the couch. She looked a little nervous, like she was ready to start a serious discussion.

"Yes, that's good," he replied, "good for me; good for us."

"I'm glad," she murmured, "because there's something we need to talk about, something that has waited too long."

He turned and looked at her like he was looking at a new Sofi. He had not heard this tone before. She'd always been very undemanding; willing to let him have his way. But this was different. "What is it, then?" he asked. "Let's hear it."

"Mahmet," she began, "I love you. Sometimes I ask myself why, but who can really understand these things. You are not good to me, and you are not good for me. You speak angrily if I don't obey you and obey is a word that is no longer in my vocabulary." She took a breath and Mahmet started to speak but she stopped him with a raised palm.

"I know that there are traditions within our culture regarding men and women, but I'm not living by those rules anymore. Your life has been your work and it would be one thing if I was included in that life but I'm not and I can no longer live like that."

Mahmet's eyes became furtive, and his face tightened noticeably. Never had Sofi spoken to him like this. Despite his rising blood pressure, he'd managed to remain silent. He could see that the woman he loved was deadly serious.

"Until yesterday," she continued, "I was ready to end our relationship. No longer was I willing to wait for you to be available. I'm not getting any younger and I would like to have a home and a husband and a family. I need that and if you cannot give that to me, I will have to look elsewhere."

Mahmet clenched everything and looked away allowing a moment for Sofi's proclamation to settle.

She continued, "When my father died, I did not cry. There was no time. My services were required, and I had to be strong. I have not cried for my brother. He was brutally murdered and left to the rats, but I was not permitted to mourn him, there was no time." She let out a long breath and drew in a slow one. "I refuse to be that woman any longer.

Peter Brandt has become a good friend and my heart has gone out to him. He's living a loss that I cannot completely comprehend. I have been helping him and I intend to keep helping him. It's something I have to do; for me as well as for him."

Mahmet turned back to her. His jaw softened. Then everything about him began to soften.

"I need your help Mahmet. I need you to love me. I need for you to let me in."

He nodded slowly. He said nothing.

"We think that Peter's wife who was abducted in Venice may be imprisoned across the strait in one of the palaces. I have a question for you and if you love me, you will answer it."

He simply looked at her. His eyes were shining. His lips trembled ever so slightly.

"Have you ever heard the name *Caribe*? Do you know which palace is his?"

Mahmet flinched and looked away. For a moment or two there was silence. He stood up slowly, and looked down at Sofi, his face expressionless. "I need another beer," he grunted.

He crossed to the fridge, grabbed a bottle, popped the cap and walked slowly back to the living room. He sat down beside Sofi, taking her hand, he took a deep breath.

"Al Caribe is the immediate neighbor of my Pasha, Ali Sandar. They are partners in business, but never in women. Caribe is the exclusive type. Sandar would not be involved in the abduction."

Sofi turned and looked at him, raised his hand to her lips and allowed her tears to flow.

Mahmet gathered her into his arms and held her like he never had before. There was tenderness in his touch and softness in his eyes. The fierceness had moved aside and if only for a moment his heart was open.

"Tell me, Mahmet," she said softly, "tell me all of it."

"Very well," he replied, shaking his head. "I must say the timing here is amazing. The mission I have been conducting came to an end just yesterday. You see, I was assigned to infiltrate an organization based here in Istanbul that has been trading in arms with the Russians, the Ukrainians, the Uzbekistanis, anyone that had what the organization wanted whether it be drugs or ancient artifacts."

Sofi's tears stopped. She pushed herself out of Mahmet's arms and sat back far enough so that he was in focus, and she could concentrate on his words. "What the hell are you talking about?" she asked, anger rising.

"I'm not actually a bodyguard." He paused and took a deep breath, "I'm actually a CIA operative." He ducked as if expecting Sofi to take a swing him.

"You're a what?" she demanded, her voice cracking.

"CIA," he repeated, "I'm an American although I was born and raised here in Istanbul, which was why I got this assignment."

Sofi held up her hand to stop him and slowly shook her head, "So all this time, you've been working undercover, and you never told me?"

He looked at her for a long moment allowing her to read him. "I couldn't tell you," he said evenly, "not just for my sake but for yours. These are very dangerous men I've been after and keeping you out of it was the only way I could keep you safe. If they busted me, they would have had you killed – you and the rest of your family. They already killed your brother. It was a warning."

"So, who are these men? Is your damned Pasha one of them?"

"Yes, he is." Mahmet replied. "He's one of the principals. His neighbor, the al Caribe guy is another. Caribe is the big boss. Just yesterday we intercepted one of their shipments in the Black Sea and it was a doozie, a game changer. The ship was carrying enough bio-chemicals to kill millions and alter the course of world politics."

Again, Sofi shook her head. This time she looked away and stared out the window. "Wow," she managed, "I don't know what to say. I don't even know where to begin. I kind of hate you for this. You've lied to me since the beginning. I now have no idea who I've been with these last two years. I've been living a lie. I'm so angry with myself right now. My instincts kept telling me something was off, but I didn't listen.

Your absolute devotion to your employer seemed irrational. I nearly broke it off with you a dozen times because of it. Do you have any idea how stupid I feel?"

"I never meant to hurt you, Sofi," he said gently. "In truth, I never meant to love you. That was never part of the plan. It could have blown my assignment."

The look on Sofi's face said it all. She'd heard enough. She rose to her feet, grabbed her purse from the kitchen counter, a jacket from the hall closet and stormed out the door.

Mahmet leapt from the couch to reach for her, but she was gone. He collapsed back down and buried his head in his hands.

***

Nora stood stock-still allowing her mind to evaluate the situation. It didn't take long to deduce that there was no way out. She pulled herself to her full height, dialed in *defiant* and began walking slowly towards the men.

Together they watched her approach without speaking a word. As she reached them, Caribe whispered something to the guard. The man nodded, turned away and headed back around the house.

Nora stopped before her captor and looked him right in the eye. Displaying no fear, she waited for him to speak.

"Well," he began, "it looks like we've had enough excitement for one day. I think it best we postpone lunch. I'll have Azul escort you back to the safety of your room. I have something to attend to this evening, but shall we say tomorrow evening for our rendezvous. Dinner at nine, I think – and wear something beguiling."

Inwardly Nora shuddered but somehow kept her revulsion to herself. A young man she'd seen before emerged from the shadows, bowed minimally and indicated that Nora was to go with him. She did as instructed without another glance at Al Caribe.

***

Mahmet was about to retrieve another beer when the door opened, and Sofi stepped through. He remained seated and watched her unsure as to how to behave. He started to speak but before he could say anything she was talking.

She seemed angry but cool, on edge but professional. "You told me an awful lot, Mahmet and it's too much for me to deal with now. As I was saying, the Peter Brandt situation is very dear to my heart, and I will deal with nothing else until I have found a way to resolve the matter. Ironically, this confession of yours could not have come at a better time. What I intend to do will require your involvement and I sincerely hope you will agree to help me."

"Of course," he muttered.

"Peter and I, through the process of elimination have come to believe that his wife was taken by Hassan al Caribe. We believe she is currently being held in his house. What an irony that the house is right next door to that of your employer, or suspect, or gunrunner, or whatever he is. I need you to help get me inside Caribe's house."

Mahmet's began to shake his head slowly from side to side. He tried to speak but wasn't in time.

"If you don't agree to help me, I will have nothing more to say to you; not one word. After the total deception you've made me part of, it's the least you can do."

Mahmet just looked at her. There was no arguing with what she was saying.

"If you help me with this and if both of us emerge alive, I promise I will let you explain everything. You will have a chance to plead your case before I turn my back on you forever."

Mahmet slowly nodded. "Actually, I think I may have seen the woman the other night," he murmured.

Sofi's eyes were now ablaze.

"Al Caribe had this dinner party, and most of the women were wearing veils. That was a first but the woman who accompanied him acted very strangely. She seemed kind of out of it, drugged maybe, and not real happy. Come to think of it she left the party early. I wasn't focused on her, so I never put two and two together. As a matter of fact, that night was when I learned about the weapons shipment going to the Crimea. I overheard al Caribe and my Pasha talking about it. That's how we finally managed to get them. This coincidence is unbelievable you know."

"So how do we get in there?"

"Well, Pasha Sandar is away. He's supposed to be meeting the shipment in the Crimea. It's such a big deal that he had to supervise it in person. He's in for a bit of a shock since we intercepted the ship with the lethal cargo, which is now on its way back here to Istanbul."

"How?"

"Well, when I overheard them talking, I made a call to Serge, my superior, simple as that. The rest was out of my hands, but I was told that the interception was a success."

"Simple as that, you say. But my little mission is not quite so simple."

"Well since Sandar is away, I can get us into his house with no problem but that's where things get tricky. Al Caribe's palace is a fortress, literally. He has armed guards and dogs and cameras and sensors. It's damned near impossible."

"We have to make it un-impossible, Mahmet."

"Wait a minute, we're going to arrest these guys anyway. Maybe we lump it all together."

"Really?" Sofi asked. "You think you're going to arrest al Caribe and Ali Sandar on Turkish soil? Are you nuts? They own the local police and there's no way the CIA will get permission from Ankara to go after them."

"I know that Sofi. But this is an international affair. Turkey and the United States have an extradition treaty. Al Caribe and Sandar will be arrested and removed to the United States."

"Even if that was to happen, and I'm not convinced, it will take time. I don't have time. Peter Brandt doesn't have time and Nora doesn't have time. Al Caribe might have tired of her already. We need to get to her before he decides to get rid of her."

"Okay, I have an idea. It's a bit complicated but the only way to control anything about Caribe's palace is to control al Caribe himself. We need to capture him."

"Before you tell me, Mahmet, I think it's only fair that we include Peter in what we know. He's in bad shape. I think he's lost all hope. I'm worried about him."

"I'm not sure, Sof," Mahmet replied, "Peter is a civilian. We're talking top-shelf police work here. It's dangerous stuff. Do we really need a rank amateur involved?"

"He is involved. That's why he's here. It's his wife we're talking about. He's the one who pinpointed where she is being held. He's good. We can keep him out of the actual operation, but he deserves to know."

"Okay, if you insist."

"I do insist, Mahmet. This is my case, and you owe me big-time."

Mahmet nodded.

"I'm going to call him. We should go and meet him at his hotel. We're not doing this over the phone."

"Okay, do it."

"There's just one more thing I have to ask you, Mahmet, before we move forward with this plan."

"So, ask," Mahmet replied as he rose to his feet.

Sofi took a long trembling breath, "So what do you know about the death of Demir? Peter thinks he saw you at the cistern the night he was killed."

For a long moment there was silence. Mahmet looked away, sighed deeply and turned back. "Yes, I was there," he said softly, "I was sent with one of al Caribe's men to see if the job had been done. I had nothing to do with your brother's death though, I swear, but I knew it had happened. It was meant as a warning and was supposed to scare you off. They were afraid that you might stumble onto the shipment. Obviously, you didn't scare off. I could have told them that, but they are not the kind of men who listen, and I couldn't let it be known that you and I are involved. There's no way that information would be good for either one of us. That is why I've been so secretive about your existence."

Sofi just shook her head, searching for words. "So, you knew and didn't tell me?"

"I'm so sorry, Sof. Please understand – I couldn't. I couldn't explain it to you without endangering the whole mission. And in truth, I hoped you would heed the warning and not get yourself killed. I love you, Sofi."

"I'm in shambles, Mahmet. I don't know what to say. I don't know what to feel. But whatever it is, it's going to have to wait."

Sofi reached for her phone and placed the call. It was answered on the first ring. She told Peter she had news and was on her way to meet him.

Ten minutes later, Sofi and Mahmet were knocking on Peter's hotel room door.

When he opened it and saw Sofi, he mustered a wan smile. When he recognized the man standing behind her, his smile faded. He stepped back allowing the visitors to enter and crossed the room to the window where he stood watching them without expression. "So, you have news?" he asked.

"Yes," Sofi replied, "but I think you should sit down before we tell you."

Immediately, all the color that was left drained from Peter's face. "Is it bad?" he whispered.

"No Peter it's not bad. It's actually quite good but it's a bit of a story."

Slowly, Peter sank into the chair by the window as the other two sat on the couch.

He stared at Sofi as if he was about to be sentenced.

"We know where Nora is," she announced.

Tears filled Peter's eyes, but he angrily dashed them away as relief flooded his face.

"You were right, Peter. She is just where you thought she was and we're devising a plan to go get her."

Peter was rocking forwards and backwards trying to contain himself. He didn't want to talk. He wanted to listen and listen he did.

By the time Sofi had finished telling the truth about Mahmet and the extent of the operation they'd gotten caught up in, he was laughing softly and shaking his head.

"You've got to be kidding me," was all he could manage.

"So, you're up to your eyeballs in this thing?" he asked, looking at Mahmet.

The big man nodded and managed a grin. "Afraid so," he responded.

"You're an American?"

"Yup."

"Well, I'll be. I guess this explains why you haven't been particularly warm."

"Well Peter, I hope you understand that I've been working on nailing this guy for almost four years. We finally have him dead to rights. We were onto a weapons shipment that would bury him, and right at that moment you waltzed into the picture. Not only that, you managed to involve my fiancé to the extent that you and your missing wife became the most important thing in her life. So now, Sofi and I are working at cross-purposes. She was about to mess up an operation that's taken years to put in place. Nothing personal, but you were not helping."

Peter grinned wryly, "I am sorry about that. But it's my wife we're talking about here. She's pretty darn important to me, more so than some shady gunrunner. I hope you understand."

Mahmet raised his hand, palm forward, "Oh I get it Peter and I'm sorry. And by the way this guy is no shady gunrunner. Al Caribe is now dealing in bio-chemical weapons. He's a world-changing monster. But we're about to get him. We're going to get your wife too."

"Thank you, Mahmet," Peter replied, breathing a huge sigh. "So, what's the plan?"

"That's the bad news, Peter," Sofi grumbled. "So far we have no real plan. If we involve the authorities, the bureaucracy will get involved. We don't have time for that. We have to get Nora now and Mahmet is going to help us."

Peter glanced at the big man and nodded.

"Our problem is the security at Al Caribe's palace. It would be like attacking the White House. So, that's why we're here talking to you. You've been very resourceful so far and we're hoping that among us we can come up with an idea. It's going to be tough, but we'll get it done. We have no choice."

Peter turned away and gazed out the window at the traffic on the strait. It took a moment for him to regain control of the storm of emotions assailing him.

The other two waited. They both seemed to realize that it was not the time for words.

Eventually, he turned back and rejoined the confab. "So going to the local authorities is out of the question and going to our government takes way too much time?"

"Right," said Sofi and Mahmet in unison.

"And the house is impenetrable," said Peter,. "Great."

"Mahmet can get us close," said Sofi. He is on staff at the house next door. He's a bodyguard for al Caribe's partner. That's how he was able to penetrate their operation."

"Wow," Peter muttered, "this is deep."

"We need to find a way in, that's all there is to it." Sofi announced.

"How about arranging for her to get out of the compound; like a medical emergency where she needs a hospital?"

"Good idea," Mahmet agreed, "but we have no way of getting a message to her. I saw her a few nights ago at a dinner party. At least I think it was . . ."

Peter was out of his chair and across the room in a flash. He dropped to his knees in front of Mahmet. "You saw her? You really saw her? You saw Nora?" He was now trembling with joy and with fear and excitement.

"It might have been her. The woman I saw was with him and she was wearing a veil but it sure could have been her. She appeared out of it, like she was drugged, and she had minders. The more I think about it the more I'm convinced it was her."

Peter was by now overcome. He threw himself back onto the rug and lay there, arms and legs outstretched, staring at the ceiling trying to absorb everything he'd just heard. His mind was bending and ready to break, but one incontrovertible truth stood out. Nora was alive!

CHAPTER 43

Nora's defiance had deserted her. The bravado she'd exhibited with al Caribe had dissolved into tears of hopelessness. Sitting propped up in the giant bed she felt lost like a little girl. Maybe it was time for the unthinkable. She had figured out a way to do it. She was afraid but determined the man would not have her, not ever.

She'd tried to marshal her thoughts, to stay positive, but it was a losing battle. She found herself slipping deeper and deeper into the shadows and wishing she could disappear completely.

***

Hassan al Caribe sat on the front verandah, staring at the water, lost in thought. He was concerned that the woman had very nearly made her escape. Such a mistake was unforgivable. At least one man would pay the ultimate price. His thoughts were interrupted by the buzzing of his phone. He looked at it and answered.

"Yes, Ali," he grumbled.

He listened for a moment.

"What the hell do you mean, missing?"

As he listened, he rose and began to march back and forth on the polished stones.

"Ships of that size do not just go missing, not in the Black Sea. It is not the bloody Atlantic Ocean."

His pacing and breathing quickened as he listened.

"You're there already, and you had better damn well find her, Ali. If it's pirates, they die, all of them and their children. They don't know what they've gotten themselves into. Find the ship, Ali. This is one we cannot afford to lose."

"What the hell is going on here?" he muttered as he sat back down and put his phone back on the table.

***

"It's got to be tonight," Mahmet announced as they drove to Sofi's flat. "We don't know how long Sandar will be gone, and we need his house to access Caribe's."

They'd decided to have a bite to eat at Sofi's while they continued devising their plan of attack.

"I suggest we go by boat," Sofi offered as she sliced cheese and cold chicken for sandwiches. "We have no chance using the elevator. I'll get an unmarked boat and we'll leave it to you to explain what we're doing there."

"There won't be more than a couple of guards. He relies more on the alarm systems when he's away. The guards will do what I tell them."

"Then what?" Peter asked.

Sofi and Mahmet looked at each other and shrugged in unison.

"I can get us onto al Caribe's property," Mahmet offered. "The door between the properties will be locked and armed but and I have the code. Getting inside the house itself is the hard part. There will be four guards and a security system. I wish I had the answer, but I don't. Maybe it will come to me. Maybe God will show us the way."

"Doesn't sound too hopeful, does it?" Peter murmured.

"We have to try," Sofi said firmly. "Our chances will be no better tomorrow. What is life without risk?"

"This is going to be as risky as it gets," Mahmet replied, "But I agree we have to try."

"What about weapons?" Peter asked. "We're going to need guns."

"I have a gun for you, Peter," Sofi said. "You've used it before."

"Silencers would help, Sofi," Mahmet interjected. "We may have to shoot the guards and the dogs without sounding the alarm."

"I can get silencers," Sofi replied nodding. "I'll grab them from the vault when I go for the boat."

"What time is it?" Mahmet asked.

Peter looked at his watch, "Six-thirty," he replied.

"Okay, here's the deal," Mahmet had apparently assumed command and there was no argument. He was by far the one most qualified for the job.

"How long will it take to get the boat?"

"An hour," Sofi said as she went about the flat gathering things they'd need. She retrieved a pistol from a kitchen drawer, made sure it was loaded and handed it to Peter along with a handful of shells. She checked her own gun and strapped on her holster.

"I hope you're prepared, Peter," Mahmet said firmly. "This is as real as it gets."

"I know that Mahmet," Peter replied nervously. "I can do it. Don't you worry."

"So, listen Peter, when we get there, I would like for you to remain with the boat. If there is a firefight you won't be of much help. Sofi and I have had experience with this kind of thing and it's going to take all we've got."

"But I want to be there. I need to be part of this."

"Oh, you will be. The boat will be our only chance for escape, and we need someone to move it from Ali's house up to Caribe's at just the right time. We'll need you to do that part Peter or we have no shot."

Peter looked at Mahmet for a long moment, seemingly weighing the options. He then nodded, "Okay," he agreed, "I can do that."

"Good man," Mahmet replied.

"So, I'm off," Sofi announced bravely. "I'll meet you guys by the mosque under the big bridge. You remember the one, Peter."

"Sure," Peter replied. "Good luck Sofi, we'll be waiting."

"Don't forget the silencers," Mahmet said stiffly.

Sofi stepped in front of him, reached up and held his big face in her hands. "I won't," she said and smiled, "You realize this is our first mission together?"

"And let's hope it's our last," he replied, struggling to smile in return.

"I do love you, Mahmet," she breathed, "and may God bless us all this night." With that she was gone.

"How about one beer for the road?" Mahmet suggested.

"Why not," Peter answered, looking a bit pale, "it might calm the nerves a little."

"Oh, you'll be okay Peter. It's always like this even after a hundred missions. When the action starts, the nerves will disappear. It's kind of like stage fright I imagine."

They sat and chatted for a half-hour to pass the time. Mahmet filled in his new pal on the reality of his work and offered some more details about his current mission. By the time he was done describing his career, Peter was feeling a little more confident about their chances. Before they knew it, it was time to go.

CHAPTER 44

Mahmet drove very carefully, aware that this would be a very bad time for a fender bender. The traffic seemed lighter than usual, and they arrived at the mosque with a few minutes to spare.

Maybe a good omen, Peter considered.

The men sat side by side on one of the wrought iron benches in the grounds of the Ortaköy Mosque and stared out at the straits. As time passed and darkness fell the boat traffic diminished appreciably. Navigating the channel in the dark was just too dangerous for rational people. The men remained quiet, each in his own thoughts, until the unmarked police boat bumped gently against the wall.

"She's here," Mahmet said softly. "Game on."

The men climbed aboard, and Peter headed for the stern bench. "Kind of a beat-up old scow," he remarked.

"And perfect for our needs," Sofi said, "completely incognito and very fast as hell if needed."

Fifteen minutes later, at 8 o'clock exactly, and shrouded by darkness, they floated up against the wall that protected Sandar's mansion from the Bosporus. Without a word, Sofi and Mahmet hopped ashore and disappeared into the night.

Peter looped the bow rope through one of the iron cleats but didn't tie it. Holding onto the rope, he sat down behind the wheel and tried to prepare himself for what would be the toughest action sequence of his career.

Mahmet led the way up the side of the house until he reached a door. He punched a series of numbers into the keypad and pushed the door open. He then entered some numbers into the keypad on the wall inside and nodded.

"We're good to go," he murmured.

They headed down the hall and turned left at the first intersection. They entered a wide corridor and Sofi followed along saying nothing. As they walked, lights came on overhead.

A couple of minutes later, they stopped at a door that appeared to have its own alarm.

"That was fifty-seven steps," Sofi whispered. "I'm like that. Good to know in case we lose the light."

Mahmet started to respond but thought better of it. "This is the bedroom," he said. "Inside we can see the security monitors. A couple of the cameras are mounted on the roof, and they scan al Caribe's property as well. We'll be able to see how many guards there are and where they're stationed. "

"Cool," Sofi replied as she watched Mahmet punch in the code.

"How do you remember all these numbers?" she asked.

"It's my job," he replied gruffly, "like counting steps is your job." As he pushed open the door, he flashed a teasing smile at her.

She was a bit surprised but attributed his attitude to the fact that he really liked his job.

As they stepped into the room, the bedside lights came on and much to their surprise they found a man standing in the middle of the room wearing a very nice blue velvet robe. He was also pointing a large gun at them."

"Mahmet," the man gasped, "what the hell? You were nearly a dead man. What are you doing here?"

Mahmet stumbled for a moment or two but managed to get a hold of some words.

"Well, I um, came to do a check. Knowing you were away, I didn't want to take any chances. I didn't expect you to be here. What are you doing here anyway? I thought you were in Crimea."

Sandar crossed to the bed and placed his gun down on the spread.

"Well, it seems there's been a snag with our delivery. Apparently, the ship's gone missing. Nothing I could do there, so I came right back to get things sorted out."

"Pasha that is terrible news," Mahmet responded. "I know how important this particular shipment was to you and Pasha al Caribe."

Ali nodded and sat down at the end of the bed. He looked at Sofi as if he'd just noticed her. "And who is this beautiful creature, Mahmet?" he asked after a long moment of perusal. "It seems like you've been keeping things from me."

Sofi was a little taken aback. Here she was in her work gear; blue jeans, a canvas jacket, running shoes and a baseball cap. She blushed anyway and offered an awkward grin.

"Oh, this is my sister, Pasha. This is Sofi. We used her boat to get here, much better than fighting traffic for an hour. She begged for a look at the most beautiful house in Istanbul and I couldn't refuse. I do hope you're not angry."

"I am not angry, Mahmet, but I didn't know you had a sister. All this time together and you never mentioned her. Were you afraid I might like her too much?" Ali chuckled and wiped the drool from his chin. The man was nothing if not obvious.

"Actually Pasha," Mahmet said evenly, "I'm glad you're sitting down because I have something to tell you. I think you will be surprised and not at all pleased." He stepped forward and reached for Sandar's gun, passed it to Sofi and pulled his own weapon from his holster.

"You see Pasha . . ." he continued speaking so softly that the older man had to strain to hear him. Mahmet had been taught that this forced the listener to concentrate. ". . . that issue you're having with your shipment of bio-chemical weapons was actually arranged by me."

In an instant, Sandar's perfect tan disappeared. He choked just once and began to tremble. As he sat in shock staring at his 'number one protector', he seemed to be having trouble processing the information that was being delivered.

When Mahmet finished explaining what had happened and what was going to happen, Pasha Ali Sandar was about as compliant as bath water.

Mahmet directed Sofi to the adjoining bedroom, where she'd find the appropriate costume for the next act.

As Mahmet waited for her to get ready he kept the Pasha occupied. He was more than happy to answer questions. The man had quite a few.

By the time Sofi returned, Mahmet had instructed Sandar on what his role would be in the upcoming scene. Sandar was staring at nothing. It appeared that he was contemplating the reality of his future.

Sofi looked spectacular in a pale-yellow kaftan and silver slippers. She'd loosened her hair and allowed it to tumble past her shoulders. She looked amazing.

Mahmet nodded and smiled. Sandar was unaware that she'd returned.

"So, when we arrive next door," Mahmet said firmly, "you will introduce her as Sofi, your new um . . . distraction. Okay?"

"Yes, yes," Sandar agreed, nodding rapidly, "as you wish."

"Very good, now call al Caribe. Tell him you must see him at once. Explain that you have new information about the missing ship that you don't want to discuss on the phone."

"But he doesn't know I'm here," Ali said sounding very nervous. "He thinks I'm still in the Crimea trying to sort out the mess. He'll be angry with me."

"Oh, he'll get over it, Pasha. Pretty soon he'll have a lot more than your unexpected return to worry about. Call him. We don't have time to waste."

Mahmet had not mentioned the real reason for getting into al Caribe's house.

The phone conversation was brief, and Ali's pallor became even paler. He ended the call, rose shakily and led the way out. Just the tip of Mahmet's pistol was showing but that seemed to do the trick. The Pasha was spent and was docile as a lamb.

They crossed Ali's grounds to the door in the wall that separated his house from that of al Caribe. Mahmet slid open a small panel, entered a code and waited as the steel slid into the wall. He stepped through and the others were right behind him.

Al Caribe was waiting for them outside on the front verandah. He was flanked by a couple of armed guards who looked less than welcoming.

"So, you have news, Ali," al Caribe asked quietly

"Yes Hassan, I received some information I need to impart to you immediately and you know we cannot trust the phones."

Al Caribe glanced at Mahmet without expression and turned for a moment to the beautiful woman at his side.

"And who is this woman, Ali, and why is she in my house?"

Ali visibly flinched but stammered a response.

"Eh, she is my new friend, Hassan, and as it turns out she has information you should hear."

Hassan again turned and this time glared at Sofi who stood perfectly still, looking completely calm.

"What is this information then?" he demanded. "Now would be a very good time to tell me."

"If we could just step inside, Hassan, if you please, where we might speak privately, Sofi will give you all the information you will need," Ali suggested.

Hassan studied his visitors for a long moment, seemingly weighing the importance of acceding to Ali's request. He decided, nodded once, turned to the door and barked at his guards.

"Stay here Haid. It seems I must deal with this alone."

He crossed to one of the glass doors, opened it and stepped through. Sandar, Mahmet and Sofi followed. He started down a wide corridor, heading for a secure area and did not notice that Mahmet had reached for a keypad by the door and pushed one of the buttons thereby locking all exterior doors.

Mahmet hurried and caught up just as they reached a small nook where a fountain splashed softly.

"Well then," Caribe said as he turned to face his visitors, "let's have it."

To Caribe's surprise, it was Mahmet who stepped forward and began to speak. For some reason a gun had appeared in his hand, and it was pointed directly at Caribe's chest.

"Mohammed Hassan al Caribe," Mahmet said calmly, "I hereby apprehend you under the jurisdiction of Interpol, in the name of the government of the United States for the commission of the crime of transporting for purchase, lethal weapons of war."

Al Caribe's mouth fell open as he struggled to form a word – none came. He simply stood there bristling. For a second, it looked like he might take a leap at Mahmet, but a casual wave of the pistol seemed to alter his thinking.

"Who are you?" he spat. "Why are you here? Do you know who I am? Have you any idea what is about to happen to your life?"

"Oh, I have a feeling I'll be fine, Pasha," Mahmet replied evenly, "despite the power you wield here in your fair city. And to answer your question, I'm a CIA operative assigned to the Eastern Mediterranean. I've been watching you and your operation for a very long time."

"You traitorous bastard," Caribe spat again and turned his attention to Ali. "You too, you sniveling parrot. You will die for this."

Mahmet interrupted just as al Caribe was getting ready to explode.

"Oh, that may be so, Pasha, but first he will have to deal with us. He is also under arrest. If all goes well, you two will be sharing a nice suite in a maximum-security prison whether here in Istanbul or in the United States. And you'll be happy to hear we're not quite done. The pretty lady here is an Istanbul police officer and a very good one. She is in possession of a warrant which allows us to search your residence." He tilted his head indicating that it was time for Sofi to speak.

She took a step forward waving a folded paper, "You, Mohammed Hassan al Caribe are suspected of unlawfully imprisoning a person in your domicile who was abducted per your instructions in Venice, Italy, and delivered to you here in Istanbul. Ironically, the *Izmir*, the vessel you commissioned to transport both Mrs. Nora Brandt and the bio-chemical weapons and is now re-named the Luxor, was intercepted in the Black Sea and is now under the jurisdiction of Interpol."

Al Caribe reacted like he'd been punched in the stomach. He staggered backwards and collapsed onto a chair, gasping for breath. He started to reach into his pocket, but Mahmet waved the gun at him and shook his head.

"I need my inhaler," Caribe wheezed.

Mahmet nodded permission and watched carefully as the man clutched his inhaler and sucked in two deep puffs.

"You and your partner will be transported from here to a safe location from which you will be taken to an American facility where you will be secured."

Al Caribe simply stared at the ground. It was unclear whether he was fighting for breath or for clarity.

"In the meantime," Sofi interjected, "we need to find the woman you've been holding captive. We can search the entire house and maybe break some things in the process, or you can direct us to where the woman is being held."

Caribe just sighed. It was as if he was unable to articulate a sentence.

Ali made the decision for him.

"The woman is in one of the second-floor guest suites. I'm not exactly sure which one but it's either the second or the third one on the right from the top of the main staircase."

"Thank you, Pasha," Mahmet said. "My partner will go and find her while I wait here with you gentlemen. Perhaps you should remain seated, Sandar. It might take a minute or two."

Sofi turned to him, "So how are we going to get past the guards? Obviously, they know something is up and from the looks of them they could be a real problem."

"You're right. And unless we can get al Caribe to stand them down, they'll do whatever it takes. I'm sure they are excellent shots, and we won't be able to bluff them by threatening to shoot their Pasha. Maybe I'll go have a word with them. I might be able to persuade them that it's in their best interest to take the rest of the day off."

"They'll shoot you as soon as you step outside. There won't be much talking."

"I'm thinking that if I use my ex-employer as a shield they might listen before shooting."

"Worth a shot I guess," Sofi agreed.

"Okay, so you wait with Caribe here and stay on your toes. Don't fall for his defeated act. He's a mean bastard and people like him don't give up."

"I'll be okay, thanks."

Mahmet took Sandar by the arm and led him away. As they walked, Mahmet gave him a warning, "I know you to be a reasonable and astute man, Pasha. This would not be the time to consider heroics. You were good to me all the time I was in your employ but if you try anything stupid, I will have to kill you and the other men as well."

"I understand, Mahmet. I am aware that the game is over, and I will accept whatever Allah has in mind for me."

"Thank you, Pasha," Mahmet said softly. "I'm glad you understand."

They reached the door to the verandah. Not surprisingly, the two guards Mahmet had locked out were waiting for them with guns drawn."

Mahmet punched in the code, opened the door and pushed Sandar through in front of him.

"Unfortunately, Haid, your master al Caribe is under arrest. The truth is I'm not exactly the man you thought I was. I'm a CIA agent and I've been investigating Caribe's activities along with that of Pasha Sandar here for years. They are both now in American custody and will be out of business for a very long time. That means that you two no longer work for al Caribe. You are now unemployed which might not be a bad thing at this moment. If you agree to call the other men and leave the premises immediately, it will not be necessary for my team to come looking for you and arrest you as accomplices. Or we can start shooting at each other. But I don't see how that can work out well for any of us. What do you think?"

Haid glanced at his partner and without a word holstered his weapon. His pal, Riza, immediately followed suit. Haid then pulled a radio from his pocket and spoke briefly. He nodded and waited. Within a couple of minutes, the other three guards arrived on the scene, and waited for instructions.

At Haid's direction, they followed him to the boathouse. As Mahmet watched, the large doors swung open, and a small speedboat materialized from the darkness. Without a word, the men boarded the craft, Haid started the engines and within seconds, the boat picked up speed and disappeared into the Bosporus.

When the boat was well gone, Mahmet directed Sandar back into the house.

When they appeared at the niche, a very relieved Sofi gave her man a happy smile and a quick hug.

"I'll wait here with these two while you go find Nora. The sooner we're out of here the better. This place gives me the creeps," Mahmet said.

"Actually, I think I should go fetch Peter first. He deserves to be a part of this moment and she doesn't know us. She won't know what to believe. What do you think?"

"I think I'm not going to argue with whatever you want to do. It's gone pretty darn well so far."

Sofi offered a quick grin and hurried away. Mahmet directed Sandar to a chair and backed up against the wall keeping a close eye on his wards.

***

Sofi arrived back at the launch to find Peter nearly frantic.

"It went great," Sofi assured him, "we got them both. Now it's time to find Nora. I thought you might want to help."

"Oh my God, yes," he wailed, "of course I do. Waiting here for your signal is maybe the hardest thing I've ever done."

"Well let's go get your wife. You're going to have quite the story to tell. Her too, I bet."

Peter's grin was beyond infectious. Sofi grinned in reply.

Sofi started the engine and the boat crept forward until they were floating in front of the al Caribe mansion. They tied up and headed inside.

"Follow me," Sofi whispered as she headed for the golden staircase wondering why she was whispering.

At the top of the stairs, they entered a wide corridor and began looking for a door with a key in the lock. Two doors down, they found what they were looking for

As Sofi reached for the key, Peter clutched his heart and reminded himself to breathe.

CHAPTER 45

Nora lay on her bed staring at the ceiling. She couldn't think of anything to think about. She was tired of the bountiful blueness of the Bosporus and the endless stream of boats going somewhere that she wasn't.

She'd come to accept that solitary confinement was a recipe for madness – she wasn't exactly sure when it had happened, but it had. She felt like crying but she had no more tears. Truth was she had no more Nora. Her will to live was gone. The time had come. She was ready. Then she heard a soft knock on her door, followed by the key turning.

"How rude," she whispered, "just when I had my mind made up."

She looked over as the door opened and was surprised to see a beautiful girl dressed in yellow. She'd never seen the girl before. The girl smiled and stepped into the room. Behind her was a man, a tall handsome man with salt and pepper hair. She sat up and looked at him. He looked familiar. She knew she'd seen him somewhere before. Then it came to her, and she screamed, "Peter," she howled, "Peter!"

She turned away, dropped her face into the bedcover and wailed. "No, no, no," she cried. "Don't do this. Oh, please no, I can't."

She felt a hand on her shoulder and then a weight on the bed and then there was a warm body wrapping around her and pulling her close and holding her to him. And she smelled him. She could smell him. "Oh God," she wept, "oh God."

She turned to face what was happening to her. And there he was, looking at her, smiling at her. It was him. It was her Peter.

She grabbed him, all of him that she could grab, and tried to lose herself in him. And as she did, her world went dark.

***

It was as if they were strangers. They lay together on the bed in Peter's hotel room, studying each other in the half-light. So much of life had passed in the few weeks they'd been apart, and they were desperate to connect but the task was not an easy one. It was as if one of them had been unfaithful and forgiveness was hard to find.

For nearly an hour they didn't speak. Words couldn't reach across the space that lay between them.

It was Peter who made the first move. He reached out and gently stroked Nora's hair. As he did, a tear spilled down her cheek. Gently, he brushed the tear away and tried to form a smile, but it wouldn't come. He understood that he was looking at a different Nora. Gone was the fearlessness she was famous for. She seemed fragile now, breakable as glass. He sighed and lay quietly, gazing at her beauty. That part of her had not changed.

Suddenly, an ungodly shriek ripped through the silence. They both jumped a foot and in that instant the spell broke. It was the magic hour; the call to prayers. The muezzins were delivering a banner performance.

Nora was first to let go. Her eyes began to fill with light and the laughter was quick to follow. Soon she was howling. As the tears flowed, her squeals of happiness filled the room.

Peter was soon swept into the fray and erupted in peals of joy. Together they joined the muezzins in a tumult that continued long after the prayers were over.

Then they were in each other's arms, laughing and crying at the same time, lost to the world.

They made love until dawn, alternately touching and loving and tasting, unable to get enough of one another.

As the morning light crept into the room, Nora turned her back to her husband and spooned herself into him. It had always been her favorite way to fall asleep. "So," she whispered, "how did it feel to have a virgin?"

"Huh?" Peter muttered, sure he'd heard her wrong, but he was too far gone to pursue it.

"I'll explain later," she whispered as sleep took her by the hand and led her through the mist into a fantastic new dream.